wine & dine

L.B. DUNBAR

www.lbdunbar.com

Wine&Dine
Copyright © 2019 Laura Dunbar
L.B. Dunbar Writes, Ltd.
https://www.lbdunbar.com/

Special Edition cover (2024)
Content Editor: Melissa Shank
Editor: Jenny Simms/Editing4Indies
Proofreading: Karen Fischer

other books by L.B. Dunbar

Sterling Falls
Sterling Heat
Sterling Brick
Sterling Streak
Sterling Clay
Sterling Fight
Sterling Touch
Sterling Stone

Chicago Anchors
Elevator Pitch
Catch the Kiss

Parentmoon

Holiday Hotties (Christmas novellas)
Scrooge-ish
Naughty-ish
Grouch-ish

Road Trips & Romance
Hauling Ashe
Merging Wright
Rhode Trip

Lakeside Cottage
Living at 40
Loving at 40
Learning at 40
Letting Go at 40

Silver Foxes of Blue Ridge
Silver Brewer
Silver Player
Silver Mayor
Silver Biker

L.B. DUNBAR

Sexy Silver Fox Collection
After Care
Midlife Crisis
Restored Dreams
Second Chance
Wine&Dine

Collision novellas
Collide
Caught

The Sex Education of M.E.

The Heart Collection
Speak from the Heart
Read with your Heart
Look with your Heart
Fight from the Heart
View with your Heart

A Heart Collection Spin-off
The Heart Remembers

BOOKS IN OTHER AUTHOR WORLDS
Smartypants Romance (an imprint of Penny Reid)
Love in Due Time
Love in Deed
Love in a Pickle

The World of True North (an imprint of Sarina Bowen)
Cowboy
Studfinder

dedication

For my readers, who continue to encourage me and make me want to be the best for them.

Cheers, Lovelies!

chapter 1

Runaway

[Dolores]

"Just go, Dolores," my brother says to me. I stare at him, not even able to blink. Even though Denton is two years younger than I am, he looks better than I feel. Rock star. Model. Photographer. He's lived a life while I've spent mine here—in Blue Ridge, Georgia.

"I can't just leave," I admonish, brushing back my hair. It needs a cut and a wash. In fact, I can't remember when I last showered. Since my mother's death, a steady stream of well-wishers have stopped by at all hours to check on me.

I'm fine.

"Dolores." My brother sighs. It's a crime that men age well. At forty-five, he still has sharp cheekbones, bright dark eyes, and a smile that'll warm a room. I could hate him, but I don't. I understand why he ran away when he was eighteen. Our father was a miserable man. Still, it isn't lost on me that I was the one left behind to hold together the pieces of an already cracked vase. The diner. The farm. Our mother. Our grandmother. The list has been endless for twenty-seven years. And I'm tired.

"You can leave. I'm here now."

"Until you decide to leave again," I snap, causing Denton to flinch from his seat on a stool. He sits opposite the counter, the one I've been drawing circles on while we talk. He's right about this place. The paneling is dated, and the floor looks dirty even though it's clean. Grease permeates everything. Dolores' Diner is run down, and so am I.

"I deserve that," he says, lowering his voice, "but I have no intention of leaving. I finally have Mati in my life, and I'm not letting her go."

Matilda Harrington Rathstone had been my brother's fantasy girl his entire young life. As best friends, he gave her up to their other best friend, Chris Rathstone—Rath—when they were young, but Denton got his second chance with her.

I nod in response to my brother because I don't know what to say. He disappeared again the day after our mother's funeral. Although he called me, promising he would come back, I didn't have much faith in him. When he left at eighteen, he left. To my surprise, he took my calls occasionally, but he was always busy. The road. The band. The women. He didn't listen to me about our father's death, our mother's illness, or our grandmother's declining health. All those things fell on me—the dutiful daughter.

"Look. I'm giving you my keys." Denton slides a ring of keys across the Formica countertop. "Take the Beast and drive. Get out of town. Get away from here. Get the fuck away from Rusty."

My head shoots up at the mention of Rusty Miller. Crusty Rusty— a member of the local motorcycle club Devil's Edge and my lover-with-only-lover-benefits for the past ten years. I can't even call him a friend, and he'd never allow me to call him a boyfriend. In simple terms, he's been a sex partner to me and a few other women in the area. I cringe at that thought. I typically defend my relationship with Rusty, what little relationship I can call it, but watching my brother get the girl of his dreams leaves me questioning my own sensibility in regard to Rusty. Slowly, I'm realizing I want a little more for me.

"Can't just go. Just drive and disappear." I wave a hand dismissively toward the front window of the diner. I open at six a.m., but Denton showed up and locked the door, pulling the blinds and turning the sign back to CLOSED.

"Yes. You can," he emphasized. "You can do this, and you should."

"Where would I go?" A teeny-tiny niggling of a possibility tiptoes over my chest. *Could I do this?*

"California," Denton says, his voice rising an octave, and he double taps his hands against the counter. *Bah-dum-dum.* "I'm giving you my keys. Car. Condo. It's on the beach."

Denton lowers his head to peer up at me. "Ever been to the beach, Dolores?"

I sigh. Yes, I've been to the beach. Bolton Lake is only a few miles from here, but somehow, I know the lake isn't the beach he means.

"The ocean," he clarifies as if reading my thoughts.

"Of course." I weakly smile. "When we were kids." I can't say I fondly remember the experience. It was one of the few times we took a family vacation. Like so many family outings, it ended poorly. Daddy drunk. Mother a close second. Denton getting in trouble. Had Daddy started hitting him by then? I don't recall.

"A real ocean," Denton teases. "The Pacific."

I chuckle. He's so full of himself and California. My eyes roam his face. He's going to find it difficult in this small town. Everyone will be in his business, especially when that business includes Mati, a beloved daughter of society and widow of the well-respected Chris Rathstone. Yet I see a twinkle in his eye, and a certain brightness fills his face. He looks…happy. I'm not certain I know the emotion, but if I could recognize it, I'd say Denton wears it.

"You just got back here," I remind him. His month-long absence left everything to me again. The after-funeral effects, the diner, the farm, and our aging grandmother, Magnolia. "I can't leave you."

"Yes, you can," he repeats. "In fact, it might be better for me. I need to dig in." He spreads his hands over the scrub-worn counter and then folds his fingers like he came across something sticky.

"You don't know the first thing about running a diner."

"I have Hollilyn."

"She's ready to have a baby any day," I shriek. My assistant manager and flirty waitress is due to have her first child in less than a month.

"Let me worry about that," Denton remarks.

"And then there's Magnolia. She doesn't know what to do with herself now that Mama's gone."

"Already working on that as well." He winks, actually winks, as though he knows a secret, but he isn't sharing with me.

My head tilts, and my hip juts out. I stare at him again. He fought so hard to be nothing like our father. In many ways, he isn't him, yet all I know of my brother relates to his fame and fortune as a rock star success. He looks like our dad, but not exactly. We look like siblings, but only if you look closely. His once black hair has specks of silver while mine is dull and almost a burning-charcoal color. I don't have the energy for my typical dye job, the one that gives me a hint of blue mixed with glossy black. We share similar facial bone structure, but while his is more model worthy, mine is because I forget to eat. Our eyes are the biggest difference. His are midnight while mine are a daytime blue—my mother's eyes, everyone tells me. I view the world just like her: loveless.

As if magnetically attracted to his keys, my fingers stretch as the tips tap on the countertop. My eyes focus on the metal strips with crooked teeth. *Could I do this?*

In answer to my unspoken question, my brother slides the ring within my reach. The metal hasn't touched my fingers, but they twitch as the pull grows stronger.

"Do it, Dolores." He dares me. "Run away for a while."

"I'd need to go home. Get some clothes. Close my house. Say good-bye to Magnolia."

Denton reaches into his back pocket and pulls out his wallet. My eyes widen at the wad of cash stuffed in it. He pulls two bills and then fumbles with a card. Two Benjamin Franklins and a gold card.

"I can't take your money," I admonish. I'm not some charity case. I have my own income, and my own home paid for by said income. I'm an independent business owner, for heaven's sakes.

"Consider it a loan then. I don't want you stopping as you pass go. Here's two hundred dollars and a card to get what you need."

I chuckle because he can read me. As if he knows I might take his offer but then second-guess myself when I get home to pack my things.

My hand smooths down my hip, the feel of my waitress uniform suddenly constricting me. My podiatric-approved shoes with instep support weigh heavy on my feet. Sensing my inability to move, Denton pushes the keys the final distance, and I curl my fingers around the cool teeth. He stands and walks around the counter to envelop me in his arms. I've hugged a hundred people since my mother's death. The people of this town respected her as the former mayor's widow, even if they didn't respect the previous mayor.

Denton squeezes me, and I want to feel what he's offering, but I don't. I learned long ago to distance myself from physical affection. I can give it easily because it has no effect on me.

Yet.

The comfort of my brother's arms and his praise in my ear—"I believe in you. You can do this."—do something to me. I blink, but I won't cry. I haven't cried since my mother's funeral, since even before her diagnosis. I don't cry. It shows emotion, which I don't allow myself to feel.

I weakly pat Denton on the lower back. "Thank you."

He pulls back, his hands framing my face so I'm forced to look him in the eyes.

"This is going to be good for you," he says, his voice encouraging.

"I'll be fine," I reply quietly, giving a nod in agreement. I'm always *fine*.

chapter 2

Wet Dog – That's Not A Euphemism

[Dolores]

Standing on the shore, I dig my toes in the sand. One week ago, I was preparing for Halloween in the cool mountains of Georgia. Today, I stand barefoot in jeans rolled to my ankles with a tank top and a warm breeze ruffling my hair. My arms cross, protecting myself, or maybe I'm holding myself together.

I did what Denton suggested. I left, took the Beast—his white 1967 Ford Shelby GT500 Super Snake with a blue strip—and drove across the country to California, only making a few stops along the way. A Walmart was sufficient for clothing because I was only worried about getting the essentials. A few pairs of jeans, some T-shirts, a sweater, and new shoes. Though, as my toes wiggle in the cool grains at my feet, I wonder if I'll ever wear shoes again.

I also bought a cell phone charger with the false hope that Rusty would call me. The fantasy played out in my head where he'd miss me, wonder where I was, and then beg me to return to him. I snort aloud with the thought. One week absent and I haven't heard from him. Not a text. Not a call. Nothing.

My arms draw tighter around myself.

My second stop was a hotel. Nothing fancy, but one where I felt safe. I'd never traveled alone before, and the process grew daunting as I crossed state lines. At more than one point, I was sick of myself and in desperate need of an audiobook or a new playlist. I hadn't taken the pleasure to read in so long. Most nights, I fall asleep in front of the television or pass out after a few rounds of sex with Rusty.

I shiver at the thought.

My first night alone—truly alone—outside of Georgia, I slept. Twelve hours. I haven't slept like that since I was a teenager, and even then, I didn't sleep half a day away because I worked. My grandmother was still an active owner of her diner back then, named after her mother and my namesake, and I worked there to fill my time. She taught me to cook. She taught me to manage.

Every girl should have her own finances, Magnolia would tell me. *Your place might be in a kitchen, but only if you own it.* She'd wink. She knew my father's philosophy. A woman's place was in the home, specifically the kitchen and the bedroom.

I shiver again.

In the distance, I hear a faint call. I haven't seen anyone since I arrived last night. I'm not good with the maps app on my phone and grew frustrated at the congestion of the Los Angeles area. Denton's place is actually north of Santa Monica along the beach. His condo is on the second floor, where only one other resident occupies the other half of the floor.

"Garrett Fox lives next door. He's harmless. Sort of. Just stay away from him. He's hardly home anyway, so he shouldn't give you any trouble. I'll call him to let him know you'll be staying at my place for a while." Denton really came through and took care of everything. His car. His credit cards. His home.

We didn't have a strong sibling relationship. In fact, I'd even consider it estranged. Even though I'd seen plenty of him in the tabloids and social media, we hadn't seen each other in twenty-seven years. His rock star status included dating models and actresses, as well as bad boy behavior, but nothing as extreme as his drummer, Hank Paige. Our cousin Lawson, who now goes by Tommy, rounded out the trio of their band, Chrome Teardrops. His sister, Kit, was their meal ticket as the lead singer. A female phenomenon at the height of rock-chick bands, her diagnosis of breast cancer cut their headlining days short. Rumor has it, Denton quit although we hadn't discussed his specific reasons.

"We were a shitstorm waiting to implode," he told me after it happened. That was over ten years ago.

Then again, Denton seems resolved in his return, and he's trying to make amends, *I guess.* It's yet to be determined how well he can handle our small town, the diner, or living with our grandmother for the time being. I have missed my brother over the years, if for no other reason than he is one of the last two living members of my family.

Another bellowed call floats to me, drifting in the echo of the breeze around me. I hear the tender bark of a dog in the distance, but I don't draw my eyes from the waves before me. The aggressive roll and crash of the salt water appears angry, despite the early hour and the lightening sky announcing a potentially glorious day of sunshine. My head tilts as I welcome the heat. I want to relax, but I haven't gotten to that point. I don't even think I know how to relax, but I'm telling myself I must learn.

Suddenly, I'm thrust to the ground, and the wind knocked out of me as something heavy and wet laps at my neck.

I can't breathe, and my eyes squeeze tight to ward off the weight over me. The most pungent smell overwhelms me.

Wet dog.

Oh God, I hate dogs.

I whimper in fear, worried the thing will bite me. Willing my eyes to open, I peek at the creature on top of me. I try to roll to my side, but I can't as the furry beast licks my face.

Gross, gross, gross.

My hands struggle to rise, wedging between the underbelly of the beast and brushing against soaked fur. I fight past my repulsion and cover my face, which does nothing to deter the dog.

"Wally!" The sharp snap of a male voice cracks near me, but the heavy panting of the animal and the sound of him salivating over me are my sole focus.

Sweet mother of all things holy, he's going to eat me.

"Wally, get off." At the sound of the masculine tenor growing louder, and the strict command, the dog gyrates.

Is he…oh my God, he's getting off…on me!

The beast dry humps my hip as I'm able to roll only the slightest under him. My elbow comes up in a desperate but weak attempt to rid him of me.

"Wally!" Another loud cry and the pressure of the dog releases a bit as he is yanked to the side. I peek through the slats of my fingers shielding my face to see the master attempting to draw this wet heap off me.

"I'm sorry. Are you okay?" the man questions. His voice sounds teasing despite his concern. "He's never acted like this before. Bad Wally." I can't see his face as the sun shines behind his head, keeping him in shadow while he rambles his apology and reprimands his pet.

Finally, my body is free of wet fur and bad breath, but I'm afraid to move. A hand comes to my elbow, and I flinch at the tender touch.

"It's all right. I just want to help you up."

I ignore his offer, pressing my hands into the wet sand and rolling to all fours. His hand comes to my lower back in silent support as I push myself upward to fold back on my heels. My hands rest on my thighs while I continue to catch my breath. My chest aches, and my breathing remains shallow.

"Maybe you shouldn't stand yet?" His rich, rugged voice curls around my ear, and I shiver at the sound of genuine concern. I shake my head, drowning in embarrassment because I've just been knocked over by a dog. Of course, this man is concerned. He's concerned I'll sue him for his wild beast loose on the beach. Unwittingly, tears well in my eyes.

"Just knocked the wind out of me," I wheeze, digging my fingertips into my sandy, denim-covered thighs. The man surrounds me in a crouched position. His bare kneecap comes into my periphery. A soothing hand rubs along my spine, crawling under my hair and pausing at the nape of my neck. He massages lightly, and my eyes close. *That feels so good.*

We stay in this position for a moment, and my throat rumbles. Did I just purr?

"Think you can stand?"

My lids flip open. Sweet lord of licorice, I moan from the touch of a stranger. My heart races, and I scramble to my feet, my entire body shaky. Sounds suddenly register too loud around me. I hear the crash of the waves pelting each other and the harsh snapping bark of the dog who races around us.

"I hate dogs," I snip.

"I'm so sorry. I don't know what came over him."

I snort, swiping at my damp, sand-covered jeans as I twist out from under his firm hand at my back. "What came over him is him coming over me." My Southern drawl grows sharp with my irritation.

"You're not from around here," he comments, stating the obvious but also asking as a question.

I look up at the pet owner.

And I forget how to speak.

My breath hitches for another reason other than the blow from his pup.

The man before me has dark sandy hair and eyes to match. Scruff covers his jaw, a patch a little whiter on his chin. A hint of tattoos wraps around one side of his neck above the collar of his faded red tee. Slowly, the corner of his mouth curls, and he chuckles.

He's laughing *at me*.

I straighten up and take a painful, deep inhale.

"You ever hear of a leash?" I snap. His chuckle grows to a deep rumble, and I don't care for the way the sound travels over my body, making parts of me pulse.

"Only use them on women."

I gasp. *Is he serious?* He's kidding, right? What a pig!

"For sex play, of course."

My mouth clamps shut. Oh. *My. God.* Creep. Get away from me, I think, crossing my arms over my chest. California is not for me if this is my welcome, and I'm ready to step around him, wondering if I can outrun him. Our sides angle toward Denton's building some fifty feet away, but I'm doubtful I can make the distance over the sand as I'm out of shape. And he's clearly in shape with his fit legs sticking out from his workout shorts, and lean, muscled arms accentuating a tattoo on his forearm. Not to mention the firm fit of his faded tee, hugging his shoulders and outlining his abs.

The throbbing between my thighs increases.

"I'm Garrett, by the way. Garrett Fox," he offers, extending a hand as if I'd touch him.

Then something registers.

The neighbor.

Garrett Fox.

He's seriously hot, in a creepy sort of way. In a I-might-like-to-leash-him kind of way. I wonder if he'd lick me instead of his dog? Which shouldn't be a thought. Shouldn't happen.

Then his dog barks, and my spell on the master is broken.

With his playful eyes watching me, I decide I hate California...along with dogs.

chapter 3

She's Hot For A Mess

[Garrett]

Whoever this woman is, she's a disaster, but when she looks at me with these soulful eyes, my stomach flips.

Well, this is interesting.

Most women blush and giggle when I mention a leash. I'm only kidding. Kind of. I mean, I've never collared anyone, but I'm not opposed to any kind of lockdown: handcuffs or straps. Although, this hot mess looks like she'd rather whip me, and it wouldn't be in any way kinky. *Damn.*

Despite her disheveled appearance, she has potential. Those blue eyes match the sky, and her legs go on for miles. With her arms crossed, her breasts truss up, the nipples peaked from the wet T-shirt she's sporting, thanks to my dog.

Nice work, Wally. Then I remember he bulldozed her over. I don't know what came over him. My chocolate lab is normally a sappy wimp, but he took off for this woman like he was ready to eat his last meal. Thankfully, he's not aggressive. He'd kill her with lapping and licking, not chowing on her. My mouth waters as my eyes lower to her breasts again. Speaking of lapping and licking—

"I'm Dolores. Denton's sister."

Screeeeeeeeeeech. There come the brakes on anything with this chick.

"Ah, Denton's sister. He told me you were coming to stay at his place." Something about his sister needing a vacation. Their mother dying. *Shit.* Say something, I internally growl, but words escape me. Her eyes make her look lost.

I scratch at the back of my neck when she doesn't say anything either. We stand in awkward silence, neither of us moving. Her attention drifts back to the ocean while she shivers. A strange odor wafts off her body. She smells like a wet dog. *Shit.*

"I'm sorry again about Wally."

"Interesting name for a dog," she says, a twang of Southern in her voice. When she isn't barking at me, it's a rather sweet sound. She eyes the pup as he races away from us and then back. He looks like a rabid animal with a face too sweet for the wild. His running reminds me I flung his tennis ball, and he didn't retrieve it. Maybe that's why he plowed into her. Dolores was blocking his ball.

Ballbuster.

I bite my lip to suppress the humor I find in calling her such a name.

"His name is short for Wallbanger," I explain.

Her head nods like she understands me, and a weak grin graces her lips, which are pink and plump although a little chapped. Then her mouth pops open with realization, and I'm thinking of a few things a mouth making such a perfect O could do.

"Incredible," she mutters, huffing on the word. Turning away from me, she shakes her head.

"That's what she said," I mumble in retort, but she does not look pleased with my comeback. In fact, she looks like she wants to skewer me, so I cough into a fist to cover the awkwardness as her head whips back to face me.

Wally circles closer to Dolores's legs, and she steps back. Her hands lower, palms held outward, as if warding my pup off before he can jump at her again. I've never seen him act so crazy. He slips behind her knees, and she steps forward, bumping into me while her attention remains over her shoulder, looking down at Wally behind her. Her hands clutch at my upper arms.

"You don't like dogs?" I question, liking the feel of her pressed against me too much despite the wet dog fragrance. *Who doesn't like dogs?* Apparently, her. Another comeback rests on the tip of my tongue until her head twists upward, and her eyes meet mine for the briefest of seconds. I can't take mine off hers, but she averts her gaze quickly and follows Wally behind me, nudging at the back of my legs. My voice croaks when I speak. My tone lower than normal as I focus on her eyes, not looking at mine. "Then that seals the deal. We'll never have sex because I only sleep with women who adore my dog."

Her fingers dig into my biceps, still clutching at me although her eyes narrow. Her mouth falls open even farther, and *incredible* is the word I want to use to describe her. Incredible things I imagine that mouth can do.

"Your dog is your barometer for sleeping partners?" she snaps.

"Well…" I shrug all smug, and then her brows pinch with another thought.

"As if you'd be attracted to me."

Huh. Not what I expected her to say although she's correct. Wally is a good judge of character, and I'm not attracted to hot messes with disheveled, sand-filled hair who smell like wet dog, even if my dog is the reason for her being messy. Prepared for a snide remark and prepped for the banter, I didn't care for the self-deprecating insult. *She isn't that bad.* I catch her eyes again. There's something in that azure color—lovely but sad—and I want to dive in to save her.

I shake my head. That's crazy talk.

My heart thumps once, reminding me I'm an ass. Why am I flirting with her? Denton's sister. Off limits. *Shit.* I place my hands on her hips and press her back, feeling strangely empty with the release of her body against mine. She drops her hands instantly, swiping them up and down the curve of her hips like she can't get them clean.

"Hey, Dorothy, I'm—"

"It's Dolores."

I stare at her. *What?*

"My name. It's Dolores, not Dorothy."

"Okay, well, either way, this isn't Kansas and—"

"I'm from Georgia, not Kansas." Her hands stop stroking her hips, fists forming on each one and then one juts out. Her eyes narrow, and I forgot where I was going by mentioning Kansas. She's a little sassy, and my body reacts to the fire in her. My dick wants in on some action. *Down boy.* We already had what we shouldn't have had last night. I shake my head, refusing to let myself think about how I gave in to Alicia Graystone of all people.

"What's the difference?" I ask, knowing full well the distinction between the two states as I'm from a small town about halfway between Kansas and Georgia.

"Purple mountains majesty, not amber waves of grain," she snarks. I stare at her another moment, and then I can't help myself. I laugh. A good belly roll, bend at the waist, hands on my knees laugh. Standing there in her prissy glare, hands on hips, with her Southern drawl, she tried to school me. The laughter is surprisingly refreshing.

"Are you laughing at me?" she bites again. Her teeth clench as she speaks, and I wonder—when I shouldn't—if she'd bite me. My dick jolts again, and I'm about to have an issue in my thin workout shorts.

"No, ma'am." Her expression sours as I pull up my expired Southern drawl. "I'd have to have a heart to laugh *at* you," I explain, still chuckling. "And I don't."

She blinks as her forehead furrows. "Don't have a heart?"

My laughter lowers to a dying huff, and I swipe at a tear. I haven't laughed like that in a long time.

"Well, then nice to meet you, Tin Man." She extends a hand, standing too formal for someone who wrestled with my dog in the sand and then pressed against me.

It takes me a moment to make the connection with what she said.

Tin Man. Dorothy. Ah, yes, Kansas, but no Wizard here.

"You're pretty funny, Dolores," I say, emphasizing her name as my hands slip into the pockets of my shorts, hoping to disguise what she's done to me.

Her lips twist. "Hilarious," she whispers, before lowering her unclasped hand and brushing past me, heading toward the condo building. "See ya around, Tin Man."

My eyes follow her retreat. The sway of her ass in skinny jeans. The hourglass shape of her hips narrowing at her waist. The muscle in her back with her hair piled on her head. I lick my lips.

Well. Huh. That was interesting.

chapter 4

Curb Appeal

[Dolores]

I've been at Denton's a week, moving from the couch to the bed and then the beach. The triangle repeats, and I find myself sleeping more than anything else. I can't seem to keep my lids open or the yawns suppressed. Then one morning, the breeze holds a chill, and I tremble. This is California. It shouldn't be cold, I tell myself. My one sweater isn't going to be enough, and neither are the knock-off Chucks I bought.

"Where's a store?" I ask Denton when I call him. I hate to admit I need him. I'm helpless in my new surroundings. He hasn't asked me to check in with him, but I feel better pretending he wants me to. For the first time in a long time, he actually asks how I'm doing. He doesn't rush me away like he used to do when we spoke on the phone. Well, when I spoke, and he pretended to listen.

"There's the Grove or Century City, or you could always go down to Rodeo."

My brother must be kidding. Me on Rodeo Drive, hardly. I don't know where any of these other places are located, and I don't think my concept of a mall matches my brother's.

"How about a Target?"

"No Target, Dolores. Shop at a real store." There's nothing wrong with Target, I want to snap.

"I don't think I can find those places on my own." I hate to admit my incapability, but the traffic congestion around here isn't like Blue Ridge. It's fast-paced, crowded, and busy, and I don't trust myself to drive.

"Take an Uber."

I'm quiet for a moment. I don't want to tell him I don't know how. We don't have Uber or even taxis in Blue Ridge. We don't need them in such a small community. Thankfully, he seems to understand my hesitation and offers me instructions.

"Download the app on your phone. Use my card for the charges. Then order a driver. It's actually pretty easy."

Maybe for him, but I don't know how I feel about letting a stranger drive me around an area that's foreign to me. I've heard stories. What if he turns out to be an ax murderer or worse? I quiver with the horrid possibility.

"I can call Garrett and ask him to help you." My brother's the one to hesitate this time, and I shake my head even though he can't see me. I haven't seen Garrett since our literal run-in on the beach. I've heard Wally bark once or twice, and it's the only sign he's in the condo next to me. Then there was the other night and the sounds coming through the wall.

"I don't think that's necessary. I'll figure it out." I run a business, I tell myself so I can download a freaking app.

Only I don't find it so easy as I stand on the curb outside Denton's condo in my jeans, a light sweater, and canvas shoes, freezing. When did it get so cold? My fingers tremble as I try to download the app, which seems to be taking a long time to load. As I wait, my phone pings in my hand.

Tonight.

I stare at the singular word.

Rusty. It's about damn time, I want to curse, but realize with sadness the request implies he doesn't know I'm not in Blue Ridge.

I'm not home. I text back, fingers trembling on the reply.

When you get home.

It's rare for Rusty to reach out to me. Typically, I'd go to Ridged Edge, the biker bar just outside of town, and find him there with some of his club friends. We'd play this cat and mouse game where he'd circle like he hadn't seen me and then he'd come in for the kill and ask me to go home with him. We didn't date. We fucked. My lips twist as I admit the truth and stare at his command. *Doesn't he know where I am?*

I'm in California.

Three dots appear and then disappear. Then a question pops up. **What the fuck you doing there?**

There are so many ways to answer this question and so many statements to make. Has he not realized I'm gone? Has he not noticed my absence? Has he not missed me? With all that happened in the past month, does he not understand my need to leave? I can answer all those thoughts without asking Rusty. No. No, he does not realize, notice, miss, or understand anything about me. We have no emotional tie to one another. Well, at least he has no emotional tie to me. I, on the other hand, have given my body to this man for nearly a decade which has pulled my heart along for the bumpy ride.

Staying at my brother's.

I thought your brother was here. I can almost hear the sharp intake of his breath with this comment.

Strange how he knows Denton is in town but doesn't know I'm not.

Sorry to disappoint you. Although I'm certain he'll believe the disappointment is mine. I'm not itching to get laid, but a little physical comfort would be nice.

The thought makes me pause. *Since when has sympathy ever come from Rusty?*

Only disappointed I won't get to taste your sweet—

I look away. Not exactly a romantic gesture or declaration of missing *me*.

"Whatcha doing?" The teasing tone curls around my ear, and I sharply inhale. Only my nostrils fill with the fresh scent of a male. Manly, bayberry, and woodsy. I might not have noticed him sneak up on me, but what I do notice is how close he stands. As if I could lean back, rest my head on his shoulder, and relax into him. Instead, I stiffen.

Why am I having thoughts like these about someone like him?

A leash. I choke on the reminder of our first meeting. Garrett Fox might be hot, but he's a sex-fiend and obviously a player. *Already have one of those, don't need another, thank you.*

"Nice language," he mutters, and my eyes fall to the open screen on my phone with the text message on display. I press the home button and spin, only my arm knocks his chest, throwing me off-kilter as I balanced on the edge of the curb. My ankles give, and he catches me at the elbow.

"Whoa." He chuckles, adding his other hand to right me. My cool palm comes to his firm chest, absorbing the warmth of his dress shirt. He's wearing a suit without a tie. On reflex, I gently press the freshly starched material, feeling the firmness of his pec underneath the shirt. His eyes widen, a mischievous gleam in the sandy coloring.

"Hey." His lip curls in the corner, and a playful grin grows. His cheeks hold more scruff than the day we met, and I'm rendered speechless like on that day. His eyes twinkle like multiple grains of sand—russet and copper and tawny. The expression on his face good-naturedly teases me. His handsome features literally take my breath away.

"Hi," I squeak, removing my hand like I didn't mean to touch him after awkwardly smoothing down his shirt. His hands still hold my elbows, but I lift my arms to release myself from his grasp. He takes the hint and drops his hand, slipping them into his pant's pockets.

"Whatcha doing out here?" he asks again.

"I'm trying to figure out Uber." I blink. "I mean, I'm waiting on an Uber." I don't want him to think I'm incompetent. What forty-seven-year-old woman can't order an Uber? My shoulders fall with the thought. I hate admitting defeat, but I'm suddenly exhausted. Rusty's text has me wound down. Maybe I'll just go back to the condo and take a nap. I can get a warmer sweater or better shoes another day.

"Denton called me."

"What?" I snort. "Why?" I should be infuriated with my younger brother for meddling, but a small sigh of relief fills my clogged throat. He's trying, I tell myself. He wants to do nice things for me for some reason. I hate to question, *why now,* or feel like it's too late. I want to give him the benefit of the doubt, or maybe I just don't want to think at all. For once.

"He asked me to direct you to a salon. *Make her pamper herself*, he said." His eyes twinkle when he speaks.

"Oh, I don't need pampering," I say, waving a dismissive hand between us. Then a piece of my over dry hair falls in my face from the messy bun on top of my head. I don't think I can afford a salon around here anyway. I'm trying not to abuse my brother's generosity and only pay for things I know I'd afford at home.

Home. *Georgia.* I'm caught in this weird juxtaposition of wanting to miss it but not missing it yet.

"I'm heading into LA. I can drop you off at Nordstrom. I have a friend who works there."

I bet he does. I bet he has many friends, I think, as I eye his sharp royal blue suit which makes his eyes look like whiskey. I could get drunk on those eyes. I blink and look away.

"I don't want to trouble you. I just need a Target. I was going clothes shopping."

His nose scrunches as if he smells something bad.

"Ah, yeah, I don't exactly know where one is." He reaches for the back of his neck and scratches. He did this the other day on the beach, and I'm curious if it's a nervous habit. Or something he does before he wants to laugh at me.

I turn away from him and take a few steps before a hand covers my elbow again. With a sharp tug, I'm spun to face him.

"Hey, where are you going?"

"I don't need your help," I snap. He responds with a flinch of his head and a rapid blink.

"*Okay*," he draws out the word. "But I'm heading to the city anyway. Don't waste your money on an Uber. I can drop you wherever you need to go. You can Uber back here later."

I exhale, and my shoulders fall. It does sound like a better plan than trying to figure out where to go or how to get somewhere on my own.

Thinking of the noises coming from his apartment the other night, I can trust Garrett has no untoward intentions toward me.

"Fine," I mutter.

"Perfect," he replies too chipper, dropping my elbow and waving a hand forward for the garage. "And while we drive, you can tell me all about your boyfriend and the dirty things he says to you."

"You are incorrigible." I gasp. "And how do you know he isn't my husband?"

"Is he your husband?" he questions, a brow rising while the expression on his face morphs into something I can't read. I respond too quickly with a disparaging snort.

"I didn't think so." His playful grin returns, but I'm offended by the comment.

Why? Am I not marriage material? I've been told that and certainly felt that when James Harrington never asked me to marry him. He asked Evie instead.

"Why not?" I snap.

"No ring," he replies with a shrug, forcing us both to look down at my long, empty fingers, the ones with chipped polish and veins sticking up the backside of my hand. I have my grandmother's hands. Worker hands. "A woman like you should have a ring if she were taken."

I want to ask what he means, but we stop walking, and I glance up at his car, forgetting about my naked finger.

Of course, it's a Porsche.

Incredible.

chapter 5

Stunned

[Garrett]

"Incredible," she mutters under her breath as I pause next to my car. I'm not certain if she means me, my snarky comments, or my vehicle, a 2019 Porsche 911 Limited Edition Early Release convertible. Either way, I open the door for her and hold it as she folds herself into the leather seat. Even covered in jeans, I have a sense of how long her legs are, and I imagine them shapely and sleek beneath the denim.

I close her door and round to the driver's side. Slipping in, I fire up my little piece of pride. The sweet purr always excites me, but for some reason, the excitement intensifies with Dolores next to me. She's a captive audience in my sports car as we drive down Highway 1 to the city. There's no escaping me like she did a week ago.

I've been busy this week and haven't had the chance to cross paths with her. I'd almost missed Denton's phone call this morning. If Dolores saw last night's visitor, she hasn't mentioned anything. I had to practically force Alicia out my door.

We need to talk, Alicia pouted. Her presence on my doorstep was unprecedented, and a further reminder the previous weekend had been a mistake. Alcohol was involved then. Alcohol was involved last night. Alicia was drunk. A longtime friend, we'd already shared the benefits thing years ago, but when Alicia grew too clingy, I had to cut her loose. I wasn't marriage material. It's why I'm still single at fifty.

After I was raised by a mother and three sisters, a woman fussing over me full time is the last thing I want. Freedom rings in my ears. That's what I took when I left River City, Missouri. With a small inheritance from my granddad, I built the empire I now run—Fox Investors. I don't invest in emotions. I invest in things. Things that make me money. Lots of money. The thought shifts my eyes to the woman next to me.

Clearly, Dolores doesn't care about money. She hasn't said anything about my Porsche, the Italian leather seats, or the high-tech surround sound stereo system. Her request for a Target has me doing a second take at her clothing. Are those Chucks a knock-off? Is her sweater a brand of *anything*?

"Why don't you have a jacket?"

"Uhm…" Those pink lips open and then twist like she's locking in a secret. "I forgot one. It's California. It's not supposed to be cold here."

I scoff. "It's not Hawaii."

"Aren't they practically the same?"

My head swivels in surprise. Her brother's a former rock star, how does she not know the difference?

"Prefer the East Coast, huh?" Easterners can be snobs like that, with their loyalty to the original colonies. *Those* people love their ocean, thinking it's better than the one out west. Patriots, I inwardly chuckle with sarcasm.

"I've never been to the coast."

My head twists again, but her eyes stay focused on the houses we pass, those that line the very coast we are discussing.

"Well, I went once," she corrects. "But I try not to think of that time."

Huh. There's a story there, but I don't ask. I don't need her sad history. I'm giving her a ride because I'm trying to be a nice guy, and Denton asked me to. He's gotten me out of more than a few binds with women at the condo. We aren't best friends, but I like to think we understand each other. We've watched a game or two together. Gone to a bar or three. Thankfully, we've never shared a woman. The thought draws my eyes back to the one next to me. *His sister.*

She still looks like a wreck even without a damp T-shirt, sand in her hair, or the scent of wet dog permeating from her. Her dried out hair is pulled up in a messy bun. She wears no makeup and a sweater that looks two sizes too big for her. She needs a personal shopper and spa treatment, and even that might not wipe the sorrow off her cheeks. I should offer condolences for her mother, but if she cries, I'm a goner. It's my one weakness. I'm a sap in that area, and as soon as a woman knows this secret—that I'm defenseless against tears—the challenge is on. Alicia pulled it on me, and it's how she ended up in my apartment. *Twice.*

Dolores and I ride in silence for a bit, but as we near the city, the traffic pulls us to a halt. I press five on my touchscreen speed dial. My mother and three sisters take up the first four numbers.

"Nora, it's Garrett. Can you set up a personal shopper at Nordstrom for me and then make an appointment at Beverly's around one?"

"Sure thing, Mr. Fox."

I sense Dolores's eyes on me as the phone disconnects.

"Mr. Fox? You sound important."

"I think *incredible* is the word you mean." Her arms cross, and her lip pouts.

"Impossible," she grunts under her breath, and I scoff.

"I run Fox Investors."

"Never heard of it," she says, not judging but not impressed either. Just making a statement.

"Think *Shark Tank.* Ever see that show? I'm a behind-the-scenes guy. Invest in things to be bought and sold. The money man." She nods like she understands but doesn't probe me for more information. I'm taken aback as most women start questioning me, sniffing around for my net worth, which can easily be found in *Forbes.* I was once entrepreneur of the year and earned the decree of the most successful man under fifty.

I wait for a beat and then reconsider my accolades. *Maybe you don't want her to ask.*

"I own a diner," she says matter-of-factly. I'm surprised, and my head swivels in her direction again. "A woman's place is in the kitchen, my father would say, but my grandmother disagreed. She said a woman should only be in the kitchen if she owns it. In my case, I own the diner, thanks to her." She pauses and turns to face me. "I suppose now you'll say something snarky about me running a small business as if it doesn't compare to your big one."

"Actually, no. Small business was the foundation of this country. It's how I got my start as well. I invest in a startup company, help them grow, and then either sell off my portion or help them sell their business."

Her lips curl outward, and for once, she seems impressed, but what shocks me is how impressed I am with her. For as disheveled as she looks, she sounds intelligent.

I clear my throat.

"So, let's talk about your boyfriend, not a husband, right?" I tease. She hadn't answered my question about the missing ring, and it's on principle that I clarify. Denton hadn't mentioned his sister was attached to anyone, and I don't know why I'm digging. However, that text raised the hairs on my neck and not necessarily in a good way.

"Neither," she states; her voice low and disinterested.

Single. Okay, interesting. But he was someone if he was mentioning her unmentionable.

"Friends with benefits, then? I'm cool with that." I had Alicia although she was a leash...on me.

"Not exactly that, either." Her hands disappear into her sweater, and she hugs herself tighter.

"Sex buddies?" I joke. I don't picture her as the casual type, but we all need to get off somehow. My eyes drift to her legs, curious about them wrapped around some guy. Strangely, I don't like the thought.

She doesn't answer me, keeping her lips closed, and her thoughts quiet. We fall into a tense silence, and I wonder what she's holding in over there. I shouldn't care. I don't, really, but she seemed put off when I joked about her being the type to wear a ring. I just meant some man should put one on her and claim her as his. I'd do that if I had a woman with legs like hers...if I did that kind of thing, that is, like marriage.

My eyes wander to her legs again. Damn, I'm curious about them. I shake the thought.

Denton's sister.

Off limits.

We finally arrive at Nordstrom.

"Ask for Lana. Give her my name."

Dolores nods without a word. She stares out the window at the three-story building.

"You okay to go alone?" The question rings in my tone. I don't know why, but I'm worried. This is not my thing. I leave the shopping up to Lana. But I have a strange feeling I shouldn't leave Dolores.

"I'm good alone." Her comment is cryptic. She steps out of the car, but stands on the sidewalk, holding the door as she peers up at the store. Then she quickly turns, something filling her face, and I anticipate her asking me to join her. My heart races as I almost want her to say *come with me*. Instead, she says, "Thank you for the ride."

Huh. Not what I was expecting.

"Here, give me your phone," I demand, reaching across the passenger seat with my open palm. Her forehead furrows. "I'll give you my number in case you need anything."

She hands me her phone, and I enter the digits. "Now text me." Her brows pinch, but she does as I command. "Now I have yours." Her lips twist, but it isn't disapproving. She seems to be fighting a smile.

A car honks behind me, and Dolores jolts. The door closes without another word from her. She stands with her back to me, and my stomach swirls. *I should go with her*, but the asshole behind me honks again.

Coasting forward, I flip up my middle finger at the anxious honker. I roll up to the corner, willing myself not to look back, but my eyes are pulled to the rearview mirror. Dolores is still standing on the sidewalk, staring up at the building.

"Come on, sweetheart. One step in front of the other," I mutter aloud in my empty car.

As if she heard me, she moves forward, and I turn into traffic with a sigh of relief.

+ + +

Tonight lover?

Alicia's text is like something out of a bad comedy. I'm not her lover. I'm not her anything. Unfortunate for me, I'm a decent guy sometimes, and I let her in my condo last night when she Uber'd over. One too many drinks and a sloppy drunk later, and I had a new cushion on my couch for the evening. She tried to make a move for me, but I don't get it up for sappy Sallys, and even when I tried to pump myself later, the release was weak. Strangely, it wasn't the bleach blonde on my couch filling my fantasy in the shower but a certain brunette neighbor. The aftereffects left me shivering. I cannot be interested in Dolores.

As for Alicia and me, been there, done that, and every man knows you don't tap what you don't want twice. Only, I'm an idiot. A week ago, I was the one with too many drinks and a sorry pick-up line, leading me back to Alicia's place, tapping where I've already been one too many times. Years ago, Alicia filled a void. I don't like to think about what happened, with who, or why. Just one night, Alicia was there, willing and a little too wild. She was everything opposite…*nope*, not going to think of her. We'd been friends. I wanted to add benefits. Alicia wanted more, and that was when it was time to dismiss Miss Clingy.

Only I'd made the mistake of being with her again, and now, I get this. I toss my phone on my desk and lean back, taking in the view of the LA skyline. I love this city despite the fact even on a clear day you can't see it clearly. Smog. Forest fires. Pollution. It's so different from where I grow up but no less murky. I left behind a factory town and traded up to another more expensive one. Still, I have the money, and speaking of, I had hoped Dolores was the one texting me. I wanted to hear how excited she was to be made up. A caterpillar metamorphosing into a beautiful butterfly. Not that I think Dolores is beautiful. I mean, she's cute in a disheveled kind of way, but those eyes. It's like she sees into me when she looks at me, and I want to see inside her. The sadness in her eyes is mesmerizing.

Which it shouldn't be.

I straighten up, righting the tilt of my desk chair and spin for my computer.

It's been a hectic morning, but the glory of owning my own business and working for myself means I call the shots on my schedule. And today, I clear my afternoon, deciding to leave early to pick up Dolores, who still hasn't called me. Instead, I call the salon to confirm she is still there, and I tell Beverly not to let Dolores leave.

"She's a beauty," Beverly says in her heavy Eastern European accent. I snort as I don't know what she could possibly see in the woman with split ends, dried hair, and the start of a skunk streak down her part.

But her eyes, something inside me whispers.

I enter the salon, walk past a woman waiting at the counter, and stop to speak to the girl working behind it.

"Hello, Mr. Fox," she purrs. She's eyeing me like she knows me, and I mean more than my name. *Shit*. Have I slept with her? If I haven't, she looks willing, but she's a bit too young for my taste. I'm trying to stick with the over-thirty crowd.

"Hello, Ginger." I smile, reading her name tag, and then turn to the woman next to me, feeling her eyes boring into the side of my head.

"Hey," I say, tipping up my chin, and turn back to Ginger. "I'm here to pick up Dolor…" Her name fades as I slowly turn back to the woman next to me. Leaning against the counter with her mile-long legs casually crossed and arms folded over her chest stands Dolores.

With silvered hair.

Which is so not my thing.

I like younger women, yet I can't stop looking at her. Her dark hair is nearly gone, the ends cut, and in its place is a shimmery sterling color interwoven with inky black and a hint of blue in gentle waves. I didn't even know how long her hair was as both times I've seen her it's been pulled up, but it cascades down her back. The silver makes her eyes brighter along with a touch of red lipstick accentuating the dip and curve of her pouty lips.

"Dolores?" I choke on her antiquated name, and then I swallow. She straightens and smooths her hand down her skinny jeans, which hug her hips and outline her hourglass shape. On her feet, she wears suede booties, and her top is more fitted than the too-large sweater she had on earlier. A deep V accentuates her breasts, hinting at the cleavage in the middle of the exposing material.

She's been holding out on me.

"You look…stunning."

I've never seen a woman turn so red, and watching the heat crawl across her skin makes me want to chase it. Where does it begin? Where will it end?

"You don't think it makes me look older?" She's worried about looking older when she just looks breathtaking.

"No. No, I definitely think you can pull this off."

She nods with a weak smile. The blush returns.

"Are you ready to go home?" I ask, hardly recognizing my own voice. She nods again and bends for two shopping bags near her feet.

"Here, allow me." I step around her, awkwardly brushing against her hands as we reach for the bags at the same time. We stop and turn to one another, our faces close, our lips not close enough. I swallow again as I find I want to kiss her. I want to taste those rich red lips and run my fingers through those multi-colored waves of silver and ink.

"Thank you," she says, slowly standing. My eyes follow hers. When did they start to sparkle? "For everything." Her voice is so sincere it nearly fills my hollow heart.

Dammit. What is she doing to me?

chapter 6

Confessions Of A Sort

[Dolores]

Garrett drives us back to the condo building but hardly speaks. His initial reaction to my appearance was shocking but sweet. His eyes wouldn't pull away from my hair, and I worried he really did hate it although he said otherwise.

You look stunning.

No one has ever said that to me.

Then I reconsider his opinion. What do I care if he likes my hair? Yet I couldn't stop running my fingers through the smooth texture or curl the ends around my index. It *felt* different along with appearing different. I never considered allowing the white to show, but the beautician convinced me I could wear it. *Own it.*

You have a young face, and silver is all the rage. She even convinced me the streaks of black won't make me look like Elvira but enhance the edgy style. I like it.

When we pull into the garage, Garrett removes my bags from his trunk and then carries them up to Denton's place. As I turn the key in the door, he finally speaks, blurting out his request.

"Take a walk with me."

I'm too startled to think, so I stare at him for a long moment.

"I need to take Wally for a walk." He clears his throat. "Come with us."

Ah, the dog. "Sure," I say. "Just let me put these things away."

"No problem. I want to change. I'll meet you out back in ten."

Wearing his power suit from this morning, he still looks just as handsome as he did hours ago. I wonder if he even expels any stress running his investment company. By three o'clock at the diner, I'm a sweaty mess and exhausted.

After closing the door, I take off my new booties and find my flip-flops since the day has heated up a bit. My long-sleeved shirt accommodates the coolness of the store, but with the afternoon warmth, I search for a regular T-shirt in my new wardrobe. I bought three of the same style in different colors. I tried to keep things within a strict budget and not splurge too much so I could pay Denton back when I return home.

The thought of going home doesn't settle well with me, but I'll have to return someday. *Soon-ish*.

For the time being, I have a few new clothes, and it really does make me feel better about being here—and about myself. The personal shopper told me nothing baggy.

You still have it all tight, lady, she teased. *Form-fitting was made for your body.*

I stroke a hand over my hip-hugging jeans and smooth down the casual T-shirt in solid white. I take one hesitant look at myself in the mirror in Denton's guest room and then head to the back entrance of the condo building where I find Garrett and Wally waiting for me.

Wally goes crazy upon seeing me, jumping up like he wants a hug. Thankfully, Garrett intercepts him before he gets his dirty little paws on my fresh new tee.

"Wally," Garrett admonishes, and then sheepishly adds, "I think he likes you."

"I bet he likes all the girls," I tease, reaching out hesitantly for the back of the slobbery canine's ears. I don't really like to touch animals, but there's something about the way Wally looks at me—almost begging me to scratch him—that I can't resist.

"Who's a sweet dog?" I say in my best false-impression of a dog lover. "Are you a sweet dog?"

Wally's tail wags so fiercely his whole backside wiggles.

"You're a pain in the ass, aren't you?" I'm still using the whiny tone as I insult him, and he continues to wag away. His owner laughs.

"Let's walk." Garret whistles and throws a tennis ball from a plastic stick out toward the water. Wally races after it, and we begin our stroll. Dutifully, Wally returns the ball, dropping it at his feet, and then looks up as if begging Garrett to toss it again.

"Did you have a good day?" It feels odd to ask him but also strangely appropriate. I don't know what else to say.

He shrugs, staring off after Wally. "The usual."

Earlier, he seemed excited to tell me about his company. Fox Investors. It sounds important, buying and selling and producing, but I don't really have the business mindset for products. I'm more into service, food service. Still, he didn't mention details, and I fully expected him to start bragging about all he's bought and sold and produced.

We continue in silence until Wally drops the gnawed ball before me.

"See? He likes you," Garrett teases. "He wants you to pick it up."

"I'm not touching that nasty thing. It's been in his mouth where he slobbered all over it." I shiver violently, exaggerating my repulsion. "He's probably been drinking out of your toilet all day and licking his—"

I don't get a chance to finish my thought before Garrett grips my wrist, forcing my palm open, and places the ball in it.

"Ewww." I shudder. I'm so frozen in gross-out horror I don't consider I can just drop it.

"My dog does not lick his own balls."

"He's male. Every guy likes to get himself off." I squeal. "Or is he like his dog-daddy, seeking pleasure from others?"

Garrett's eyes open wide. "And what would you know of my sex life? Not that I'm hiding anything. I'm a healthy man." He pats his stomach, which isn't the region of his body most healthy, I imagine.

"Oh, I bet. I heard you through the walls."

His pouty mouth pops open, and his eyes sparkle. "Yeah. What did you hear?"

I don't think I can repeat it, but with the teasing challenge in his eyes, I give in. "You know, the usual generic sex lines. *Right there.* Get it, get it. And yes, *yes*, *YES!*" My voice accentuates each positive cry, my chest heaving as I grow louder. My eyes close, emphasizing the false pleasure of some woman in his bed. Not that I think of him in his bed. Or a woman with him in it.

When my eyes open, I find Garrett watching me. The mocking gleam is now a flicker of flames.

"I can guarantee no woman sounds like that in my bed, nor do I call out such weak commands."

When did we step closer to one another?

"Incorrigible," I mutter. Another retort rests on my lips. What *do* women sound like in your bed? Only, I don't want to know. Not really. Not about other women.

"Incredible," he murmurs with a gleam to his light eyes as he watches me. I bet he is. *Do you want to be in his bed?* The tone of his voice merges with my thoughts, and for a moment, I wonder if he's asked me that. Our eyes lock in this weird way like we're trying to look into each other. Around the mind. Down the hatch. To the heart.

"If you don't want to hold his ball, just toss it. Don't tease me by playing with the ball." Garrett clears his throat. "I mean, him. *His* ball." Garrett chokes again. I look down at the nasty, ratty dog toy in my hand. Weakly, I throw the ball forward, and Garrett chuckles.

"Another reason I shouldn't be handling his ball."

Garrett's laughter sputters as he mutters *ballbuster* under his breath. He's behind me, and once again, I feel his presence like a warm blanket over my shoulders. He's close—*so close*—and I inhale. The salty air mixes with his fragrance. Bayberry and ocean—a heady combination.

He steps away too quickly when Wally returns for another toss. The sexual innuendos dissipate with the throw, falling flat in the wind.

I can't be attracted to Garrett. I'm not here for a hookup. I have Rusty. The thought makes me sad, though, because I don't really have him. And I'm no longer certain I want to consider having him. At all.

Garrett seems to sense my thoughts are a thousand miles away, and he begins to chatter as we walk. The weather. The ocean. The Los Angeles area. The sound of his voice and the trivial conversation give me the distraction I need from my thoughts.

After we return to the building, I thank him again for the ride and including me in his walk. He escorts me to Denton's door, and for half a second, I have a sense of him kissing me, like a good night kiss after a date. I don't think I've ever been kissed at the door, though. The only doors I've seen have been opened for me to walk in and follow a man for more than a kiss.

"I'll see you later," I say, disrupting my own displeasing thoughts, and Garrett tips his chin without a word. As I slowly close the door, willing myself not to ask him inside, I watch him until he's nothing more than a sliver behind the wood. He remains in the hall, watching me in return, our eyes locked in that strange manner until I finally shut Denton's door. Once closed, I lean on the barrier and tilt back my head.

Like a lingering bad dream, Rusty fills my thoughts again. What would he think of my hair? My new clothes? My comparison of him to the man across the hall?

He wouldn't care for any of it. He wouldn't even notice my hair. He'd remove my clothing too quickly to note I had new things. As for another man—I was his—although he'd never said as much. He'd never called me his; I'd made myself the label. And he certainly didn't belong to me. He belonged to many women.

Was that really good enough for me? Why do I think about these things?

You just shared an innocent walk with a flirty man who did something kind for you, that's why. It's nothing more, Dolores. Don't daydream.

I press off the door, shaking away my thoughts of Rusty…and Garrett.

I'm not much of a drinker. In fact, I don't indulge because of my father, but I find a bottle of wine and decide one glass won't hurt. After filling a bulbous crystal, I walk out to Denton's balcony. He explained to me how I could wirelessly connect my phone to his speaker system. With his step-by-step coaching and a frustrating phone call, I figured it out. Now, the rich voice of Otis Redding fills the balcony, telling the tale of a person who left his heart in Georgia and sits on a dock wasting time.

Am I wasting time? I wonder. I stare out at the waves crashing into each other. I have no idea what I'm doing here. It's been a week, and other than sleep, I've done nothing productive. Yet I find I'm content. I've never just sat, and for a moment, I feel relieved. *Is this what relaxing feels like?*

I also feel…pretty. My new cut and color flits in the breeze, and my clothes feel foreign but flirty. I've propped my feet up on the edge of the railing as I sip wine at four o'clock in the afternoon.

"Hey." Garrett's deep voice startles me. With his condo as the other half of this floor, his balcony is only a few feet from Denton's. "You like Otis?"

It takes me a moment to comprehend his meaning. The man. The song.

"I love this song. I love older music." I don't know why I offer the information. Rusty hates older tunes, preferring heavy metal and the like. He especially hates when I try to make him dance to classics or any music, for that fact.

"Like who?"

Etta James tops the list of those I rattle off while he smiles as I speak. He doesn't offer commentary; he just listens, so I keep talking.

"When I was a girl, my mother loved to dance. My father never took her, although she claims that's how they met. She'd make me dance with her in the living room. Swing dance was her favorite. Big band." I huff a laugh with the memory. "I was never very good, but she made me practice over and over. I never knew how much I loved it until I didn't do it anymore." The memory is sadder than I recall. As I grew older, the last thing I wanted to do was dance with my mother. I wanted to dance with boys instead. For years, I did, and then I fell into Rusty's bed after James. Neither man would dance with me.

"I'd love to dance again," I say, and then my head swings in the direction of Garrett who balances on his forearms against his balcony railing. "I have no idea why I told you that."

His mouth curls, and he tips his head. "I'm glad you did."

We look at one another for a moment like we did earlier on the beach and in the hall. We aren't exactly staring. We're just looking— eyes focused on eyes. *What does he see when he looks at me?*

"Let me…" Garrett begins, but then his phone rings. He frowns at something on the device and holds up a hand for me, signaling one minute. Then he turns back for his condo with the phone at his ear.

Let me come over, I foolishly thought he'd say, but there would be no reason for him to ask.

When he's gone for more than five minutes, I decide I've had enough of the day. Taking my wine and my music, I go back inside Denton's condo and head to bed.

+ + +

Garrett and I spend several days in a routine. Every day around four, he comes to the door and asks me to take a walk with him. Wally is growing on me. He gives me this doggie look with his strange blue eyes, and I pretend I'm offended, exasperated at the interruption to my not-so-busy life, but I always give in, secretly pleased to spend time with both of them. I don't want to admit it to myself, but I look forward to the time.

"Hey, can you dog sit for me?"

"What?" I've stopped in my tracks at the request as we walk along the beach.

"I have to go out of town for one night. My usual dog hotel can't take him on such short notice."

"There's a dog hotel?"

"Yeah." He looks at me like I have two heads for never hearing of such a thing, and I look back at him, equally puzzled at the concept. "So will you?"

"I can't dog sit."

"Why not?" Garrett asks a bit surprised, his eyes shifting sideways when we begin walking again.

Because I hate dogs, I want to remind him. I watch Wally race into the waves and then chase a sea gull, kicking up sand at his feet as he runs. Dirty. Smelly. Dog.

"It's only one night. I need a sitter."

"What do you do when you have one-night stands?"

Garrett scoffs. "I don't have them. Wally is my excuse not to stay."

"Interesting," I mutter, without realizing I've said it out loud. "What about a girlfriend?" I saw the blonde come and go from his apartment the first week I was here.

"Don't have one of those either." His voice lowers, and I glance over my shoulder at him.

"Ever?" I'd be shocked. He's too good looking, too smooth not to hold a woman's attention.

"Had a few. They didn't stick." He refuses to look at me, and I'm wondering if there's a story. Of course, I have my own. I loved James Harrington. He was my knight in chrome armor. The bad boy my dad disapproved of, and I gave everything to him although his heart was never mine. Then came Rusty, who was a rebound when James went for Evie. Eventually, Rusty became my regular. In a small town, there aren't many options once you're over thirty. I was thirty-seven when we began hooking up. The thought makes me shudder.

"Where are you going?" I ask, my voice laced with complaint. I shouldn't ask. I shouldn't care. I don't want to sound needy, but I look forward to four o'clock each day.

"Atlanta. Why? Want to go home?"

The question throws me off as much as him asking me to dog sit, but I don't stop walking this time although my feet stumble in the sand.

"I don't think I'm ready," I reply quietly. It's not that I don't want to go home ever again. I'm just not ready to return to who I was despite feeling a little lost in California. With Mother gone. With the condition of the diner. With Magnolia's crumbling house. Rusty. My life feels like it's all been for naught, and I'm relieved when Garrett doesn't ask for an explanation.

"Still searching for the ruby slippers, Dorothy," he mocks, and it takes me a moment to register the reference. "I get it."

He finally stops walking and looks at me. "But the yellow brick road doesn't always lead to the Emerald City. And Dorothy had the power to make decisions all along."

He's quiet as he looks off in the distance.

"My granddad invested in me, my future, and I ran with it. Searching for my own ruby slippers in a masculine, non-threatening, I like women way." He smiles, and I chuckle at the clarification. "I try to remember his gift of a chance, his gift of faith in me, and I never want to let him down. Well, at least, the memory of him. So I understand the idea of chasing after something, even if it isn't clear what you're looking for."

The words sink in, but something stands out. *Let him down.* Am I letting others down by not returning? I shake the thought, reminding myself how much I've done to support Mother, Magnolia, and the diner. Even Rusty. It's time for me to invest in myself…only I don't know what that means.

"My grandmother took a chance on me, too. The diner was hers. When I finished college, she gave it to me as a graduation present. I was the first woman with a degree in the family." *I'm just not sure the diner is the right fit for me anymore.* Fear shivers down my spine as I admit the thought to myself.

Garrett's eyes open wide. "Wow. I was raised by my mother and three sisters. They all went to college."

He isn't insulting me, just stating the difference between us.

"Three sisters. Whoa."

"I know. Each one thought they were my mother even though they are all younger than me."

"And they've made you the man you are today," I mock.

"Something like that." He chuckles, but it lacks humor in response to my teasing. We continue walking, heading back toward the condo, and my heart sinks a little. I've noticed feeling the same sensation each time our walks near the end.

"Okay," I mutter.

"Okay, what?" he asks, tossing the mangled ball for Wally one more time before we reach the door.

"I'll do it. I'll dog sit."

Garrett's face lights up like a kid on Christmas, and he leans forward to kiss me on the cheek.

"You're the best," he whispers as he pulls back, and I snort.

"Yeah, right." He probably says that to all his dog sitters. Still, my face heats where the imprint of his lips linger despite the swift brush on my skin.

Dog sitting? What have I gotten myself into?

chapter 7

Dog Sitting And Some Petting

[Dolores]

Despite worrying about Wally running away from me and having to tell Garrett I lost his dog, the time was spent no differently than what I do every day. I binge watch television, read a book, and try to remember to eat. Garrett gave me a quick tour of his place before he left. It's a mirror replica of Denton's. Open concept kitchen-dining-living room with double doors leading to a balcony off the living room. Three bedrooms, one of which is an office. Master bedroom with another set of double doors but no walk-out balcony, only a decorative railing.

I'm not supposed to let Wally on the couch, but when he hops up next to me and puts his head on my thigh, I don't kick him off.

"That's what you get for asking me to dog sit," I mumble aloud as if Garrett can hear me all the way in Atlanta.

My hand finds Wally's head, and I stroke his soft fur. The motion is strangely soothing. I doze on the couch, the television still on. The monstrosity nearly fills the wall adjacent to Denton's apartment, and my mind drifts through everything and nothing. Eventually, I decide I should sleep in a bed even though I told myself I'd stay on the couch. Garrett told me I could stay in whichever bedroom I was most comfortable. Out of curiosity, I wander into his room.

His dressers are masculine: one is a chest of drawers, the other a low double set with another large television over it. The rustic black wood tone surprises me, considering his flair for expensive, sleek, and modern. Two nightstands flank the king-sized bed. He's neat for a man. Unlike Rusty's place, nothing is out of place, on the floor, or covering the dressers. It's also extremely clean, almost fresh, with the bed made and vacuum marks on the carpet. Rusty's bed is constantly disheveled. The floor remains littered with clothing and an alcohol bottle or two, plus maybe a glass and an ashtray rest on the rickety furniture. I shiver with the comparison. The contrast between the two men is one end of a spectrum compared to the other. I always thought I wanted the bad boy until I had a few. Somehow, I sense Garrett has bad boy tendencies, but he just disguises them under a suit.

Opening his bedside table confirms my suspicion. Sex toys.

An eye mask. Some silk blindfolds. A box of condoms. A set of metal balls. A vibrator.

I've seen nothing to suggest Garrett swings both ways, though I don't know him well enough. Considering the object is pink-tipped with rabbit ears, with one longer than the other, I'm assuming he uses this to pleasure his women friends. Not one-night stands. Not girlfriends. So maybe friends with benefits?

Sex partners? I'm good with that.

The thought makes me a little sad. I'm tired of a sex partner, but I don't even think I could handle a friend with benefits. I'm emotionally drained in all aspects of my life, so it would be nice to have an emotional connection with someone. Sex partners doesn't exactly have that kind of ring to it.

I close the drawer and coast my fingers over the dark pattern of the duvet. The material is soft, and based on how Garrett dresses, I imagine he sleeps in only top-of-the-line sheets. Testing my theory, I draw back the duvet. The cool sheet under my palm feels nice, tempting, and my skin gets goose bumps. I wonder how the fabric would feel everywhere.

"Don't look," I mutter to Wally who lies on the floor near the bedroom door. I strip out of my clothes, making the room a little less sterile, set my cell phone on the nightstand, and then slip into Garrett's bed.

"Nice," I murmur, drawing the coverings up to my neck. My legs swish, and my arms spread. I'm making a snow angel across his sheets, relishing in the way the material kisses my skin. It's decadent like chocolate drizzled over a strawberry. My nipples peak, and my fingers twitch. I think of the drawer of toys. I don't know where any of them have been, but the thought alone heightens my imagination. My palms flatten on my belly, skimming over my hypersensitive skin until they reach my breasts. Cupping each swollen globe, I squeeze until my fingertips find my nipples and pinch.

A moan escapes, and I hear Wally shuffle in his sleep by the door.

My hands lower, skating down my stomach again. My abs quiver, and my lower belly pools with flutters. Finding the curl of coarse hair at the apex of my legs, I stroke lower, heading farther south until my cell phone goes off. I retract my hands like I've been caught with them where they shouldn't be. My head rolls over the luscious pillow, and I check the caller ID on the screen.

"Garrett." I exhale his name as I answer, drawing out the harsh syllables in frustration.

"Dolores." He chuckles. "Whatcha up to?"

My head falls back to the pillow, and I try to regulate my breathing.

"I'm in bed," I say, my voice still shaking and a touch too high pitched.

"Oh. Sorry to wake you. I just wanted to…" He pauses a beat. "Whose bed?" His voice drops.

I can't answer him.

"Dolores, are you being a naughty doggie sitter?"

His choice of words makes me giggle. I've been caught with my hand nearly in the cookie jar, and shame washes over me.

"You know I have doggie cams." His tone draws serious, and I panic, rolling my head left and right, searching for a hidden camera.

"Wally's fine," I offer, my voice a squeak. *Can he see me? Does he know what I was about to do in his bed?*

"I'm sure he is. And you know I'm teasing, right? About the cameras."

My eyes close. "You suck," I mutter.

"Hmm…only if you ask me nicely." He has no idea what his suggestion does to me, and my fingers slip over my bare thigh under the now-warm sheets. Tenderly, I stroke my inner thigh—so close, but not quite where I need.

"Dolores." His voice dips when I don't reply. "Whose bed are you in?"

I swallow the lump in my throat. "Yours."

Garrett groans through the phone, and my fingers trace closer to the prize at the center of me.

"What are you doing in my bed, stunner?" He has no idea what his words do to me. *You look stunning*, his rugged voice whispers in my memory. I can't tell him what I'm doing. I can't tell him how close I am to touching myself. How it's been so long since I've felt this way. Desirable. Pretty. Turned on.

I don't answer with anything other than a moan. I mean it to signal I can't speak, but he groans in response, and I hear a shift through the phone.

"Are you touching yourself?" His voice cracks, and I immediately say, "No." My fingers withdraw, but my sex pulses, aching for attention. The sheets suddenly feel scratchy, weighty, wanting. I spread my legs, and the material falls through the valley I've made. Cool cotton caresses my inner thighs, resting over a part of me which feels like it's beating faster than my heart.

"Are you thinking of me touching you?" He swallows. "In my bed."

God, yes. My fingers return to my thigh, curving over my prickly skin. Another shuffle whispers through the phone as if he's removing something. A shirt. A sheet.

"Tell me where you are," he demands, his voice deeper, richer.

"I'm in your bed."

"Give me more details."

"I'm in the center—"

"Dolores," he drags out my name, and I'm forced to respond.

"Naked."

"Fuck," he mumbles. *Was that a belt clanking in the background?*

My fingers dip, stroking over my wet folds, which pulse after just one stroke. It won't be enough, and I continue circling. Garrett's breath increases in my ear. The silence ticks between us a beat.

"Tell me more," he commands. "What are you doing?"

"I'm touching myself." My eyes close as I admit the embarrassing truth, but the sultry sound of his voice, the commanding tone, and the hitch of his breath urge me onward. I can't stop.

He moans into the phone. "How does it feel? Details."

"Wet," I tease. "Warm," I purr. "So good." I don't recognize my voice. I've never sounded like this with anyone else. I've never done this with someone else.

"Fuck," he groans again, and the hum forces me to rub harder, stroke faster. "Stunner, are you about to come on my sheets?"

"I…" My breath catches. I'm so close. "I think so," I mutter, a little surprised with myself, surprised he's listening to me do what I'm doing. *So close.*

"Do it," he demands, and I let go, moaning incomprehensible things into the phone as my head tips, and my fingers delve. My release drags out, slow and sweet, and long overdue. I fall back to the pillow, eyes closed with exhaustion, and I hear Garrett grunt. As I settle down from my high, I giggle, feeling naughty. *Did he just get off too?*

"Are you misbehaving in Atlanta?" I admonish without a trace of disapproval in my voice. *Did we just have phone sex?* I slap my dirty hand on my head, catching a whiff of what I've done.

"So misbehaving. I think you need to punish me when I return." He chuckles, deep and satiated in my ear, and I roll to my side, inhaling his pillowcase. Bayberry and woodsy. *Garrett.*

Oh God. I'll never be able to face him.

"Hey, Dolores."

"Yeah." My voice remains dreamy, giddy even, as I swallow back my mortification.

"I wish I was a Wizard." His voice lowers again, and my brows pinch.

"Why?" I wonder, tugging the Garrett-scented sheet over my shoulder and relaxing into the comfort of his bed.

"I'm thinking there's no place like home right now."

Home. I'm not sure I know where that is anymore, but his sentiment is very sweet.

chapter 8

Classics On The Big Screen

[Garrett]

After a weather delay in Atlanta, I finally arrive home to find my condo empty. It wasn't like I thought Dolores would still be in my bed even though there is such a thing as wishful thinking. I actually didn't know what I'd do if I found her between my sheets, especially after my meeting in Atlanta. *Damn Denton.* He put all kinds of ideas in my head upon my visit.

However, Dolores doesn't seem like a clinger, and last night certainly wasn't any contract. We got off together. *So what?* Although, I admit I don't think of it quite so flippantly. Despite my history, phone sex isn't normally my forte. And Dolores seems different.

I struggle with my tie as I head to my bedroom. The sheets are clean and not the same color as the ones when I left. For some reason, my heart drops a little at the thought. Not that I want dirty sheets, but I wanted the evidence she'd been in my bed. The scent of her. The imprint of her.

I walk to the glass doors of my room and notice a woman racing down the beach with a chocolate lab jogging after her. She stops short and bends over laughing as Wally continues running, not able to stop his trajectory with his speed. He sprints back to Dolores, and she jumps left and then right. Still laughing, she takes off jogging again. Wally follows at her heels.

I haven't heard Dolores laugh since I've met her. Hell, I've hardly seen a real smile. She's always giving me false ones or weak ones. I wonder if she smiled last night. I still can't believe she did what she did—that *we* did what we did.

My lips curl as I recall her voice—breathy, dreamy, satiated. I quickly strip as I watch her chase Wally and then Wally chase her. It's an image I could easily get off to, but I'd prefer to see her up close. After changing into jeans and a T-shirt, I head out to the beach.

"Hey," I call out.

"Hi," she says, out of breath. She stops short before me, but her body vibrates with the energy of racing Wally. She wears black yoga pants and a sweatshirt. Her cheeks are flushed, and she looks beautiful.

"Seems like you two have become fast friends." Dolores bends at the waist, her breathing heavy.

"The only thing fast is him. I can't keep up. I'm so out of shape." From the shape I see, I'd disagree. Her legs are long and firm. Her hips hold just the right curve, and her ass—heart-shaped. She's a dream in those form-fitting pants.

"Looks like you're doing a decent job."

"Decent?" she mocks. "Do you know how hard it is to dog sit? Watching Netflix and reading a book. It's difficult work." She looks up at me, and the blue in her eyes shimmers. She doesn't look as hollow as she did when I first met her. Her lips curve into a genuine smile as she teases me, and the desire to kiss her comes over me.

"You're all right." I shrug. She stands, fists coming to her hips, where she juts one out.

"All right? I thought I was the best," she states, recalling what I said when I asked her to dog sit. Her voice lowers as she twists her lips. I can't help myself, and I step closer to her. My fingers reach for loose silver hair whipping over her cheeks in the breeze.

"That has yet to be determined." My tone drops as well. Her breath hitches, and then Wally squeezes between us. Dolores steps back, and her arms flail as she stumbles. I reach for her but miss.

"Ballbuster," I mutter to the dog as I reach down to pet him. "Are you turning traitor on me?" A lick across my face tells me he still loves me, but he's got a crush on Dolores. I might, too.

"How was Atlanta?" she asks, the playfulness of her voice receding. Atlanta. It's always interesting to go there. Guilt washes over me as I was close to home but didn't take the time for a visit. My mother has understood over the years. When my granddad passed, it was hard to return to River City, not to mention my sisters are always wondering why I'm not married or at least procreating with all my sexual waywardness as they call it. No children, thank you. Wally is my baby.

"Atlanta was business as usual." Though that isn't quite true. I've been thinking of a new venture. Something I haven't done before. It would be more than investing in others. It's an investment in myself, actually. *For my retirement*, I say although I have no intention of retiring anytime soon. I could, though. I have plenty of money, but it's not about the money—at least, not in this case. This would be all mine. I don't know what I'd do with myself if I didn't have a business to run. Netflix and books all day are not on my agenda. I should tell her I saw Denton in Atlanta, but I don't. I don't know why, but I hold the information in for another day. Maybe I don't want her thinking of home. Not yet.

Dolores nods, and we slowly follow Wally back to the condo. A tense silence falls between us when I don't want it to be awkward. Having an orgasm in my bed without me is unusual, but nothing I'd condemn her for doing. Still, she's quiet as we stroll.

"Thanks again for watching Wally. I really appreciate it."

"It was nothing," she says, waving a dismissive hand. Her arms have returned to wrapping around her middle.

"Was it fun?" I tease.

"Let's not push it." Push it is exactly what I want to do, so I ask what I've been thinking since last night.

"I'd like to take you out. A thank you for dog sitting." *It's not a date*, I tell myself.

Dolores peers over at me, her brows pinching. "You don't have to do that. It was no trouble, really."

"I want to," I say, stopping her with a hand on her upper arm.

"Is this about last night? Because we don't have to do this." Her voice sounds weak, her tone one of defeat. Her eyes can't meet mine, and she brushes a wayward hair behind her ear.

"No." *Yes.* "Let's go out. It will be fun." I've noticed she doesn't do much. She's in the California playland, and she hasn't been anywhere yet. The night will be unseasonably warm for November, and I have the perfect place in mind for her.

+ + +

I arrive at her door at six o'clock. It's growing dark, and the bonus of early nightfall is the timing of where we are going. I've packed a simple picnic, not finding much in my fridge. Dolores doesn't look like she eats, and she's mentioned forgetting the necessity. Her cut cheekbones attest to good bone structure, but she could use a little meat on her.

When we pull up to the park, Dolores leans forward, squinting out the front window.

"Is that a movie screen?"

"It is," I say, stepping out of the car and rounding it to open her door. Her eyes still focus on the large screen cutting into the night sky. After helping her from the car, I walk to the trunk to remove blankets and a bag.

"We're watching a movie in the park," she says as if questioning it while confirming it at the same time.

"You said you liked classic music, so I thought you might like classic movies. Tonight's showing is *It Happened One Night.*" I hesitate as we walk. Maybe this wasn't such a good idea.

"With Claudette Colbert and Clark Gable?"

"Are you familiar with this one?" My shoulders lighten a little with the possibility.

"It's one of my favorites."

Twisting to peer at her, I'm rewarded with a genuine smile. Not the forced one. Not the sheepish one, but a full watt, teeth exposed, red-lipped smile.

"Are you okay?" she asks as I stumble on my own feet.

"I'm good," I mutter, my heart thumping. Huh. *What was that all about?*

We find a spot although it's farther back from the screen than I'd like and spread our blanket. Dolores sits, eager to see what's in my bag.

"It's the best I could do." I don't want to add *with short notice*. I typically plan these things ahead of time. Expensive wine. Imported cheese. A catered dinner. Although, on second thought, I've never done something like this before. Knowing Dolores isn't impressed by extravagance, I brought a bottle of wine from a Napa winery, a variety of cheeses, a box of crackers, and a sausage roll. The collection looks weak once I have it all laid out.

"This is perfect," Dolores murmurs as she takes the red wine I offer her, and I relax a little.

"What should we drink to?" I ask, holding up my glass. "In my family, we always drink to something on special occasions."

Dolores's face falls a little, and she holds her plastic wine cup with both her hands. "Sounds like a nice tradition." She pauses a second and then lifts her cup to mine. "To dog sitting."

I chuckle. That isn't what I had in mind, so I add, "To stunning company."

Her face heats like it did the day she transformed at the salon, and I want to trace each blush of pink on her skin.

"You're very charming sometimes," she says before taking a sip. Then she redirects the conversation. "Oh, this is good."

"Do you like wine?"

"I'm not really a connoisseur, but I won't turn down a good glass." Her lips twist while she considers something, and then adds, "My father was an alcoholic. A bad one. Not that there's a good one, but he was an evil man. Watching him and then my mother hide in drink turned me off to heavy drinking."

I stare at her. We've mainly kept our conversations casual, but every once in a while, she throws in something personal. Not for the first time do I note she seems like a well of secrets.

"My dad ditched us when I was eight. Guess he didn't want a wife and kids anymore. My granddad helped my mother raise us. He was a major influence in my life."

Dolores smiles one of her weak smiles. "What did he teach you?"

"How to go after what I wanted. Do things he didn't do."

"He didn't teach you to be a man?" she teases.

"Nope, remember three sisters. I constantly heard how to treat women, how to act, and was reprimanded if I didn't behave accordingly."

"Do they live around here?"

"We're scattered. Jane is in Chicago. Mae is in Michigan. Lindee still lives near my mom in River City, Missouri."

"Missouri?" She laughs. "I thought you were from here."

"No one is really from here. I moved to California after I graduated from Missouri State University."

She claps once, another laugh escaping.

"What's so funny about that?"

Sobering, she says, "Nothing. Absolutely nothing."

Suddenly, the movie screen lights up, and an old-fashioned countdown begins. The opening credits roll, and we settle into snacking while we sip the wine and watch the classic black and white movie.

At some point, we move closer to each other, slipping the second blanket over our legs to ward off a chill in the air. My arms support me, resting at my sides, with one hand behind Dolores. If I twitch my thumb, I can rub her ass, but I don't. I don't want to make this anything more than it is. Dolores and I are becoming friends. It's not that I don't have female friendships, but I tend to ruin them by stepping back or fucking them. The thought reminds me of Alicia. I haven't called her in a week although she's been burning up my text messages.

Dolores yawns beside me.

"Tired?" It isn't late. Maybe she's bored.

"Just comfy," she says, lowering herself to her side. Her elbow bent, she perches her head on her hand to continue watching the movie. She laughs occasionally, and I find I like the sound. *I like her.* The emotion isn't unheard of. I've liked many women in my time. Heather Robinson. Tracy Dean. One was my high school sweetheart and the other, my college one. Both wanted a hometown boy to settle down with while I wanted to be more than River City. Then there was Kathryn Cole. I shiver at the memory of her.

Without thinking, I scoot over and tug at Dolores's forearm, forcing her head to rest on my thigh.

"What are you doing?" she mumbles toward the screen.

"Making you more comfortable." Or maybe I'm making myself comfortable. I want to touch her somehow. Holding her hand doesn't work well in our positions on the blanket. With her down on her side, this seemed like the best solution. My fingers find the ends of her hair and gently stroke the tips. Occasionally, I brush down her back. She doesn't flinch away from the caress, but she doesn't give in to it either. As the movie draws to an end, the credits roll, and people clap. Dolores remains still.

"Dolores," I softly speak. My hand risks combing through her hair at the side of her head.

Well.

"Dolores, sweetheart, the movie's over." I gently shake her shoulder, and her eyes flip open. Seeing the screen go black and a spotlight snap on to guide movie watchers for the exit, she sits upright.

"Goodness, I fell asleep," she groggily states the obvious. "I'm so sorry about that."

"Don't worry about it." I liked her head on my thigh. Her comfort. Her closeness. "Not sleeping well?"

She shrugs noncommittally as we gather up our things. We walk in silence back to the car, and I open her door. On the ride back to the condo, her head rolls on the headrest, and she watches me as I drive. Her hands are tucked between her thighs, and once again, I want to touch her.

"Like what you see?" I tease.

"You are kind of pretty, but you already know that," she playfully snarks. "But you're also sweet. Tonight was really nice of you."

"I fed you wheat crackers with Gouda." I scoff.

"I didn't find anything wrong with that."

My palm sweats on the steering wheel. "Well, don't be ruining my reputation. Tin Man, remember." I pat my chest with a flat hand.

"Your secret is safe with me," she whispers, her eyes drifting toward the front windshield.

Too quickly, we arrive at the condo, and I'm walking Dolores to Denton's. As we stand outside, I lean my shoulder against the wall while she unlocks the door. Suddenly, I can't take it anymore. I drop the blankets and the bag to the floor. The sudden noise in the otherwise quiet hall draws her attention to the objects.

"Dolores," I say, and her eyes drift up to me. "Thanks for going out with me."

Her head tilts, and her lips twist like she's thinking. My thumb comes to the corner of her mouth, and I tug the tender skin. The pad of my thumb rubs over her lower lip.

"We should kiss," I say, sounding awkward and fifteen instead of fifty. "I mean, we gave each other orgasms. We should at least kiss. Once."

"I was hoping you'd forget about that," she mumbles, her eyes leaving mine.

"No chance." Last night was sexy as hell, and my dick jolts at the thought of her getting off in my bed. I only wish I had seen it, felt her while she went off.

"Technically, we gave ourselves orgasms," she corrects, and I chuckle. I step closer to her, cupping her cheeks so she has to look at me.

"I don't think this is a good idea," she whispers while her eyes lower to my lips, and her tongue slides out to licks hers.

"I think this is the best idea," I retort, watching the roll of her throat.

"It's not," she mouths.

The brakes hit. "Why?"

"You have the blonde, and I have Rusty."

The blonde? Alicia? I'll speak with her tomorrow. "The sex partner?" My voice cracks. I don't want her to have a sex partner. I don't want her having a Rusty. *Is that his name?*

"Yes."

"No," I reply. *No, no more sex partner.* Then I have another thought. "Why isn't he here with you?" Dolores tugs back from my grasp on her face.

"Because we aren't like that."

"What do you mean?"

"We…we don't spend time together like that."

I stare at her, questioning.

"We don't exactly date, okay? We just…we just have sex," she huffs, her eyes closing and her face heating. This isn't the flush from a blush but irritation. Embarrassment.

What the fuck?

"What if someone wanted to date you? What if someone wanted to spend time with you?"

Her eyes lower. "I'm not looking to add more partners who can't commit."

Can't commit? Does he fuck others on the side? I might not be single-minded, but I'm loyal. Everyone knows up front, so I'm never accused of being unfaithful. I'd never cheat on someone. Not to mention, I don't want to join some list for Dolores. She doesn't strike me as the type to have more than one partner anyway.

"Kiss me," I say again, pushing her to give in. My hands return to her cheeks. "Just one." I'm not asking her to marry me, just for her to give me an end of the night taste.

"Garrett," she exhales.

"This isn't Kansas, Dorothy. Kiss me."

She laughs good-naturedly, and I need to capture the sound. I'm not sure who stepped into who first, but my lips meet hers, drawing her into mine. Our mouths cover each other, tugging slowly at one another and dragging out the tender brushstrokes of connection. My lips trace her mouth, savoring the taste of her.

Then she opens. Her breasts crush my chest as her arms wrap around my neck. Her tongue delves forward, the thick muscle tangling with mine as her body presses flush against me. She's kissing me back like a starving woman. She's kissing the fuck out of me.

My dick jumps. He wants inside her. Our joined mouths won't be enough, and just as my hands start to roam the outline of her body, she pulls back abruptly, releasing me. I fall against the hallway wall, stunned and breathless. She doesn't look at me. Instead, she turns for her open door and steps inside. I spin to follow her when the door closes in my face.

What the hell just happened?

chapter 9

Kiss And Miss

[Dolores]

I shouldn't have kissed him back.

Shaky fingers come to my lips as I slump against the door. My body vibrates with desire. My sex screams for attention. A tremor ripples up my center.

I couldn't help myself, I argue. I don't know who stepped first, but once his mouth brushed mine, it's like he unleashed a suppressed beast, and I took his mouth, hoping to devour him.

I haven't kissed like that in years.

I haven't *been* kissed like that in years either.

Rusty's kisses are open-mouthed and sloppy, and his lips too wet, often from drinking. I don't like to kiss him, and I allow it to last only seconds. I'm not a shy sexual partner. I take what I want, which is one thing Rusty appreciates about me. Unfortunately, the relationship stops at sex. No emotions. No friendship. Just sex. And I thought I could handle that when it started, but after ten years, I'd like something more. My brother just got a second chance with the girl of his dreams. I want my turn, only there's no boy of mine.

When James Harrington fell for Evie, I lost faith in men. As the boy next door and forbidden fruit, he was my first everything, but he wasn't loyal to me. My trust in the opposite sex was already on shaky ground because of my father and his unfaithfulness to my mother. I didn't know what a stable relationship should look like. George Harrington and his wife, Elaina, are my image of a perfect marriage, but even they had issues, especially when it came to their son and me getting caught in his bed when we were eighteen.

My thoughts jump back to Garrett.

Is he still standing on the other side of the door? I'm afraid to look through the peephole.

Garrett is a player, like the other men in my life. I've seen the blonde although I haven't seen her lately. Still, I have no reason to believe Garrett isn't without someone in his life. Like I told him in the car, he's rather pretty. The wave to his hair. The scruff on his jaw. His light brown eyes. He's perfect—to look at.

Would I trust my heart with him?

Absolutely not.

Although he was sweet tonight, allowing me to rest my head on his thigh. His fingers traced down my spine and twirled in my hair. For a moment, I forgot we were friends. Only neighbors, actually. His kind gesture was a way to thank me for watching his dog. It wasn't a date. It wasn't anything more than what it was—a movie in the park. A classic black and white movie on a dark fall evening with a spontaneous picnic. A romantic comedy about a girl who runs away and the man who needs a news story. It happens to be one of my favorites. The decision to take me to such a place, have such an experience, was thoughtful and considerate.

But it didn't mean anything.

Garrett takes care of women. His sisters were excellent teachers. Their tutelage of him has paid off. The details in scheduling my shopping trip and the salon experience are a testament. His respectful distance each time we take a walk is another. Tonight, Garrett was a gentleman beneath the good looks and playboy status.

And then he kissed me.

Finally, I press off the door. Not one to typically drink alone, I head for the unfinished bottle of wine I opened before I dog sat. I turn off the lights and press the bottle to my aching chest. Falling onto the couch, I stare out the dark balcony doors. I'm suddenly exhausted.

Tired of Rusty Miller. *Why isn't he here with you?*

I miss my mother.

She didn't approve of Rusty and our arrangement. Her bitterness toward men suffocated me.

I loved a man once, she said. It wasn't my father.

Men are meant to disappoint, she added.

Sometimes, I think she meant my brother, who took off at eighteen and never looked back. I didn't fault him, though, because he had his reasons. Sometimes, I faulted her. She should have stood up for us better. On the other hand, she was one of my best friends, and I sympathized with her plight.

The duplicity splits me in two most days, reminding me I'm tired of my life.

+ + +

The next day, I awake with a new outlook. I can't keep rotating between the bed and couch. I need to see Los Angeles and the surrounding community, so I devote the following days to an adventure. Finding the courage to use the Uber app, I travel the city. The Chinese Theatre. The stars on Hollywood Blvd. The Santa Monica Pier. I take in the sites of the entertainment playland.

I miss the four o'clock dog walks on purpose. Instead, I take long walks on the beach in the early morning hours.

I consider calling my cousin, Tommy Carrigan, and his wife, whom I haven't met.

But I don't.

It's late November, and Thanksgiving is in a few days, but I won't be home. There's no one to cook for without Mother. Denton says he'll take Magnolia to the Harrington's. Rusty and I don't celebrate holidays. There would be nowhere to go.

Despite days of avoiding Garrett and travels around the West Coast city, I'm sad. Mostly, I'm terribly lonely. It's as if I've never left Georgia. Everything I've done the past few days I've done by myself, just like at home.

Then one afternoon, I see the diner. An old railcar tucked off the popular path. The neon sign advertising its name radiates bright pink in the gloom of the day. From the outside, I can see the booths along the steamy windows and the thin counter with stools before it. It's similar yet different from my place. The sharp fluorescent lights inside scream *come on in* like the welcome sign by the door. I bet it's warm. California has swung back to cold, and I shiver in my sweater. I forgot my coat in the condo.

A waitress walks the length of the place. She wears the stereotypical waitress outfit in turquoise, playing into the persona of the restaurant—a 1950s dining car. The menu board proudly displays all their specialties and features of the day. The place looks fresh, sparkly, and clean.

Moisture fills my eyes, and I realize it's raining. Rivulets of water stream down the outside of the windows before me. The condensation blooms on the inside of the panes. The droplets tap in a steady rhythm on the chrome exterior of the building, and the sound mesmerizes me.

Then I feel him. The rain that has been pelting my body and stinging my cheeks for I don't know how long disappears as an umbrella covers me. His breath hits my damp hair as his body stands near mine. I hear him shuffle behind me. Something heavy and warm covers my shoulders. My eyes close for a second, melting into the comfort, but the water continues to leak from my lids.

"Sweetheart, whatcha doing out here?" he asks, but I don't know how to answer.

I have no idea what I'm doing anymore.

chapter 10

Tears

[Garrett]

"Sweetheart," I whisper, stalking up behind her in the pouring rain. Her hair lays plastered to her head, dark and dripping. Her too-large sweater hangs below her hands, nearly to her knees with the weight of the water. Her suede boots are soaked as rain puddles around her feet.

What is she doing out here?

I glance up at the building before us. *On the Go* is an old railcar turned diner. If I hadn't been aimlessly staring out the window of my hired car, thinking of her, while we wound down this side street, I would have missed her standing on the walk, melting under the rain.

The past few days have sucked dog balls. Dolores has completely ignored me, avoiding our daily walks. It surprised me at first how much this agitated me. I didn't realize how much I looked forward to four o'clock each afternoon until she wasn't there, rolling her eyes as she pretended to be inconvenienced in her busy day. I like her sass.

She's been avoiding my phone calls as well. I've missed the teasing banter and flirtatious innuendos of our nightly chats. It's been surprisingly refreshing to talk on the phone, but her current silence cuts deep.

I hate it.

Because I miss her.

She didn't seem to hear me as I approached, covering her with an umbrella. Her attention remains fixated on the diner before us. *She's so wet*, and I don't mean that in a sexual tease. I struggle to remove my suit coat even though I know it won't be enough to warm her up. She's shivering.

"Sweetheart," I repeat. "Whatcha doing out here?"

She remains silent, misty air emitting from her nose. Her lips are bluish, and her skin looks pale.

How long has she been standing here?

It's purely by chance we turned down this street. Traffic is a beast. People cannot remember how to drive in heavy rain. The day is dark because of the storm, matching my mood. I'm wound tight as a deal I've made wasn't going as planned. The initial investment was minimal but enough to get the product started in a mass-production plant. On the first day, the equipment stalled, and maintenance isn't coming together to repair the line. I'm furious although it isn't directed solely at the management team.

I've bounced from my office to the plant, so I have a driver today, and I was headed back to the city. I'd spent too many nights home alone, thinking of Dolores and our kiss. Her mouth is made for sin, and I realized that the second we separated. She's a genie in a bottle, and I want to let her out. I'll give her anything she wishes.

The sensation had been coming on slowly. A sense of not liking to be separated from her. Our daily walks haven't been nearly enough. I like hanging out with her. Then we had our date, and the kiss fucked it all up. I had planned to meet up with a few friends downtown tonight, hoping to blow off some steam. I don't intend to fuck a woman. I cut off Alicia the day after Dolores and I kissed although, in hindsight, I dropped Alicia weeks prior to that night.

"It looks like my diner," she finally speaks, interrupting my thoughts, and a breath I'd been holding for days releases, like setting free the oxygen trapped in a balloon. "But not really."

I want to reach for her and draw her to me. Her shivering freaks me out, but I'm afraid she'll shatter into a million pieces if I touch her.

"How does yours look?" I work to keep my voice steady. I don't want her to stop speaking, even if all she does is describe her place.

"It's old. Worn down. Like me."

"You aren't old," I say with a chuckle lacking humor. Taking on a more serious tone, I add, "You aren't worn down, either."

"My diner has this drab paneling that's cracked in places, and tile floors that don't look clean even after I scrub them. The chrome is dull. The kitchen dated." Her voice fades, but I sense her mentally checking off the things she doesn't like about her business. "I never had the money to fix it up. I didn't consider it run-down until Denton returned."

That bastard. What did he know? He told me he hadn't been home since he left at eighteen. What a way to treat his family.

"He's right, though. It's dated. Like me. Like my clothes. My hair. My everything."

"Dolores," I say, softening my voice as I touch her chin and force her to look at me. That's when I notice the tears streaming down her cheeks like the rainwater against the windows of *On the Go*.

"Why are you crying?" My voice remains low, level, concerned. She seems so strong to me, so I don't understand.

"I'm crying?" she asks. "I can't remember the last time I cried. I didn't even cry when my mother died."

Shit. Shit. *Shit.* Her mother's death, which she's hardly mentioned, must have been weighing on her more than she thought. She's been holding it in. Then her brother's comments about her business. And this trip across the country. No wonder she was a hot mess when I first saw her. Okay, Wally may have been part of the issue as well, but still…

"You haven't cried about your mother?" I ask, and the saddest blue eyes I've ever seen look up at me. Deep lakes and drowning oceans did not compare to the depths of those hollow eyes and the sorrow filling them. She shakes her head, and I can't take the distance any longer. My arm envelops her, drawing her against me.

"I miss my mother," she says into my chest, and then the real shaking begins. Soul-rattling sobs occur against my chest. Her hands come up to cover her face, and I struggle to balance the umbrella over her while keeping my coat on her shoulders and my arm around her back.

"Shh," I soothe. "It's okay to miss her." I don't know how to comfort her other than to kiss her rain-soaked hair. Waterworks on a woman is my weakness, but she's not using them to play me. She's not crying because we're breaking up or I canceled a date. She's legit crying over something that has nothing to do with me—and I'm heartbroken for her.

The rain continues, and the pelting spray near my ankles has soaked my pant legs. Dolores continues to shiver and sob against me, and I realize I need to do something.

"Fuck it," I say as I collapse the umbrella, feeling the downpour cascade over both of us. I scoop her up and jostle her once to get a better hold on her. "Hold on, sweetheart," I tell her, and she wraps her arms around my neck. Her cold nose nuzzles against my skin.

I walk us to the waiting car and set her down to guide her inside. The second I close the door, I pull her back to me, tugging her onto my lap and tucking her head against my neck. I bark out my address to the driver. Screw my day. I'll handle the production plant later.

With Dolores on my lap, her wet attire seeps into my dress shirt and suit pants. A chill comes over me, but it's nothing compared to the cold of her skin. Her nose is ice against my neck. I reach for her hands lying limp in her lap.

"You're freezing," I say, kissing her forehead. She doesn't respond as the tears continue. Her head remains lax against my shoulder.

Once we arrive at the condo building, I lead her to my door. It's an awkward walk as I keep both my arms around her, and half the time, I have my lips pressed to her temple. My mind sends mental messages to hers.

Don't cry.

I'm here for you.

It's going to be okay.

As we enter my place, I take my coat from her shoulders. The suit might be ruined, but it isn't my primary concern. Dolores needs warmth. I drape my suit jacket over a stool in the kitchen and guide her back to my bedroom. We walk directly into my bathroom.

Although she's still crying, she's unaware. Silent tears are the worst.

"You need a shower to warm up. I'm going to undress you," I warn her. "No funny business, okay? Don't be throwing yourself at me," I tease, hoping to lighten the mood. Hell, even a fake smile would be something, but she doesn't crack one bit. Her eyes remain downcast as do her lips, which are almost purple.

I reach for the faucet and turn the shower on hot, hoping to steam up the room before she enters the stall. Leaving the shower door open, I tend to her clothing. The heavy, water-laden sweater slaps on the tile floor at our feet. *That thing must go.* Next, I slide her shirt up her torso. Through her soaked bra, I see dark nipples peaked from the cold. I drag my eyes away. There's nothing sensual about the moment, but my dick isn't getting the memo.

My fingers find the button of her jeans, and I unsnap, then unzip. The skinny jeans are even skinnier when soaked and adhering to her hips as I struggle to remove them. Eventually, she helps me by leaning against the counter and kicking off her booties. The suede shoes are destroyed. Silently, she pulls off her socks and then takes over to finish removing her pants.

Holding out my hand, I wiggle my fingers for hers. When she places her hand in mine, I tug her forward.

"No funny business," I say, reassuring her I'm not coming onto her. I'd love nothing more than to bury myself inside her in hopes to distract her, but it doesn't feel appropriate. She nods, acknowledging she heard me. I step behind her and unclasp her bra. I don't look as I push it forward, and she lowers her arms to release the material. Her own fingers curl at the edge of her underwear, and she slips it downward. I back up, allowing her space. I tell myself not to look, but I can't help myself. My eyes are drawn to her.

Her backside is perfectly heart-shaped like I called it before. A tramp stamp covers her lower back, something her rebellious self probably did in college. No one gets tattoos there anymore, but my fingers twitch to outline the design. With a hand on the curving ink, I gently press her forward. I swear I won't look at any other part of her. I want her under the spray so she'll warm up.

"I'll be right outside the bathroom door," I tell her, letting her know I'm not leaving while still offering her some privacy. She doesn't look back. She doesn't respond. The only sounds are the rush of water from the showerhead and the click of the glass door cutting her off from me.

chapter 11

Shower Me

[Dolores]

Once the shower door closes, the tears fall in earnest again. I haven't cried this hard or for this long as far back as I can remember—not in front of someone else and especially not in front of someone I hardly know. Keeping my emotions to myself has taken years to perfect. James Harrington was the first to teach me this lesson. My heart cracked when he didn't return the feelings of love I had for him, but it wasn't fully broken. Rusty finished the shattering with his cavalier attitude about our relationship—or lack thereof one.

My mother was the one to teach me to keep my feelings in check. *Never let a man know how you feel. He'll use it against you at every turn.* Spoken like a woman truly scorned, I never wanted to be bitter like her. Somedays, it was difficult to contain my emotions. I'd reveal a little bit of myself, ask for a little bit more from Rusty, and demand a little compassion from my mother. Magnolia tried to sympathize, but she was a woman near eighty, and her Victorian ideals sometimes clashed with the modern era.

My palms lay flat against the cool tile wall of Garrett's shower. A glass box on three sides large enough to fit two. Water streams down on me from an overhead rain shower. The droplets burn at first as my skin is colder than I realize. My fingers curl into fists as I can't seem to control the tears or the wracking sobs in my chest. My heart literally hurts.

My head lowers, allowing the spray to wash over the back of my neck and down my spine. I want to scrub off my skin and the pain of loneliness that goes with it. I also want the heartache of feeling unaccomplished to swirl down the drain.

I'm almost fifty, and where am I in life?

I didn't hear the shower door open, but suddenly, I sense his presence. Garrett's like a shadow, one I find comforting and endearing just when I need one.

"Sweetheart," he whispers behind me, and I stiffen. I can't do this right now. I can't have sex with him, and the tears fall harder. I don't even know if I want to have sex with him.

As if reading my mind, his hand comes to my lower back.

"No funny business, okay? Just…I don't know how to help. Let me help." He pauses, his fingers tickling the base of my spine lightly. "Stay as you are, facing away from me. I have my boxers on. Just let me…" His voice drifts as his hand travels up my spine. He reaches around me for the shampoo bottle on the ledge, and I hear the cap snap open. Then fingertips touch my scalp.

With a gentle massage, Garrett scrubs at my hair, piling it high and rubbing the nape of my neck. He whispers shushing sounds and mutters words of sympathy. *I'm here for you.* The pleasurable pressure on my head is too difficult to deny, and I willingly let him wash my hair. He guides my body forward and back to rinse the sudsy tresses. It's messy as it flows down my face, and I swipe at my cheeks to find I'm still crying, but I'm no longer sobbing.

"I'm sorry," I say, though I don't know what I'm apologizing for.

"No need to apologize." His forehead comes to the back of my head. "Just try to relax, okay?" His hand brushes down my spine again, and then he reaches for the soap. Firm fingers press into my shoulders, thumbs digging into tense muscles, spreading suds across my shoulder blades and lowering to the curve of my ass. He doesn't slip below a line, staying respectful and courteous. In some ways, I don't want him to be polite. I want him to take me up against this wall, thrust into me, and make me scream. However, I know seconds after something like that happens, I'll feel just as empty as I do right now.

He pushes me forward so the water travels down my back as it rinses the soap clean.

"The water's getting cool. Almost ready to step out?"

I nod, and he reaches around me for the faucet. "Stay here. Don't turn around." His sharp tone warns me he's struggling. I mean, I am a naked woman in his shower. With the shower off, I shiver and fold my arms across my breasts.

Within seconds, Garrett is behind me again. "Lift," he demands, and my arms spread. A towel wraps around my back, and I take the edge to secure the thick terrycloth material around me. Garrett spins me to face him, and his hands come to my cheeks. He swipes his thumbs over them and then steps back for the open shower door. When I step out, he points at a large white robe hanging on the back of the door.

"Put that on. I just need a minute."

Reaching for the robe, I hear the slap of wet material hit the shower floor. I will myself not to look as I hear the shower turn back on. I risk a peek to see water streaming over Garrett's firm body. Rivers slither down his back and spread over his solid ass. He scrubs quickly at his hair and the raised arms flex, displaying his strength. I recall how he carried me to his car.

"Thank you," I whisper even though I know my voice doesn't carry loud enough over the spray. He turns his head to see me still standing in his bathroom, and a sly smirk comes to his lips.

"Have a seat in my room." He nods toward the door, but his eyes hold mine. He isn't staring; he's begging me to step out.

I turn away and enter his room. On the stand next to the bed sits a bottle of amber alcohol with a cup of tea next to it. I fold myself onto his mattress, propping up pillows behind me and tucking my feet into the end of the robe. Warmth surrounds me as I brush back my hair with my fingers. I reach for the tea and take a sip. It's still hot and smells sweet. The taste tickles my tongue.

"I put whiskey in there. Drink up. It will warm you from the inside." I stare up at him as he stands just outside his bathroom door. A towel similar to the one I used drapes around his hips, exposing a thick trail of fine hairs to his belly button. *He could warm me from the inside out.*

"Thank you for all this," I say, my voice low and rough from crying. "I don't know what came over me."

Garrett crosses the room to one of his dressers and removes some clothing. "Stay right there," he commands, not addressing my comment. "Be right back."

He returns minutes later dressed in a pair of loose gray lounge pants and a white undershirt. *He's so good looking*, I think for the millionth time. He makes sleepwear look sexy. Crawling up next to me on the bed, he spreads out on his stomach and props himself up on an elbow.

"What were you doing out there?" He isn't judging me. He's curious, concerned even. I can't remember the last time someone worried about me.

"I was wandering the city as I've been doing for the past few days. I decided I needed to get out and see some of the famous places. I may never get to California again."

His brow furrows at my statement, but he remains quiet.

"I turned a corner, and there was the diner. And it reminded me of home."

"And it made you sad."

"Sad is the wrong word." I lower my gaze to the cup in hands. "It reminded me I'm alone. I don't have anyone. I can't count on Rusty, and Denton didn't like the diner. He didn't intentionally hurt me, but he made me feel like the place was a pit." I sigh. "He's right. It is. It needs a facelift, but I can't afford it, which makes me feel like a failure at running my own business."

His hand reaches for my covered ankle. "Hey, none of this. You own a business, right? Is it in major debt? Things happen, but there are always solutions."

"I'm not in debt, but I'm not making a killing either. The locals love the diner, but the community is shifting. The brewpub down the way attracts much of the younger people moving into the area. The tourists find my place, visiting the diner nearly as old as the train depot because it seems like the trendy thing to do, but I can't count on tourists for steady business."

My palms absorb the heat from the mug, and I take another sip. My blood slugs through my veins as my body melts into the pillows at my back. I'm starting to warm.

Garrett's lips twist like he's considering a thought. "Tell me more about Rusty." His tone deepens, a hint of a groan in asking.

"We're nothing to tell. Honestly, we have sex. Ten years of only having sex. It's a small town, and I'm over forty. Hell, I'm almost fifty. When he came onto me, I was vulnerable. He's seven years younger, and I guess I had the cougar thing going when I met him at thirty-seven." It sounds pathetic when I think about it.

"I've got no room to judge," he tells me, jiggling my foot as he gives me a false smile.

"When my mother died, I saw his true colors. He didn't even come to the funeral." My head falls back, and I stare up at the ceiling. It's hard to admit I mean so little to him.

"Were you close to your mother?"

"You could call it a love-hate relationship. She was one of my best friends, but she constantly had her moments when she didn't hesitate to remind me she was my mother. Judgment was her middle name, next to bitter and alcohol."

He nods as if he understands, but by the hints I've had of him with his mother and his sisters, I'd say he probably doesn't. His eyes jump to the bottle next to the bed.

"Sorry about that. I just thought it would help."

I don't want to lie. Seeing alcohol sitting next to the bed made me think of Rusty. The constant bottle near his bed and the amount he would consume. But I also appreciate Garrett's intentions. He really is trying to help me.

"You're a good man, Garrett Fox."

A hint of pink covers his cheeks, and he nudges my foot. "Now, don't go ruining my reputation."

I chuckle softly. "Somehow, I think you've ruined it all on your own." I look down at the monogram on the thick robe. "Ritz-Carlton? Let me guess. Weekend rendezvous, and you stole it as a souvenir."

"Ha-ha. I didn't steal it. They allow you to take them and then charge you a small fortune for one."

"You left out the weekend rendezvous."

"She was expensive as well," he teases, but then he flips onto his back and looks up at the ceiling. "I don't want to share all my escapades with you, though." His head rolls to the side to face me. "This isn't about me tonight." His eyes remain on mine as if he's digging, as if he's *excavating* for my soul. I swallow a lump in my throat.

How many women has he been good to like this?

"Want something to eat?"

"I'm not really hungry." I stifle a yawn.

"Tired?" he asks, his voice softening. "I'm not judging, but you sleep an awful lot."

I nod again. "I do. It seems I'm making up for years of not sleeping."

"Are you depressed?"

"Maybe." There's nothing wrong with depression. I know many people suffer from it, and many women my age develop it. I just hadn't considered it for myself.

"When my dad left, my mom was depressed. She was anxious, too. She thought we were all going to leave her or die. She had to take pills to keep herself on track. It's not a bad thing," he adds, leveling his eyes on me. "She's better with them."

"I'm just going through something…" My voice drifts off. I've actually read about it this week. Adjustment disorder. It's when a major change in your life occurs—by natural circumstances or unexpectedly—and the body can shut down, or emotions run deeper than regular. I'm not self-diagnosing, but it sounds more likely that I have this condition. I don't want to blow it off as a phase, but some recommendations include exercise and staying busy—neither of which I have been doing until the past few days.

I'm not certain keeping busy helped.

"How about some mindless television?" Garrett rolls for the remotes on the opposite stand and clicks on the television. The sound comes loud, filling the room.

"Sorry about that. I play *Fortnite* when I can't sleep."

"Isn't that a video game for kids?"

"I'm a child at heart."

I stare at the flat screen as he lowers the volume and switches to the guide.

"I heard you through the wall one night."

He stares back at me. "Playing *Fortnite*?"

I shake my head. "With Blondie."

"Alicia?" His eyes widen. "You think…" His voice halts as he chokes. "I don't have sex in here." He's almost appalled at the suggestion.

"What?"

"This is my domain. I don't share this space with hookups." His crass explanation startles me, and I blink. He scrolls through the channels as he asks, "What did you hear?"

"Something about *get it* and *go left. Right there*, I think."

He laughs in response. "That was definitely video game speak. No one says *go left* during sex."

I'm a bit mortified we're having this conversation, so I keep my lips clamped shut for a second.

"And for the record, Alicia and I aren't a thing. We were once upon a time, but not now and never again."

"So no hookups in here?" I say, looking around the room. He must be lying. I've been in here. I've even had an orgasm in this bed. Granted, I was alone but still. "What about me?"

"You're not a hookup, sweetheart," he says, narrowing his eyes as he glares at me.

Of course not, I think. *I'm a hot mess. Why would he possibly want to hook up with me?*

chapter 12

Gratitude Is The Attitude

[Garrett]

I can't get her to eat before she grows drowsy from the warming whiskey. However, I'm starving, plus I need to take Wally out, so I excuse myself to make a quick sandwich and eat it while I walk my dog. When I return to the bedroom, she's sitting on the edge of the bed, her hands gripping the mattress.

"What are you doing?"

"I should go," she says, her voice groggy and rough. "It's getting late." She presses off the bed and stands on wobbly legs. Her hands smooth down the thick terrycloth. Her clothes are ruined, so she'll have to cross the hall in the robe.

I'm not a cuddler. I don't hold women after sex. If I spend the night, we separate, each to our own side of the bed. So it's a shock when I don't hesitate to step forward and wrap an arm around Dolores's middle. I speak into her hair at the nape of her neck.

"Don't leave." She stills under my embrace. "Just let me hold you tonight."

Her breath hitches, and her stomach flinches under my forearm. I don't want to remind her again, *no funny business*. I promise myself I won't touch her below the waist. Though it was nearly impossible not to get a glimpse of her sweet tits in the shower. I'm a man, what can I say? I peeked, but I didn't react. Okay, I did react, but I didn't touch. I swallowed back my desire and willed my dick to settle. Keeping my boxers on helped contain my erection from nudging against her naked ass. Her fine naked ass. Her fine heart-shaped ass.

"Okay," she whispers.

Thank fuck. I give a little internal cheer of victory. I'm convinced her Rusty might be like me. Well, at least in the cuddle category. But tonight, I'm making an exception to many rules. She's going to stay in my bed, and I'm going to hold her to me all night.

I pull back the duvet, and she climbs under the sheet. She's still wrapped in the robe, which won't be comfortable to sleep in, but I don't want her changing out of it. Heaven help me, she can't sleep naked. I crawl over her and scoot under the sheets as well. Molding my body along the curve of hers, my knees bend, my arm drapes over her waist, and my face nestles into her hair. She smells like me, from my shampoo and soap, and I find I like the scent on her. I'd like other scents on her—like our bodies mingling and sweat mixing—but not tonight. Tonight, I tug her to my chest and squeeze my arm around her as if I can't get her close enough. Which I can't.

She's fitful in her sleep, muttering and grunting, and I want to settle her dreams. Eventually, she presses my arm off her.

"What's wrong?" I ask as she sits up.

"I'm too warm, and the robe is hard to sleep in." She rolls her neck near the thick folded material.

"Top drawer. I have T-shirts and boxer shorts if you'd like."

The room is dark, but I see her nod. She presses off the mattress and stands. I watch her cross my room and then open the dresser drawer. She removes one item and bends at the waist, stepping into my boxer briefs. Suddenly, the robe slips from her shoulders, exposing her back to me like it was in the shower. She's pear-shaped—bigger hips that taper inward at her waist—and I want a bite. Her spine cuts a river up her back, and I want to lick the path. She slips a T-shirt over her head, then pulls her hair free. I could watch her dress for the rest of my life, and the thought startles me.

She spins in my direction, then bends down to pick up the robe and returns to the bed. She folds herself back into the space she left, reaching for my arm to cover her waist. I smile to myself as I breathe her in again.

"I think you're starting to unrust," she murmurs.

"What?" I chuckle.

"That heart you say you don't have? I think I hear it ticking, Tin Man."

I press a kiss to her covered shoulder and snicker. "Don't get your panties in a twist, Dorothy. It's only temporary."

"Good to know," she says, but then she pauses. "But thank you all the same."

"Anytime, stunner." I smile into her back.

"Why do you call me that?" she asks in a sleepy voice.

"Because you're stunning."

She chuckles softly. "I'm a hot mess."

"Hot being the appropriate word," I mutter. She twists to look at me over her shoulder, causing her backside to press against me. The slight brush of her ass against my lower region causes an immediate reaction, and my hand comes to her hip.

"I'm trying really hard to be a gentleman," I say, leaning forward to press a kiss to her shoulder. "So stop squirming."

"What if I don't want you to be decent with me?" Her voice is hardly a whisper, and I stare at the outline of her body in the darkness. She can't mean what she asks.

"Dolores. Not like this, sweetheart." I don't even know why I say that. I could take her, make her lose herself for a little bit, but I don't think she needs that. She needs me to prove I can control myself.

I nudge her with my nose at her shoulder, and her body shifts. She turns away from me and stiffens as she tries to settle under my arm.

"Of course not," she mumbles. I don't ask. I just want to hold her, which is so unlike me.

+ + +

The next morning, I'm making breakfast when Dolores enters my kitchen. She's wearing my forest green boxer briefs and an old band T-shirt with the robe open over her. I removed my T-shirt when I woke, not used to sleeping in a shirt, so I'm bare-chested as I cook bacon. Dolores's eyes catch on my chest, widening as she takes in my skin, my abs, and lower. I try to keep fit for someone fifty. It takes more work than it did when I was younger, but I'm proud of the effort. Apparently, so is Dolores because her eyes linger, especially at the treasure trail leading into my pajama pants.

"Like what you see?" I mock, holding my arms out wide for her to take a better glance. Her face heats, and not for the first time, I want to lick the path blossoming on her skin. She turns away, and her breath hitches as she notices my television.

"It's Thanksgiving!" she shrieks, and her hand lifts to her lips as if she's horrified. "How did that happen?"

"It's typically the fourth Thursday of November," I deadpan. Her head swings back to me, narrowing her eyes at me. My attention drifts to the Thanksgiving Day parade broadcast on the screen. I was supposed to go home, but I missed my flight this morning. I had scheduled it for six a.m., finding the time easier from LAX to Missouri. As if reading my mind, her eyes widened.

"You aren't supposed to be here, are you?"

I shrug. I don't like to spend the holidays alone, so I typically head back home. Sometimes, I spend the time with friends in the area. She steps forward, her hands bracing on the island that separates my kitchen from the living space.

"Oh my God." She panics. "You need to go. I should go." She steps for the front door, but I'm quick to round the counter and envelop her from behind. My chest leans against her back.

"Look, it's not a big deal. I missed my flight. I'll never get out of here now."

"But it's a holiday. You should be with your family."

"What about you?" I ask, still speaking to the back of her head. Her hands grip my forearm around her waist.

"What about me? I'll be fine."

"I'm not leaving you alone."

She stills, straightening from her bent position. "I need to go," she whispers.

"Or you could stay," I suggest. "We'll make a day of it. We can watch movies, hang out. I'll cook."

"You don't have a turkey," she snorts, looking over her shoulder at me.

"I'll get one. There has to be a store open or a delivery service running."

"It's Thanksgiving," she screeches again as if this wasn't the reason for our crazy conversation in the first place.

"I'll figure it out," I say, standing taller and forcing her to spin and face me. "Just don't leave." I'm starting to sound desperate as I almost beg her not to go.

"Let me cook then," she says, her arms trapped at her sides as mine wrap around her body, holding her flush to me.

"Deal," I say, and I can't help myself as my lips quickly brush hers. I don't linger like I want. I don't devour like I crave. Just swipe and step back, leaving her stunned.

"I need to head home for some clothes." She looks down at her attire and tugs the robe closed.

"We could make it casual Thanksgiving. You don't need to change." I wiggle my brows at her, allowing my eyes to roam her body. I like her in that robe, in my boxers, in my condo.

"You're unbelievable," she mutters, stepping toward the kitchen island.

"Undeniable is what I prefer," I say, passing her and swatting her ass. My hand wants to grip the tight globes and then press her to the cabinets, but I don't. *I'll behave*, I promise myself. "I need to take Wally out. I'll be back in fifteen."

I turn back to her, walking backward down the hall toward my room. "Can I trust you not to leave me?"

Her mouth curves, a genuine smile hinting behind her lips. "You can trust me."

chapter 13

An Act Of Appreciation

[Dolores]

He can trust me, but I want a real shower that will leave me smelling like myself and not the scent of him. The fragrance is too much because it makes me crave him. My body hums from his swat to my backside and the too-quick kiss. Waking in his bed seemed surreal and a bit déjà vu. When I woke a week ago after dog sitting, I'd had the same restful sleep and peaceful comfort—something I hardly experience alone.

We agree I should change clothes. I can't spend the day in his underwear. I've already moistened the center because of the soft, worn material rubbing against my core. I need a rub myself, or I'm not going to make it through the next few hours without throwing myself at him.

When I return to his place, I find him unpacking grocery bags. A small turkey. Boxed stuffing. Potatoes. Cornbread mix. I typically wouldn't use products from a package, preferring to make things from scratch, but I won't complain. Again, I feel guilty he missed his flight home.

"I'm sorry about you missing your family."

He spins to face me. "I'm not." The sentiment shocks me, but he's smiling as he speaks.

"How can I help?" I ask, wanting to make myself useful. Then I pause. "Are those Target bags?"

"Yeah, there's one a few blocks from here."

Silence falls between us as he realizes what he's said.

"You liar." I laugh. Stepping toward him, I reach for a spatula on the counter and wield it like a weapon as I approach him. Raising his hands in defense, he laughs as he steps around his kitchen island. "You said you didn't know of a Target within fifty miles."

I'm still chasing him as he jumps over the back of his couch. Wally joins in, yipping and barking at the chaos in his space. Garrett is full-on laughing as we shift left and then right with the couch as a barrier.

"You didn't need Target. You needed an overhaul."

"Ah," I gasp, attempting to head over the couch like he did, but I don't have the same stretch as him nor are my legs as long. One leg gets stuck over the back of the furniture before Garrett reaches for my arm. He yanks me forward, my back falling until I hit the cushions, and then he's over me, straddling my stomach. My wrists are cuffed above my head as Garrett leans forward.

Kiss me, he said when we went to the movie.

Kiss me, I beg.

But he stops himself like he did last night.

"Are you saying I look drab?" I mock.

"I'm saying you had potential."

"That's so mean," I pout.

"Yet look at you now." His eyes roam over my body. Flannel shirt rolled to the elbows, unbuttoned enough to reveal a cami underneath. A pair of skinny jeans. Flip-flops because we'll remain inside. "You're stunning."

"I'm a mess, remember?" I snark, losing steam.

"A beautiful mess," he says, his voice catching on the comment. *Kiss me.*

He's lowering, and I swallow, my mouth watering for another taste of him. A real taste of him. His hold on my wrists above my head no longer seems playful but seductive. His thumbs stroke over the sensitive skin. I want him to keep me like this—his captive.

Instead, a loud buzzer beeps, drowning out our panting breaths.

"Oven's hot," he mutters, pressing off my arms and shifting off my body.

Me too, I think, but it's probably for the best I not mention it. He's allowing me the honor of spending the day with him, and I shouldn't mess it up by adding anything sexual to the mix.

He lowers a hand, offering to help me stand, and I reach for his. As he tugs me upward, our eyes meet in the way they do, where we seem to be looking, searching, digging for something inside. Then he releases me and scrubs at the back of his neck as he walks toward the oven.

It's better like this, I remind myself again as I follow him.

We spend the remainder of the day preparing food, sipping wine, and watching a combination of football and movies.

"What's something you'd really like to do while you're in California?"

"I don't know," I say honestly. I've seen several of the tourist hot spots, but I don't know what's left.

"Okay, forget California. How about in general? What's something you'd like to do? Experience? Something you wouldn't go for in Georgia but really want to try."

I shrug, shaking my head.

"Come on," he says, bumping my shoulder with his while we sit on his couch waiting for our dinner to cook. We sit close enough that our arms touch, and my skin prickles with desire. My fingers want to tiptoe over his forearm and trace the tattoo.

"I'd like to take dance lessons."

He chuckles until he sees I'm serious. "What, like ballet? Tap?"

"Tango."

His wine glass pauses halfway to his lips.

"I already know how to swing dance from my mom, but I always wanted to learn something…sexier."

He bites his lip.

"You want to laugh again."

"I don't," he says, his voice rising as he chokes on a chuckle.

"You do." I snort, smacking him on the shoulder.

"No, really. That sounds cool. You should do it."

I shake my head again. "I wouldn't know how or where, but yeah…that's something I've always wanted to learn."

Garrett grows quiet after that, and we return to football until it's time to eat. When dinner is almost ready, Garrett asks if we should change. "We could dress up," he offers.

I suppose it would be nice, but this day has been so carefree that I don't want to make things awkward by forcing us to be formal. I don't want to feel like we're on a date.

"I'm comfy, though," I say, sticking out my lower lip to pout.

"Me too," he says, his eyes catching mine as a smile spreads across his face.

Casual Thanksgiving it is, then, and we stuff ourselves.

"I can't move," Garrett says, slouching back on his couch after we finish eating. He's propped his feet up on his coffee table and slouches into the cushions. I throw myself down next to him.

"I can't breathe." I laugh, a hand covering my stomach. I haven't eaten this much in weeks, and I feel full, warm…and almost happy.

Garrett flips the channel on the television to land on another classic movie.

"*An Affair to Remember*. Another favorite," I announce.

Garrett groans and rolls his eyes in a teasing manner. He's indulged me all day with black and white movies between football games. Two minutes into the movie, when he tugs my arm and pats his thigh, I fall over to rest my head on his leg. Garrett's hand comes to my back, and he begins stroking along my spine with his fingertips. I relax under his touch until his fingers fall from my back. A gentle snore sounds behind me, and I smile. I snuggle into him and continue watching the movie about a couple destined to be together but only after a catastrophe.

I've never had a man search for me like Cary Grant tries to find Debra Kerr. No man has chased me half as much as I've chased him, and I'm saddened by the thought. What's happened to romance? Or is it only in the movies? As the movie nears its end, Garrett's hand returns to my waist, and I sense his other hand scrubbing down his face.

"Nice nap?" I mutter. He doesn't respond, so I roll my head on his thigh to look over my shoulder. His eyes remain closed, but I feel something at the back of my head. Slowly, I continue my rolling to face him and then press myself upward.

"Garrett," I whisper, stroking the ridge bulging in his sweatpants with a finger. He shifts his body, and his fingers, loosely resting on my hip, tighten. My fingers curl into the band of his sweatpants, and his lids open a bit. A sly smile curves his lips.

"Whatcha doing?" Hooded eyes peer down at me, mischievous and daring. Keeping my eyes on his, I tug at the waistband and slip my fingers inside his pants, palming him over his boxers.

"Dolores," he groans, his head falling back in submission. My exploration continues. He's long, firm, and ready. *How was he hard so quickly?* I refuse to compare him to another. He's so much more than anyone I've been with even hidden under his tight boxer briefs. I know this for certain. I curl up on my knees to get a better angle and tug his sweats lower on his hips. Garrett's hand comes to the back of my head, and his fingers comb through my hair.

"Dolores, what are you doing?" His voice remains lazy.

I don't answer him. I'm on a mission. He's been so nice to me all day. He held me all night. I just want to give him something in return. My fingers curve around his thick shaft, and I squeeze. Garrett hisses.

"You don't have to do this," he says, but his fingers tug at the ends of my hair. I lower and kiss his exposed tip.

"Fuck, Dolores. Don't tease."

I answer him by forcing his briefs lower and then swirling my tongue around the mushroom ridge. Then I open wide and draw him deep. His hand fists in my hair, twisting the tresses around his closed hand near the nape of my neck. I drag my lips to the tip and then fill my mouth with him again. Back and forth, I work him, sucking, licking, savoring. Working over him is working me up as well, and I'd love to touch myself, but this moment is for him.

"Sweetheart," he warns, his fist tugging gently. "I…" His voice falters as I take him deeper. Fighting past the gag, I bring him to the back of my throat, and he explodes. His lips mutter a litany of curses like a prayer of gratitude. Pulling back slowly, I swallow every drop of him and sit up.

"What was that?" he asks, sitting straighter and scrubbing at his face with both hands. I still don't answer, and then his hands reach for my face. He tugs me toward him, but I stop him with a palm on his chest.

"Wait."

"What?" His voice rises an octave.

"You don't want to kiss me after that." Rusty never allowed us to kiss after he'd come in my mouth. *I'm not fucking tasting myself.* I learned early not to go for him after taking him in.

"Fuck that," Garrett says before his mouth crashes mine. I'm pressed back as his lips seize me. The kiss devours my lips, sucking them into his mouth before opening and delving forward with his tongue. He sweeps the inside of my mouth as his fingers slip into my hair, and he fists the strands again, tilting my head to tangle my tongue farther with his mouth. He's consuming me, and I want to be swallowed whole.

A vibrating noise sounds from the coffee table.

Garrett continues kissing me.

Then the buzzing begins again. Garrett pulls back, and I realize it's my phone.

"Maybe it's Denton. I wanted to talk to my grandmother tonight." We both look at the phone at the same time to see it isn't Denton.

The caller ID reads *Rusty*.

chapter 14

Rust On The Heart

[Garrett]

Fuckity, fuck, *fuck.* Not him and not now. Holy…what the hell just happened?

"I…" Dolores's voice falters as she stares at her phone. I use the moment to tuck myself back into my sweats. The day has been casual, and I've let myself go by staying comfortable the entire holiday. When she pouted at me about changing, it was so cute that I didn't want to disappoint her by dressing in more formal attire. Remaining as we were, the holiday was more special than any stuffy dinner I've ever attended.

Then…then she gives me head like I've never had, and I want to devour her.

So why the fuck did he call? Why now?

"Are you still talking to him?" I snap as old insecurities fill my veins. Is she cheating on him *with me*?

"No," she bellows. "No. I haven't spoken to him since before I came here."

"What does he want?" I ask, frustrated.

"I don't know." Her voice lowers, eyes still focused on the phone. "I should go."

"What?" I snap. How can she leave? She just gave me the blow job of all blow jobs. I mean, what man doesn't want to wake up to be taken by a sexy vixen looking up at him with lust-filled eyes and a salivating mouth ready to draw him deep? It can't only be me. She just fulfilled a fantasy of mine, and now she wants to walk away.

"I think I should leave," she repeats, uncurling her legs from my couch and standing. "I've had a wonderful day, Garrett. The best Thanksgiving ever."

I don't understand. *What's happening?* She's shutting down, and I get that, but I don't want her to go. We were just getting started. We can skip Rusty. Fuck him. I'll take her back on my couch with her head on my leg watching movies.

Just. Don't. Leave.

"Fine," I mutter instead, falling back on the cushions.

"It really was a great day," she offers, trying to salvage what can't be salvaged as she reaches for her phone.

"Uh-huh," I murmur, scrubbing both hands down my face again. She steps around the couch and reaches down to pet Wally.

"Be a good boy, smelly Wally," she purrs to him in the false tone she uses to insult him. He traitorously wags his tail, banging it on the tile floor. The *slap, slap, slap* sounds desperate. He doesn't want her to leave either. I stand and round the couch, coming up behind her.

"Help me understand what happened here?" I'm almost begging her for an explanation. She stands upright and spins to face me.

"I just wanted to give you something special." Her eyes lower as if she's ashamed. I don't want her to feel bad about what she's done. I love what she did. I want more of what she did.

"Let me reciprocate," I suggest, my lip curving at the corner although my smile can't reach a full curl. She's going to shoot me down. I can see it when her lids lift, and her blue eyes find mine. Without answering, she pats my chest.

"Thank you for everything." Then she turns and lets herself out.

Fuck.

What the fuck?

+ + +

I work from home the next day, avoiding my family who called to make sure I was all right. I called them on my way to pick up food yesterday and explained how I missed my flight.

"Are you sure you're okay?" my mother asked.

"Yeah, Ma." *I've never been better*, I thought as I rushed through the store picking up items to make the day as special as I could for Dolores.

I wanted to give you something special.

She'd certainly done that. My dick jolts with the memory. Her lips. Her mouth. Her tongue.

Then that man called. Her asshole sex partner. Has he fucked her there? He better not.

I want to be her sex partner.

Then I stop. In all reality, I don't want to be her sex partner. I don't want to be her fuck buddy or friends with benefits. I'm falling for Dolores even though I promised myself I would never fall again. I like her. A lot. She's funny and sexy without realizing it. She's stunning when she smiles, and I want to freeze-frame each moment she gives me a rare grin.

I thought we'd made a breakthrough after her cryfest and spending the night in my arms.

She's broken, and I want to glue her back together, but I can't if another guy is in the picture. Then again, Dolores doesn't live here. Her home is in Georgia. He's in Georgia. Eventually, she'll want to go home. I keep forgetting this fact.

I throw down my pen and tip back on my couch. My hand spreads on the cushion where she sat all day yesterday. My fingers separate as if they can feel the curve of her hip. My chest aches at her absence, and I don't like the sensation.

I'm a guy. I've fucked around. I've left women. I've had my way and moved on.

Somehow, with the positions reversed, I don't like it one bit.

"Fuck this," I mutter aloud for the millionth time and lean forward for my laptop. It's then that I notice an email I've been hoping to find. A waitlist finally had an opening, and I'm in. There's a place I want to visit for investment purposes. I'm hoping to scope out the place as I'm still looking for that one thing for myself. That one investment. For the first time in a long time, I thought I might like to share my secret interest with someone else, but after last night, I'm no longer certain.

I can't go through this heartbreak again.

Memories of Kate fill my head. It was years ago, but the reminders still sting. I know better than to get attached.

chapter 15

Rhythm Of The Heart

[Dolores]

Two days pass without communication from Garrett. It's totally my fault, and I own it. It's just…I'm too embarrassed to go to his place and apologize. I shouldn't have taken advantage of him, which is what I did. He was so sweet all day long, and then I had to go and take it one step too far. I just wanted to give something to him, and guys like *that*. Not to mention. the moment I felt his hard-on, I wanted to explore him like I've never wanted to explore.

I'm a sexual being by nature. It's one reason I was with James, and then Rusty, for too long. I love the physical contact. It's been a struggle to keep my emotions out of the mix, but I've worked hard at suppressing them over the years. When you're stung a few times, you get the hint. *Put up or get out.* With Rusty, it's been more put out and shut up.

Garrett is different, and this is my problem. I'm making him into something he's not. He's a good guy with a big heart—and a big dick—but we shouldn't get involved. We won't get involved. The other night would have led to a one-night stand, and I don't need one of those. I need a friend, which Garrett has certainly been since I got to California.

But now I've ruined everything.

When Rusty called, I freaked out. He never calls me. What did he want? Why would he call at precisely the moment he did? How could the universe be so cruel?

Yet it was a reminder my home is far away and waiting.

"Where you been, baby?" Rusty drawls through the phone when I give in and return his call. A drag of a cigarette, or possibly something else, hisses through the line.

"I'm in California." *Remember?* I've been missing for almost a month.

"It's been a long time. When you coming back?"

Does he want me back?

Then another thought occurs.

Do I want to go back to him?

The deeper question is: can you return to someone who isn't yours? I belong to Rusty. He's told me on many occasions, but it's not in a romantic, you're mine manner. I'm property to him and the club by way of him. Rusty belongs to Devil's Edge. Not a ruthless one-percent MC, but a riding club all the same with some pretty hefty rules. No other man could date me. No other man would risk it.

In Blue Ridge, not many eligible men exist. Sure, there are several Harrington brothers, but I've learned my lesson with James. Not to mention, the others are too much like brothers *to me*, so I can't hook up with them. The Duncans are another crew of bachelors, but they are distant cousins, so just…*no*.

"I'm not sure when I'll be home." I take my time to answer Rusty, who's pulled a few more hits of whatever he's smoking on the other end of the line.

On a heavy exhale, he says, "Guess I'll see ya when I see ya." Then the line goes dead.

I don't know why I called him back. A hint of false hope he'd say he missed me and wanted me to come home to him muddled my decision-making. Fake optimism stole the content of a great day with Garrett, and I hate myself for it.

These are my thoughts as I go for a long walk along the beach despite the dropping temperatures of late November. I miss Wally, which shocks me. I miss Garrett, which doesn't.

As I stand before Denton's door, unlocking it after my walk, I feel the presence of Garrett behind me. I want to lean back and press into him—like when he held me in his bed—but I don't. I freeze, unable to turn and face him.

"I have something for you," he says, reaching around me and offering me an envelope. I spin but can't look up at him.

"You didn't have to do anything." I have no idea what the envelope could contain.

"I thought you'd like it." My brows pinch, and my chest aches. He's too good to me, and I don't know why. I have nothing to offer him…but decent blow jobs. I'd willingly drop to my knees if he asked me to, but somehow, I think I've crossed a line he won't want crossed again. On the other hand, Garrett's a smooth talker, and I bet he's used to getting what he wants from a woman and letting her go when he's finished.

The thought makes me sad.

"Thanks," I say. Waving the envelope between us, I'm still not able to look up at him, but he surprises me when his fingers tip up my chin. His eyes find mine, and he looks at me in that way he does—not a stare, a search. He wants to understand what I can't even explain. I don't recognize myself when I'm with him, and I can't decide if that's good or bad.

He nods and then steps back as if he's found his answer. He watches me as he walks backward to his side of the hallway and then turns to enter his apartment. Without a glance back, he closes the door.

+ + +

On Tuesday, I find myself inside the Movement Mystique. The mystery gift is a voucher for four nights of dance lessons.

Don't disappoint. A picture of a Tin Man stands in the corner of the cardstock paper.

Did I disappoint him?

Having nothing to wear, I've arrived in yoga pants, a sweatshirt, and tennis shoes.

"No, no, no," a flamboyant male says to me after I identify myself. "This will not do." He eyes my attire. "You are too striking for this." He waves a hand up and down my physique in disgust. Reaching for my hand, he tugs me to follow him through a curtained doorway and into a dance room.

"Umm…" This seems a little unorthodox. A man I don't know, who clearly won't have interest in me, drags me to a corner of his studio.

"Peter. My name is Peter, and this is for you." He stops short and points to a wrap dress in black and a pair of female dance shoes, size nine for my bigger feet. Color—ruby red. I turn to him, aware I'm staring at him.

"What's this?"

"If you want to dance the tango, you must have the proper attire."

"The tango?" I choke. "I don't want to…" *Tango*. It's a sensual dance, and being up close and personal with this man—or any man, for that fact—will be a bit awkward.

"What kind of dance did you think you were learning?" Peter asks.

"Swing or something like that, which I already know."

"You know how to swing dance?" He taps his foot like a movie diva, crossing his arms over his thin chest.

Crossing my arms in response to his shocked demeanor, I snap, "I do."

He eyes my outfit again. "Quite." He's mocking me. Crossing the dance floor as if his ass holds a pen between his cheeks, he practically sashays to the opposite corner. *Swish. Swish. Swish.* He's gliding as he nears a giant stereo system. After he presses a button, the room explodes in big band music.

"Let's see," he says as he spins and saunters back to my side. With a few snaps of his fingers, we break into stride. I'm rusty at best. It's been years since I've practiced or even participated in the steps. My mother was the one who loved it, but I fall into line with Peter as my lead, and for a moment, I'm sprung back in time to our living room on the Lane. My mother's smile. Her wiggling hips. The kick of her feet. If I wasn't laughing so hard at myself, I might burst into tears with the memories. However, it feels good to remember her in a happier light than the years of disapproval and closet drinking.

I'm bent over out of breath as the song ends, and Peter steps back to give me a one-time clap. His hands clasp together in surprise, but another set of hands continues slow applause behind me.

Oh, God.

I spin and face him.

"What are you doing here?" My face flushes from the exertion but also the possibility Garrett saw me dancing. I don't need an audience.

"Thanks for warming her up," Garrett says to Peter without breaking eye contact with me. The sandy brown of his eyes roams my body and then flashes to the dress. His lips twist, and then he nods. "Okay, then."

He steps forward, and my hands come up to stop him. "What the…?"

"Sweetheart, you didn't think I was your partner," Peter teases. "I'm the instructor."

"But. I thought…" I can't finish my thought.

"You might want to change," Peter suggests, whispering as he leans toward me like he's sharing a secret.

"She doesn't need to change. She's perfect as she is," Garrett says, his eyes not leaving mine as his voice lowers.

Oh God. I'm melting.

"You don't have to do this," I say quietly, but Garrett has my hand in his and squeezes.

"I know, but I want to." We pass another minute gazing at one another before Peter clears his throat, and I break away to change. My sweatshirt is rather bulky, and the sneakers clunky. Not to mention, the shoes aren't conducive to sliding over the wooden floor. Peter shows me to a changing room, and I stare at myself before the mirror after I slip into the dress. Hugging my body, it accentuates my hips and highlights my breasts. The crisscross over my chest cuts low, but snug. One wrong move and I may be on display, but I feel…pretty. Sexy even. My hands coast over my hips, and I note the bright red heels. *Ruby slippers.*

If I click three times, will they transport me home? I may never leave this city, and Garrett might give me a good reason to stay. I smile slowly at myself and then step through the changing space curtain.

Ignore the man behind the curtain, rings through my head. As I stare back at Garrett, who wears his own set of dress shoes, fitted suit pants, and a shirt with sleeves he's rolling up his forearms, there's no chance I can ignore him. *Tin Man, my ass*. He's definitely the Wizard.

"May I have this dance?" he asks after fixing his sleeves and stepping up to me.

Take them all, I want to say.

"You may," I tease, and in less than a second, I'm in his arms, tugged to his chest, but held off just the teeny-tiniest bit. The dance stance. We're so close but not close enough, and it's the sexiest position I've ever been in. Hesitation and anticipation balance between us.

Peter explains how he wants us to move. It's a simple eight count, and I follow Garrett's lead as Peter coaches him. Garrett's a fast learner and an amazing dancer. His hand on my hip. His fingers coasting up the side of my body. His palm stroking under my arm.

"What's the matter, Dolores?" Garrett mutters to me as we practice this sultry move, and I shiver. I'm Baby in *Dirty Dancing* when she laughs at being tickled.

"Nothing," I mutter, though I lie. I'm so turned on when I'm supposed to be concentrating. "Just lead."

I follow where Garrett takes me, spinning us, gliding us. Our legs tangle. Our hips collide. Our cheeks brush, and I want him to kiss me. We take another turn, and then his nose drags along the corner of my lip. My eyes close, and I falter. Garrett catches me.

"Sorry," I mumble, growing flustered and wet. So wet. The aroma—and the aura—of sex lingers between us. I want him like no man I've ever wanted. Not James. Not Rusty. I want Garrett to take my body, and I'll do anything he asks.

Peter snaps out another direction. "Dolores, stand at his back. Wrap a hand around his chest. Garrett will capture it, and he'll do the rest."

I roll around Garrett's shoulder and stand directly behind him. Normally, he's the one to sneak up on me. Garrett shivers as I exhale.

"What's the matter, Garrett?" I singsong in the tone he used with me. He chuckles.

The music starts.

I do as Peter directs. My hand starts on Garrett's bicep and then skims forward to press into his chest. My fingers spread before they are captured by Garrett, who sways us to the side. I step around him to place my body in front of his, and he tugs me into him. His hand splays on my lower abdomen, his fingers so close to the promised land, but I will myself to keep steady as Garrett dips me back and then tugs me forward.

My body screams for his.

He spins me out and pulls me back. We glide in the not-close-enough dance stance a few paces until he turns me so my side leans against him. His fingers spread just under my breast. When he nudges upward, I'm certain that's not part of the dance. We step one, step two, and then he faces me. His one hand rests high on my back; the other lowers for my hip and then drags up my side in the move we've been practicing. His palm skates under my arm to my wrist as his nose traces down the side of my face.

Oh, God. I might orgasm from this.

We bend at the knee and then more steps. *Step. Step. Turn.* I'm lost to his lead until he tips me backward. His palm flattens on my throat and skims down the front of my dress, between my breasts and lower, narrowly missing my center again.

Take me already.

He slowly pulls me up, and my eyes freeze on his. The melody beats in tandem with my heart…and my sex. Garrett stops moving, and then he kisses me. Tender. Light. Too quick.

The music halts, and I step back. Peter stands in the corner, fanning himself with his hand.

Tell me about it.

"Let's take five." Peter points with his thumb over his shoulder. "I'll just be a minute." Judging from the sweat on his forehead, he might need more than five, but I'm not concerned with Peter. I turn back to Garrett, who steps into my dance space and cups my cheeks. His eyes volley back and forth, searching mine.

"Come away with me this weekend."

My mouth pops open. *What is he saying?*

"I have somewhere I'd like to show you. Get your opinion on something."

My cheeks, already flushed, heat further.

"Okay." I have no willpower to refuse him. His lips curl at the corner, and then his mouth falls to mine, hungry, eager, divine. I'm so worked up from the dance I can't deny him. I open and take him in, matching his lead once again like a ravenous hussy. I want him to take me on this dance floor with the mirrors so I can watch us. His hand skims the side of my body like it did while we danced. When he reaches my hip and tugs me forward, I'm rewarded with the pressure of his excitement against my lower belly.

"What are you doing to me?" he mutters against my mouth before pulling back and resting his forehead on mine.

Same thing you're doing to me, Tin Man. Finding my heart.

chapter 16

Wine And Dine

[Garrett]

A weekend away seems like the perfect thing for Dolores. She needs to see another part of California before she returns home, though I don't like to think of her going back to Georgia. Not to mention, I want to visit the winery for ideas. My personal investment? I'd like to own a vineyard. It gives me a way to honor my granddad—who invested in me and always wanted land—while creating something long term. A retirement plan even though I'm way too young to retire. I still have a lot of buying and selling inside me yet. My next purchase, though, needs to be a long-term purchase for me.

"Where are we going?" she asks as I enter her brother's apartment. It's hard to remember it's his as we've spent the past few nights in here. I'm feeling like a teenager each night as we kiss and kiss and kiss some more with wandering hands but respectful boundaries. I don't need to cross the line, but I want to with her. What's that saying: *parting is such sweet sorrow*. The hardest part of each evening—is leaving. A weekend retreat will allow us to spend the nights together.

"Napa."

"As in Napa Valley?" She stops pacing to her suitcase and spins to face me.

"Yes. Wine country. Did you bring a dress?"

"I didn't know I needed one." She actually doesn't, but I'd like to see her in the black dress I had sent to the dance studio again, and if we eat at the restaurant, she may want to dress up.

"Bring the black one I bought you." She stares at me, folding something over her hands.

"You need to stop buying me things. You kind of spoil me." She isn't being coy like some women can be, or even encouraging me to spend more on her. She's stating a fact, but I find I enjoy spoiling her.

"It's my pleasure," I say, stepping up to her and removing the item from her twisting fingers. It's a T-shirt material, and I ask her if she needs it. It looks extra large, like a sleep item. Reaching for it, she folds it and stuffs it in the suitcase.

"What about Wally?"

"He's going with us. They have a place to keep him while we stay at the inn."

"An inn," she states. Now she does sound coy. "How quaint."

"I'm hoping so."

As we drive north, she asks about my upbringing in southern Missouri. I ask about her diner. She has a wealth of knowledge about the food industry, and I'm glad I asked her to visit the winery. She might have an eye for things I won't notice, but I haven't told her my dream yet. I'm nervous. I want her to like what I have planned.

One thing we have in common is a deep respect and admiration for our grandparents. I tell her more about Granddad before he died.

"He was a spirited old coot." I throw my voice to add a Southern drawl. "He always told me nothing was impossible."

"Sounds a little like Magnolia. She didn't believe everything was for everyone, but she did believe in me."

"You've never told me, why do you call your grandmother Magnolia?"

"When we were young, her mother was still alive and Magnolia didn't want the same title as her mother. It made her feel old." She chuckles and I smile.

"So, what do you mean *everything for everyone*?"

"Magnolia knew love had limits."

I don't like the sound of that, but I also know all too well she's right. I'd been in love once. I'd never do it again.

"Some people just don't get the love they deserve," she adds.

"Wow, what a downer."

Dolores chuckles. "I guess it is."

"Have you been in love?"

"I thought I was. His name was James, and he was the boy next door with a bad boy reputation. We fooled around a lot, but then he fell in love with someone else."

She shrugs, and I want to take her hand.

"What about Rusty?" I swallow back the bile mentioning him brings me. I told myself I would not ask. I'd take the time she gave me and accept she might go back to him.

"Love does not exist with Rusty."

"More fooling around," I tease although there's no humor in my jest.

"Can we maybe not talk about him?" She looks out the windshield, her eyes narrowing at the traffic ahead. This time, I do reach for her hand and pull it to my lips.

"Definitely." I don't want to talk about him either, but I'd like to know where I stand. As much as I want to suppress the thing, my hollow heart feels an echo of a beat.

Dolores and I have spent a lot of time kissing this week. We've made out on her couch with some pretty serious petting for lack of a better word. Grinding at our seams with our hands groping, I haven't allowed us to cross any lines. No bare breasts. No naked pussy. Nothing but mouth on mouth.

It's strangely juvenile and hot as fucking hell. Dolores knows how to kiss, and her body moves like sin even if we aren't getting down to business. I separate from her each night with a hard-on that could hammer nails, but after a whack or two inside my front door, I'm done. She winds me up like no one I've known. She's wound too. Denial is the best foreplay, and I can't wait to finally watch her implode.

Once I know what Rusty means to her.

+ + +

We arrive at Vineyard Inn roughly around dinnertime. I made a late evening reservation, although the availability of the restaurant ebbs and flows. Being a week after the holiday, I assumed it wouldn't be busy, but the room overlooking the dark vineyard is packed. As the first weekend of a new month, the First Wives Club is present.

"They're a group of women who celebrate their divorces. They're the first wives," I explain after we are seated for dinner. The last hour has been rough.

First, I only had one room because the original reservation was for me. I had planned to arrive alone until Dolores.

"We can't stay in the same room," she mutters.

"Why not?" I ask, my eyes shifting to Isabelle Vincentia, the elderly woman who owns the place with her husband, Francisco. The couple has been together for an eternity, and I've seen them interact. Francisco looks at his wife like it's the first time they've met. He'll stop and touch her hair or kiss her temple. It's love incarnate, and I wanted a love like that once.

"Because we aren't..." Her voice falters.

We aren't what? I want to snap, but with the owner as our audience, I don't.

"Could you give us a second?" Taking Dolores's elbow, I guide her to the center of the lobby. "Look, this place is known for discreet affairs. The rich and famous hang out here...to hide. The owners are used to couples not being *together*-together."

Dolores's eyes widen, and she scans the empty lobby as if she'll find a couple in a nefarious act.

"Oh," she drones. "Is that what we're having?" The question feels like a slap. We better not be having an affair. I'm not into cheating. Her or me. My teeth grind.

"What we are having is a weekend away because I want to show you something."

She nods, a bit contrite, and leads us back to the concierge desk. Waving a hand over the counter, she allows me to complete our registration.

The second issue is still the room. Dolores goes into the bathroom to change, and when she steps out, all shower fresh and done up in her dress, I can't breathe. Maybe one room was a mistake. I'll never be able to contain myself. However, I realize, if I only get to hold her again, it will be enough. I've missed her in my bed, which surprises me. I don't snuggle, but I want to with her.

I'm turning into a sap.

So here we finally sit. A glass of wine before each of us, and she demands more details about the First Wives Club.

"They're mainly from the Hills as far south as Laguna Beach. Their rich husbands cheated on them, and they received a large settlement. Typically, they come together when a new one joins the rank."

"How do you know all this?"

"I've been here before when they've been present." I take a deep breath. Pain riddles my chest with this admission.

"And all the affairs here. Like who? What?"

"Hollywood producers and young upstart actresses. Or rock stars hiding out from their wives. Or…"

"Not you," a deep voice from my left catches me off guard.

"Or high-profile MMA fighters who own the joint."

"This isn't a joint," he snaps. Dolores sits back and looks up at him. He's a beast of a man with short hair cropped close to his head and bulging biceps. To my surprise, Dolores doesn't seem impressed.

"Dolores, this is Cain Callahan. His wife's family owns the winery."

"And the vineyard and the wine distribution. And the place is not for sale."

I hold up a hand because I'm no longer interested in buying. I've already gone that route, wanting a piece of the place. Instead, I want to scope it out, appreciate the view, and maybe enjoy my company a little better this time around.

Cain points at me. "No scenes." He's making one himself, but I understand. Dolores eyes me, and I know I won't have a choice in the matter. It's time to come clean.

Thankfully, a little girl skips into the restaurant with a very pregnant woman toddling behind her. Sofie Callahan must be a saint to be married to such an intense man. She's a doctor, so I suppose she's close enough.

"Daddy," the girl with wild dark ringlets calls out, and Cain's demeanor shifts. He turns to catch her when she leaps, and he hikes her up to his hip. She nuzzles her head into her father's neck but keeps her eyes on me.

"Hello, beautiful," I say, but Cain's eyes snap back to me.

"You have your own beautiful woman before you. Don't be hitting on my daughter."

"Cain," Sofie admonishes, catching up to her husband and daughter. "Mr. Fox, nice to see you again." She offers her hand to Dolores as if she hasn't seen me here before with another woman. "I'm Sofie. It's a pleasure to meet you."

"Dolores Chance, and I have no idea why I'm here." Her dark eyes fix on me, and Cain chuckles.

"No scenes," Cain mutters.

"Ah, coming from the pot, I don't think the kettle will listen," Sofie teases, brushing back her daughter's hair. "Let's let them eat in peace."

"Enjoy your meal," she says to Dolores, then tugs at her husband's bicep to lead him away.

"That was interesting," Dolores says as soon as they walk away. She picks up her wine and takes a hardy drink. Her eyes focus on me over the rim of her glass.

"I've been here before."

"I've gathered," she interrupts. My eyes catch hers, and she goes silent. It's going to take a lot to explain everything.

"I was in love once, or so I thought. Kathryn Cole was her name. Kate. I brought her here, ready to propose. Got down on my knee and everything. Then she told me no. In front of the crowded restaurant, she said no. The First Wives Club had a heyday, encouraging her to step away. Then later, one came to hit on me. It was a total shitshow."

"Oh my God," Dolores says, reaching across the table for my hand. I don't return her squeeze.

"That wasn't the worst part. As if I hadn't been humiliated enough, I went after her a week later. I went to her home, which I'd never been to. One year of dating. How had I never been to her place? I didn't question it like I should have." I swallow. "She was married. With children."

"My God, Garrett, that's awful."

I lift my glass and drain my wine.

"We'd met in an airport. It was like something out of a movie. A delay. A one-night stand. Only she was my meeting the following morning. My next investment. We'd meet on the road. Coordinate our schedules. I even brought her home to meet my family."

A shaky hand comes to my forehead.

"My sisters didn't like her, and my mother sensed something was off, but I didn't listen to any of them." I swallow again and look up at Dolores. "When she refused me, I thought it was karma for leaving my high school sweetheart who thought we'd get married and we didn't. Someone had done to me what I'd done to another. Only it was so much worse."

My eyes stay on Dolores. "A husband. And two kids. I hated myself. And I eventually hated her."

I look away and find Sofie watching our table. She stands behind a bar, and I wave my hand. We need another bottle of wine.

"I don't love him," Dolores says, and my head snaps back to her. "It sounds horrid to call us sex partners. Fuck buddies. We aren't even friends. Ten years I've given to him because…honestly…there's been no one else. I live in a small town where I work sixty-plus hours a week and take care of my mother and grandmother. I didn't have time or energy for anything else. And while he was a rebound from James, he just sort of stuck."

Her elbow slams on the table, and her fingers brush over her lips. "I sound pathetic, don't I?"

"Actually, no." I get it. Being too busy to commit, too busy to invest in more with someone else, someone better. I didn't try after Kate. I played the field over and over and over again. My hand reaches for hers and brings it to my lips. "I'm sorry you fell into a rut."

"I'm sorry she duped you."

"I'm sorry you're here with him," Cain interjects beside us while he unscrews the cork from another bottle of the fall red.

"Oh, go away." Dolores smirks, and we both look at her. Cain lets out a deep chuckle.

"I like her. She can stay." He turns back to me. "You, I'm watching. We aren't selling." He leaves us alone, and Dolores has more questions. I can read it in her eyes.

"Just start talking, Tin Man," she teases.

"Well, *Dorothy*…I've explained to you how I'm an investor, like *Shark Tank*. I buy and sell products I believe will make me a profit. It's all about market demands and the economy. Items come and go. I want something stable." I lower my voice and meet her eyes. "I want something for me. Long term."

Her eyes widen, and she leans forward, crossing her arms on the table. "So you want this winery?"

"Not anymore." I won't add how the bad memories make this a place I'd rather burn than invest in. "But I did at one time. Now, I think I'd like to find an existing property or available land. I want to build something from the ground up."

"Didn't you already do that with Fox Investors?"

"I did. But it's always been volatile. I want something permanent. For me." I take a deep breath, offering her even more of myself. "It's about my granddad. He worked at the mill near River City, making products to be bought and sold, but he didn't reap any benefit from what he produced. He always wanted land. He wanted a place of his own to produce his own items to be bought and sold, like a farm. He gave up his dream for us. His daughter and her family. When he invested in me, I promised myself that one day, I'd give him what he wanted most."

"A place of his own," she says quietly. "I understand." From what she told me of her grandmother, I believe she does.

"Will you move?" she questions, and this is the reason I brought her here. *This* is one of the questions I've been asking myself. I want her perspective. She's going to ask me the right things and hopefully make suggestions, and thankfully, we spend the next hour and our entire meal discussing possibilities and plans.

"You'll need something like this. A restaurant and maybe a resort. Make it an experience for people."

She's right. I don't want mistreated wives and clandestine affairs, but people who want a getaway…maybe romance.

I'm definitely becoming a sap.

"Tomorrow, I booked us a private tour of the vineyard and the winery. I'd like you to join me. I want your ideas."

"Mine?" she shrieks a little too loudly, drawing the attention of a few First Wives.

"Yes. You have a business mind, and I'd like your opinion."

Dolores stares at me, her hand on her throat, and I'm distracted by the way her fingers stroke her neck. She wore the black dress I gave her for dancing. The color sets off the sapphire effect of her eyes and accentuates the silver-gray streaks in her hair. Bright red lipstick highlights her lips. She's a bottle of wine herself, and I want a sip.

A chuckle from my left causes Dolores to release me from our locked eyes. We do this. Just look into each other's eyes. Hers still look sad sometimes, and I want to dive in and pull her to the surface. Lately, they've become more playful, almost mischievous, and I like how she looks at me. She's thinking. Decoding. I only hope she can't decipher too much. She'll notice that as much as I fight it, I'm falling for her. Falling hard.

"I think one of the First Wives is looking to be *your* first," Dolores says, leaning in as if to conspire with me.

"I'm not really into sloppy seconds," I whisper in return. Dolores sits back. Her hand stills at her throat.

"What am I?" Her voice is rough as her eyes blink.

"You're definitely a first for me."

chapter 17

First Place

[Dolores]

Garrett signs the bill, and we leave. We could have danced. I would have loved to dance with him again, but the First Wives looked hungry, and Garrett is a delicious dessert. With his hand on my lower back, he guides me out of the restaurant without one glance at any of them.

We pass Cain Callahan one more time. "Smart man," he mutters without looking up at us. Garrett chuckles beside me and flips his middle finger. I don't think he should tempt fate. Cain looks like one seriously rough guy, but I've seen worse. Devil's Edge in Georgia contains some scary characters in their MC.

We continue down the hall, remaining quiet since Garrett made his statement.

You're definitely a first for me.

He's a first for me as well. I've never known men with not only so much wealth but who are also so considerate. He's like a dreamy candy bar. Crisp and decadent on the outside, but nuggety good on the inside. I don't know how to respond when he compliments me. It's like I'm tongue-tied or distrusting, which isn't really true. I trust Garrett more than I trust most people. Maybe because I know he has nothing to lose in me. I'll go home, and he'll carry on. I *trust* him to do such a thing.

As for me, I've been thinking more and more about how I need to make a decision. I need to set a date and figure out what's next. All this talk of restaurants and wineries has me reconsidering my diner. I suppose I could get a loan and begin renovations to rejuvenate the place. A pick-me-up to the diner might be just what the restaurant needs. It's certainly been what I needed as a human being. After a month in California, I'm starting to feel like a new person—a new me—a better me.

Garrett opens the hotel door for us, and I walk in first. As I near the bed, I slip out of my shoes—the red slippers Garrett bought me. I turn to make a comment about our sleeping arrangements when Garrett tackles me to the mattress.

I land on my back with his arm over my waist as he lies on his side. We laugh as we bounce but then settle into silence. My head rolls to look at him, drinking him in like the delicious wine we drank throughout the evening. I'm tipsy and warm but not drunk. I'm inebriated on him, instead, and the honesty of what he told me. The excitement of his future investment. The way he looks at me.

"Let me hold you tonight," he says, his voice low and rough. A bit shaky. He's referring to my breakdown the day before Thanksgiving. I've been too embarrassed to mention it, and he's been gracious enough not to speak of it either.

"I thought you didn't do cuddling," I tease, remembering him telling me such at one point.

"I like holding you." His raw honesty makes me want to kiss him. All we've done for days is kiss, and I'm so worked up by his mouth. He's left me steaming and aching for three nights in a row, and the second he leaves the condo, I've been at myself for relief. I imagine his hands on my breasts and his fingers over my clit. I think of his tongue in either place.

The thought immediately makes me wet.

"I'll change first," I say, and Garrett releases me. I sit up, feeling shaky and shy. He's held me before, so tonight should be no different. But it will be. Sexual anticipation fills the air. I wish I had something nicer than the scoop neck nightgown I found at Target. I hadn't considered a sleeping partner in the evenings when I bought it. I chuckle at the thought and then assess myself in the bathroom mirror.

The silver hair makes me look older, yet I feel years younger. My eyes glisten from both alcohol and contentment. Garrett Fox makes me...happy. My hands roam over the cotton material. My fingers curl and cup my breasts, pressing them upward. Not as perky as they used to be, but they're still round and lush, and pebbled as I squeeze. I don't know how I'll sleep next to Garrett.

I like holding you.

I like him holding me.

When I return to the room, Garrett has his suit jacket removed and dress shirt missing. His pants hang on his hips as he's loosened his belt. His abs are sculpted at his waist, and the hint of hair leading downward teases me.

My eyes leap up to his. He's been equally taking me in, roaming down my short nightshirt which drifts off one shoulder. My peaked nipples on display. One hand smooths down my hip. I'm nervous when he looks at me like this.

"I'll be right out," he mutters, passing me for the bathroom. I slip into bed. The sheets are luxurious against my skin, which prickles and tingles. Knowing Garrett was waiting for me, I didn't touch myself in the bathroom, not to mention I feared any murmur I made would hint at what I was doing. Now, I'm suffering under the weight of the duvet and the silkiness of the sheet against my legs, oversensitive to the slightest touch on my skin.

Garrett steps back into the main room and flips off the light. I hear the rustle of his pants as he removes them, and then he crawls into bed behind me. I hold my breath, waiting for him to touch me. His hand slips over my waist, and he nuzzles his nose into the nape of my neck.

This is not going to be enough. Not tonight.

"Can I ask you something?" We've started wiggling against one another. His bent knee straightens so his foot slides down my calf between my legs. My backside lightly rubs over his stiffening erection.

"Sure." My voice squeaks.

"When you were in my bed…alone…what were you thinking about? What did you imagine me doing to you?"

Oh, God. His knee bends, separating my legs and drawing close to my center. His fingers spread across my abdomen, and his nose swirls at my neck. I take the risk and cover his hand with mine. Guiding his palm to my outer thigh, I slowly lead him upward, bunching up the material of my nightgown as we move with collective hands.

Garrett groans.

When he meets my bare hip, his hand curls over the bone and squeezes. My leg adjusts, and his upper thigh connects with my center. I arch my back, forcing the faintest rub against his leg and pressure against the firm length at my backside. I squirm. I can't help myself. My body has its own intentions.

"More." Garrett murmurs into the juncture of my neck and shoulder. I continue to drag his palm under the nightgown, over my belly, and up to a breast. Collectively, we cover one, and I force his hand to squeeze. Garrett rolls his hips, so his firm length presses into me.

I moan.

"Dolores," he whispers. I don't respond as I force his hand to cover the whole achy globe. I squeeze, and Garrett takes over. "Like this?"

His palm cups me, massaging and tugging, forcing my nipple to nub to the point of pain. He tweaks it between his forefinger and thumb, and a pleasurable jolt shoots directly down the center of my belly. My spine curves and my backside rubs against the solid ridge nudging at my crack.

He is so much better than what I had in my imagination.

"What else did I do?"

His mouth, I think, but then he interrupts my thought with, "Show me." Following his command, I cover his hand once again and drag it down my abs and into my underwear. Over the mound. Between my thighs.

"Sweet Jesus," he mutters as I guide a finger to slide through my slippery folds. Garrett's thigh lifts, forcing my leg to shift over his hip. He's opening me to his exploration, and once again, he takes over. His fingers stroke, and then they delve. One enters me, and the thrill sends another jolt up my center. It triggers my hips to rock back, searching for more friction against his erection.

"Garrett," I whisper, my voice hoarse and wanton.

"What else did I do, sweetheart?" Does he honestly want me to tell him? His mouth comes to mind again, but when I take too long to answer, he stops.

I swallow back a protesting groan. Denying myself will not happen. I need this too much.

"You make me come," I say, surprised at the rasp to my voice. Garrett's fingers return to their exploration, diving deeper as he adds a second one. I've lost my mind *and body*. My hips take over, undulating with the pace he's set, pressing against his dick at my ass.

I want it. I want this. I want him.

Then I crack. I erupt over his fingers, my knees coming together to hold his leg between mine. His thigh lifts, keeping his hand in place, his fingers buried inside me as I ride out an orgasm which brings stars. My heart races, and I squeeze one of my breasts.

"Was that it?" he whispers, encouraging me to tell him more.

I shake my head. This is enough, I think, but it isn't.

"Tell me," he demands as my leg relaxes over his, and his fingers fall free. A trickle of my release floods my thighs.

"Your mouth," I whine. Garrett wastes no time rolling me to my back. He pushes my nightgown up to my breasts, and I lift my arms. He slips the material over my head and peers down at my almost naked body.

"Stunning," he mutters as a hand reaches for a swollen globe. He massages one while the other is met with his mouth, hot and wet. He licks and laves, sucking the entire weight into the cavern of his cheeks. His teeth nip at the peaked nub. I whimper at the sharp bite but fall back as he moves to my other breast. This is what I imagined. This is what I hoped it would be like.

His open palm skates down my stomach as he continues suckling my breast, but when his fingers connect with the waistband of my underwear, he draws his mouth back. His head lifts so he can look at me.

"What else?" he questions in command. He wants more.

"Your mouth. Lower." A slow smile curls his lip, and he places open-mouthed kisses down my belly until he reaches my underwear.

Removing the material by slipping it down my thighs until I kick it free, he massages up my legs until a finger spreads me once again.

"So wet," he says, staring down at me.

"For you," I add, and he dives again. His head separates my thighs as his mouth sucks my clit. I bow off the bed, but he holds my hips down. I thrash on the pillow as his tongue spreads me and then begins a rapid pulsing motion, entering me with a force I've not experienced before. His tongue is thick. This I know from kissing him, but he's literally making out with my lower lips, sucking and savoring, tugging and torturing until I break again.

My hands cover his head, holding him in place as another orgasm rips through me. My head comes off the pillow, and I whimper his name on repeat.

Eventually, he curls up on his knees, bracing my thighs over his. The lower half of my body rests on him. Taking his dick in hand, he drags himself through my soaked folds, coating his tip.

"Please tell me there's more."

I hadn't truly gotten this far in my fantasy. Once the images of him licking me brought me to release, I didn't dare to envision more while I stole the moments in his bed.

Garrett grips my hips, and with a quick roll, he flips us so I'm over him, straddling the hard length under my center.

"Ride me," he says, and I'm triggered. For the briefest of moments, Rusty enters my head. Drunk. Lazy. Telling me to ride him so he doesn't have to put forth any effort.

"Condom," I whisper, my voice choked. Garrett sits upright, fingers curling my hair over my ear. His eyes search mine in the dark room, pinching as he stares.

"It's only us in here, okay? Only us."

"Only us," I repeat. I lean forward to kiss him quickly, but Garrett opens immediately and finds my tongue. He tastes like me, salt and musk, and I suck at him in return. When he draws back, he peers up at me again.

"Take me." The change in command makes me feel better. "Do with me what you would have done." I press at his shoulders until he's flat on his back.

"Condom," I repeat, and he rolls his head to the nightstand. We can discuss later how he already had one ready. In spite of myself, I smile as the package I find holds three. Reaching for the foil, I open it and sheath him.

"Fuck," he growls as his fingers dig into my thighs. Linking my fingers with his, I pull them over his head.

Let me be in control, I command without words, pressing at his hands, silently emphasizing I want them to remain on the pillow. As I sit up, Garrett does one better and reaches for the bottom edge of the headboard. His body is stretched, lean, and muscular, and my fingers tickle down his abs. They flinch, and I wonder if he's ticklish.

"What are you doing to me?" he whispers, but my answer won't come with words. I stroke up his covered shaft once, and then position myself at the tip. Slipping down, I cause him to quickly impale me, and we grunt in unison at the connection. His fingers fist on the board behind his head. Mine find his hips as I use his body to leverage myself up and down.

We easily slip and slide as I'm so wet from his mouth. The pace I set takes us fast, and I race for the finish line. Garrett's eyes focus on my breasts, jiggling and thumping at my chest. Sitting upright, I roll my hips, finding friction for my clit on his pelvis bone. My hands move up my body and cup my breasts. I squeeze myself, pinching my nipples.

"You are a fucking goddess," he sputters between breaths, and I rock faster. Keeping him deep, I feel him tap inside at a place I didn't know existed.

"Garrett," I call out, my voice hitching.

"Touch yourself," he commands, lifting his head to look at where we join. My fingers drop, and I instantly find what I need. I hold him in me while I work the sensitive hood. I free-fall instantly. My channel clenches as I still, and then I feel the rush of him inside me, pulsing, beating, releasing. Briefly, I wonder what it would feel like if he wasn't covered.

I'm about to collapse when he releases the headboard and sits up again, his mouth crushing mine. One arm wraps around my back. His fingers slip into my hair, holding the back of my head. Aftershocks ripple through my body, and I tremble over him as his mouth tugs and pecks at mine. He slows the kiss in an attempt to lower our rapidly beating hearts.

Too late, I think.

Take my heart, Tin Man. It already belongs to you.

chapter 18

A Tour Of The Heart

[Garrett]

Together, we collapse back to the mattress still holding on to each other. Her legs remain wrapped around my hips. My arm still encircles her back. We lie in silence, waiting for our breathing to regulate before I slip out of her. She whimpers at the release, and I want to promise her I'd stay inside forever if she asks.

Ask the Wizard for anything, Dolores. I'll make it happen if I can.

I slip from bed to dispose of the condom, get a washcloth, and return to wipe her clean. She stares at me, noting the attention I take before dropping the cloth on the floor and slipping next to her again.

"That was sweet." I don't even want to know what she means. I don't want to think of another man not offering her aftercare. I don't want to think of anyone with her again.

My fingers comb through her hair at the side of her head. She's so beautiful in the dim light seeping through the slim edge of the curtains. Her eyes gleam.

"You're kind of incredible," she says, a smile on her lips.

"I knew you'd come around," I tease, and she swats at my chest. I catch her wrist and lift her hand, kissing her open palm. "Actually, I can think of a better word. Insatiable."

There's no way one time with her will be enough. Here's the part that sucks about being fifty, though. I need a moment before I can get it up again. I could have brought some little blue pills, but somehow, with Dolores, I don't think I'll need them.

"We're going to need to do that again," I say into her palm.

"I'm exhausted." She giggles, a genuine laugh of contentment. I like the sound from her.

"Okay," I singsong. "I'll give you twenty minutes."

She giggles again and leans forward for my lips. She thinks I'm joking, but after twenty minutes of soft pecks, which turn to heady, open-mouthed tongue-included kisses, I'm ready again. I slip over her and prepare to slide home, when she mutters, "Condom."

Right. I never usually forget them. Never. But something about Dolores makes me forget myself. When I was young, I was stupid and went bare with my high school sweetheart. It was the eighties; what can I say? But once I moved West, I've always been wrapped. Kate insisted on it, and painfully, I learned why. She already had kids. I shiver but quickly shake the thought.

I cover myself this time and easily slip inside. We're slower this round. Our hips roll in a lazy dance. Our mouths remain connected. My thoughts race to her sitting over me, holding me inside her warmth, as she cups her breasts. I meant what I said—she's a fucking goddess.

I pull back and peer down at her. Our hands explore, roaming over chests and breasts, down arms, and gripping hips. Eventually, I can't take the slower pace. Dolores wraps her legs over my lower back, and my hand slips under her firm ass. I squeeze as I lift, pummeling into her.

"Get there," I mutter, but Dolores shakes her head.

"Come," she commands, and I still. My dick jolts and jumps, jetting off inside the snug condom. Still, I feel her clench around me, holding me deep. My head falls to her shoulder.

"Shit, I'm sorry. I couldn't last." Because she's fucking stunning.

"I'm not sorry." She chuckles, jiggling us both. I reach between us, still in her, and touch her swollen, sweet clit. Her eyes drift back, and her lids close. She lets me play with her folds until she whimpers out another orgasm.

Four for her. Two for me. *Not bad, old sport.*

I lilt sideways, tugging at her to follow me. We face one another, breathing in the scent of sex and us. *Us.* Like what I told her. There's only us in this room.

I thought she'd eventually mention what I told her earlier, how I proposed to someone else in this very resort, but she hasn't. Not surprisingly, I'm relieved. It's history.

"You're quiet," she mutters, her voice drowsy.

"Deep in thought."

"That would make you the Scarecrow," she snorts.

"He didn't have a brain."

"Right." She chuckles, drawing circles on my chest with one finger. "I don't think you're really the Tin Man, either."

"Perhaps I am a Wizard, after all," I joke.

"Perhaps." She sighs. Actually, I'm more cowardly Lion because I want to tell her how I feel but won't. I'm afraid to share my thoughts and my heart. Dolores already holds them both, but when she goes home, she'll take them with her, and I can't handle that pain again.

+ + +

The next morning, the questions arrive as we have breakfast on a balcony overlooking the vineyard.

"You brought me to a place where you proposed to someone." She isn't judging me but questioning the rationale.

"I told you last night. I want to scope out the place for ideas."

She nods, not convinced. I hold her hand on the table, lazily stroking my thumb over the back of her knuckles. I can't seem to let her go. We had sex again this morning. Morning wood. Hard and fast, we lay on our sides with her back to my chest. A man could get used to waking up to that every day.

"So when do we begin?"

As if on cue, Sofie enters the balcony. She's a medical doctor in the valley, but her grandparents own this place. I learned after my attempt to purchase it that the vineyard is near and dear to her heart, and she wanted to keep it for her retirement. She's only twentysomething, so she has a long time to go, but the comment sparked the thought for myself. What would I do next? When I grow tired of the hustle of other people's companies. what would I have for me?

Like Dolores mentioned, I already have Fox Investors, but I've always been someone who wanted more. More money. More business. More anything. When I look over at Dolores speaking with Sofie, I realize the more I may be missing doesn't come with a price tag. The *more* I might be searching for may be something money cannot buy.

Huh.

Sofie explains our tour guide will be Raphael, a sixty-nine-year-old man, who clearly has the hots for Dolores. If he doesn't stop flirting with her, I'm going to be charged with harming an elder. She giggles and teases him in return, which only encourages him. It's a lesson in her management skills—she's good with people. She told me her diner caters to all the locals. Old men on Saturday mornings. Ladies playing Bunco on Tuesday evenings. Her Thursday night special of chicken salad. Dolores has an easy way about her. Being so secluded at her brother's place, I haven't seen her interact much with others. It's fascinating to watch her until there are one too many winks from Raphael.

"Time for the vineyard," I snap. We toured the winery, but a golf cart ride through the vines is another part of our day. Raphael offers to drive, allowing Dolores to sit next to him, but I object.

"I'll drive. You direct." Raphael sits next to me, and Dolores sits behind us. With his attention better focused, I begin to have my questions answered. The time it takes for a vine to produce. Conditions. Weather. Land. It's all stuff I've researched, and many days it makes me miss my granddad as he'd understand it all better than I do.

We stop in the center of the vineyard where a small table is set up with wine samples. Dolores gushes over each taste while Raphael explains how to twirl a glass, then sniff and sip. She flushes by the time we finish, her cheeks rosy and her eyes bright. I want to make love to her with this look on her face.

When we return to the main resort, we find Wally, who's been hanging out in a barn. The inn doesn't allow animals inside the hotel but has a pen of sorts in a heated room in one of the outbuildings. Wally looks like he's been pampered, but he jumps to his feet when he hears Dolores's voice.

"Where's my spoiled Wally?" she coos, and his tail thumps. His heart belongs to her like mine. We decide to walk back through the vines, Wally racing up the path as we discuss what we've learned. Dolores loops her arm with mine, occasionally resting her head on my shoulder.

I'm not certain how long we walk before we discover a river and a small sandy beach area. Dolores and I stop, and she stares at the streaming water.

"This reminds me of home," she says, her arms crossing over her middle.

"You don't talk much about it." I throw a twig for Wally, but he doesn't chase it. Instead, he collapses by a tree, panting from the long walk.

"There isn't much to tell. Blue Ridge is a small town. My father was the mayor, but he was a terrible human being."

Holy crap. I didn't know her family was in politics. Her brother mentioned how he didn't get along with his dad, who died sometime while he was on the road being a rock star.

"The town supported him because that's what small towns do. He held a position of power, but people didn't respect him. He cheated on my mother. He beat Denton."

Fuck. "Did he ever touch you?"

"Not with his fist."

"People suck," I mutter. My father left us when my little sister was born. The only father figure I had was Granddad, but I wouldn't trade him for the world.

"We lived on the Lane. Mountain Spring Lane. A dead-end strip of gravel road with three exclusive homes. Daddy wanted to be part of the history of Blue Ridge, although the Harringtons and the Conrads on either side of our house were old families. Original settlers or something like that." She sighs. "Anyway, a river edged our properties. The water was cold." She chuckles, still lost in her memories.

"Do you miss it?" I hold my breath as I ask.

"I miss the diner and some of the people. It's the only place I've ever known, so in my heart, I miss the familiarity. But I don't miss the lonely memories I have of my parents." Her head rolls, and she looks at me. I love when she stares into my eyes because it's as if she's giving me her soul. I reach for her hand and tug her down next to me. She lands with a thump on the ground.

"Ow." She blends the interjection with her laughter. Reaching around her back, I nudge her to scoot between my legs. With my chin on her shoulder, I watch the water flow in the river.

"Thinking of going home?" I question. Again, my breath hitches. I don't think I'll like her answer. She twists in my arms, looking at me over one shoulder.

"Not yet. Why? Do you want me to leave?"

I answer her with a slow kiss. My hands cover her flushed cheeks, drawing her lower lip between mine. I sip the swollen skin before releasing her and pressing my forehead to hers. "I don't think I want you to ever go."

The truth weighs heavy on my chest, and the words fill the slim space between us. Her answer comes in the form of a similar kiss. Sweet. Lasting. Longing. Her tongue sweeps mine, and that's all it takes. I have her on her back, desperate to connect with her for fear she's going to leave too soon. Fingers slip into her hair as my legs come between hers, forcing her to open for me. I press upward, my dick straining to enter her. Our clothing provides too much of a barrier.

"Why do I want you so much?" I mutter between kisses down her jaw to her neck. My hips rock, forcing the stiff ridge behind my zipper to slide over the seam of her leggings. "I want you right now."

"Here?" she chokes, her head rolling to look at Wally. He's sleeping, the lazy beast. He won't see a thing.

"Right here," I say, sitting up and tugging off my light jacket. It's in the sixties but warmer in the sunshine. My body temperature escalates to a hundred. I'm hot for her. Lifting her hips, I slip my jacket under her backside and tug her leggings below her knees—just enough so she can spread for me. She sits up; her fingers work at my belt and my zipper, releasing me from my jeans within seconds. Our mouths crash again.

"Condom," she groans as I lay her back.

Fuck. I growl. I pat my back pockets and then search the inside of my jacket spread under her. Thank fuck for secret pockets. I roll the rubber to cover me and slip into her without any foreplay. Once I'm seated to the hilt, Dolores moans, rolling her hips under me to meet me thrust for thrust.

Don't leave. I tap into her. *Stay with me.*

Her hands slip into my jeans, which are just below my hips, and hold my ass.

"Harder," she mutters. "Faster."

This woman is a dream come true. I pick up the pace, pressing up on one elbow to slip my fingers between us. I'm not releasing without her coming on my dick. I flick the nub, and she denotates quickly, digging her fingers into the globes of my ass, forcing me to remain deep inside her.

Don't worry. I'm not going anywhere, sweetheart, I think as I follow her. I'm not sure the condom can hold all my seed. I'm coming and coming and coming, continuing to thrust into her as I imagine what it would feel like to be bare and free within her.

"Garrett." Her voice hitches, hinting at another building orgasm.

"Fuck yes, sweetheart," I growl, circling harder at her clit as I remain inside her. Her head lifts off the ground, and her nails scrape across my ass. She screams my name as she falls back and removes her grip on my backside. Her arms fall to the sides, fisting in the material of my jacket as a second orgasm flows out of her.

My God, I love her. The thought races to my heart, expanding the organ inside my chest. I can't breathe, but then I look down at her, satiated and pleased. She smiles up at me, a sheepish look in her eyes, and my heart beats a new rhythm.

Don't leave me.

She giggles as a hand comes to her forehead.

"What?"

"I've never done anything like that," she admits, turning her head to Wally who hasn't moved from his nap.

"Well, I'm happy it was with me, then," I tease.

She shakes her head. "You're unbelievable." She grins with mocked disappointment.

"Yeah, but you love me."

The comment freezes us both. *Why would I say that?* It's just a figure of speech, but her eyes fix on mine, and I don't want her to respond. I don't want her to say anything, and to my relief, she doesn't. We just stare at one another. Then I pull back and right her pants. I don't have any way to clean her up, but I'm more concerned I just dirtied everything with my smartass comment.

chapter 19

It's In His Kiss

[Dolores]

Do I love him? How could I be in love with him? I shouldn't love him. That would be dangerous. We hardly know one another. First of all, he's Garrett Fox. He owns Fox Investors, which sounds important and influential. I'm Dolores Chance, diner owner in a small town located literally across the country. Which brings me to reason number two. We don't live anywhere near one another. But neither money nor distance can change my heart.

I won't tell him how I feel, though. I've learned my lesson well over the years. He seems just as surprised as me that he said such a thing. His eyes tell me not to reply to his off-the-cuff comment. *Don't ruin the moment and tell him the truth.* Don't destroy the moment and lie. Just let it be. So I do.

He quickly withdraws from me, fumbles to help me with my leggings, and tucks himself away. Hopping to his feet, he reaches down for my hands and tugs me to stand. I pull his jacket with me, and he shakes it out before draping it over his arm.

"We should probably head back," he admits, whistling for Wally to rouse from his afternoon siesta. Wally yawns, stretches, and stands, taking his time to saunter ahead of us down the path leading to the inn. We follow in awkward silence. We haven't gone far before Garrett reaches for my hand and stops me.

"Look, about that. What I said. I—"

My finger covers his lips to stop him. *Please don't say you didn't mean it.* He didn't declare he loved me. He only said I loved him. He isn't wrong, but we don't need to discuss it. I don't need to turn the tables and put him on the spot. Instead, I say, "Garrett, kiss me."

He leans forward and takes my mouth, tender and sweet. His fingers loosely touch my jaw as he kisses me like he always does. The kiss tells me nothing has changed between us. We are still wildly attracted to each other. That's all we need right now.

Slowly, he pulls back, taking my lower lip with his before releasing me. His forehead comes to mine, and once again, he says, "What are you doing to me?"

"Well, I can think of a few things, but we've already done them."

He chuckles as he looks down at me. "Oh, I have a few more tricks."

"Sounds like a treat for me," I tease, and he laughs a little harder. His arm slips over my shoulder and mine goes around his waist, and although we walk back with fewer words, I still feel good about where we are right now.

+ + +

As I only have the one dress, we go more casual on our second night at the vineyard. We spent the afternoon napping, Garrett curled around me, and I feel rested for the first time in a long time. In the evening, we head to the bar where we order another sampling of wine and dance while soft music plays. Close. Tight. Together.

Tipsy, we return to the room where Garrett stops me beside the bed.

"I want to play," he says, his voice turning darker, seductive, and rough as a finger trails down my arm. My back remains to him as he flattens his palms and trails them back up my arms.

"Okay," I whisper, trembling with excitement and possibility. "A leash?" I tease, my voice cracking. Would I consider such a thing? I think that's too much for me.

"I promise I won't go that far." He chuckles as he purrs near my ear. "Just let me lead."

Nodding in response, I turn to face him. He kisses me slowly, taking his time to outline my lips, memorize my mouth, and circle my tongue.

His hands wander as he removes my sweater and then lowers my jeans. I'd already kicked off my booties, and Garrett directs me, "Put on the red heels."

I do as he says and stand before him in black underwear and a matching bra. Nothing lacy or fancy but still black. His eyes remain on mine as he tugs off his dress shirt along with the T-shirt underneath.

"Walk to the chair," he commands, watching me with the eyes of a hungry predator. I do as he asks, taking my time, but my fingers twitch. Having his eyes on me like this and knowing he's watching me move make me nervous. The sway of my hips. The tightness of my backside. The flip of my hair over my shoulder. My skin is hyperaware he's going to touch me soon, and my sex clenches with anticipation. "Sit."

I spin and fold down into the low-armed bedroom chair. Garrett slips off his pants but leaves on his boxers for the moment. He sits on the small footrest before me and strokes my upper thighs.

"Ever been tied up?"

"No," I choke.

"How about blindfolded?"

"No." My voice softens.

"Ever consider either?" His fingers skitter down my skin to my knees. I shrug. "It's me, sweetheart. You can tell me." If Garrett wants me to spell out my fantasies, I don't think I can.

"Being tied up involves a certain level of trust." My eyes shift from his. It's not that I don't trust him. I do. But do I trust this process? I'd be so vulnerable to him, and I already feel exposed. "I'd want to touch you too much," I clarify, hoping to soothe the concern on his brow. The corner of Garrett's mouth curls. "But I'm curious about being blindfolded. It seems the experience would be heightened without sight."

"What experience?"

"You touching me." My voice drops, rumbling in my throat. I want those hands higher on my thighs. I want his mouth on mine. I want to feel him everywhere.

Garrett's lips turn into a full-blown mischievous grin. He abruptly stands and returns with his tie from the night before.

"Trust me," he says, lifting one brow before placing the silky material over my eyes. I nod as I swallow. His fingers coast down the side of my neck, and my skin pebbles, oversensitive to his touch. I hear him shuffle and then the sound of the ice bucket. Cubes of ice fall inside a glass.

"Garrett," I mutter. His presence fills the space before me like the uncanny sense of him when he stands behind me. A cold cube coats my lips until he presses it between them. Instinctively, I suck.

"You have the best fucking mouth," he mutters. "Just watching you makes my cick jump, reminding me of when you took me with it." Ah, yes, my overeager blowjob on Thanksgiving.

He removes the ice from my mouth and slides it down my chin and along my neck until he reaches my breast. My breaths accelerate. My heart races. He outlines the exposed cleavage above my bra, skating up one hill and then quickly sliding down the slope to curl up the other.

"It's cold," I say until his mouth covers the swells, licking the cool path he drew. The warmth of his tongue over the cold trail peaks my nipples. I'm sensitive to the scrap of silk over them, the drag of his tongue on my skin, and the tickle of his fingers skittering up my side. He slips a palm behind my back and unclasps my bra, drawing it down my arms. Without my eyes, I feel naked and raw, wanting to cover my chest because I know he's observing me. The chilled cube circles one nipple, bringing it to a firm nub, and I yelp, arching into the cold instead of away. Something rumbles from his throat. *Approval?* Then he moves to the other but hesitates. He doesn't cross the nipple, and my chest heaves. *What is he waiting for?* I wonder until his mouth covers the firm nub, sucking at it with a suddenly cool tongue.

"Gah." I squirm under a mess of chills and heat. I reach for his head and hold him to my breast.

He pulls back abruptly. "I don't want to tie you up, but I will if you don't keep your hands to yourself. Grip the armrests. Let me lead." I nod, slowly swallowing, and curl my fingers over the short arms of the chair. He returns to my breast, nipping at the sensitive tip, and my hips buck.

My legs are already spread to accommodate him between them, but they spread wider, hoping to find friction.

"Stunner," he mutters into the swell of my left breast. "Do you want me?"

"Yes," I exhale, breathless and panting. Another ice cube clinks in the glass, and a new cube draws down the center of my stomach. My belly quivers with the icy touch until he dips lower, pressing the cube to my core over my underwear.

"You're so hot down here, it's melting."

Oh yes, I'm burning up for him. He removes the cube, and his fingers find the edge of my underwear. Somehow, the tip of the ice hits my nipple again. Does he have it in his mouth as he undresses me? I lean slightly, inhaling the scent of him. His hair. Definitely holding the cube in his mouth.

I lift my hips to allow him to remove the last of my clothing. The red heels remain on my feet. I feel sexy and seductive—bare, raw, and ready. I'm convinced I've never been so turned on in my life, so vulnerable but willing.

A cool breath blows across my warm clit, and my fingers tighten on the armrest.

"Did you go through my drawer when you stayed at my house?"

It's a strange question, considering our position, but I also know what he's asking me.

"I did," I whisper. The vibrator. The metal balls. The clamps.

"I should punish you for being a nosy neighbor," he teases, and suddenly, the cube of ice swipes up my sex. I whimper at the cold against my hot center. "But I'm curious which item you imagined me using on you."

I gasp.

"That's what I thought," he mutters with a chuckle. "Which one?"

I don't answer him. I hadn't imagined the toys in my fantasy. I only wanted him. His skin on mine.

"I should have brought one with me," he murmurs, "but I have other ways to play with you." A new cube comes between his fingers and slips inside me. I cry out, and he lifts my leg, hitching it over the low armrest.

"Place your hands above your head. Hold the back of the chair." I do as he says, my breasts thrusting forward, accentuated for him. He tugs my other leg over the opposite arm, and I realize my breasts are the least of his focus.

"You are so fucking stunning, Dolores," he says, his voice the roughest I've ever heard from him. He returns the ice cube to my slit, and my head thrashes with the sensation of melting cubes, dripping, coating my core. Then the warmth of his tongue covers me, and I jolt. One hand reaches for him.

"Uh-uh-uh. Obey the Wizard, Dorothy," he teases, catching my wrist. I return my hand to the back of the chair, clutching at it like my life depends on it. Like my heart does. His mouth returns to my core where he laps and licks, bringing me close to the brink but then stopping short. He pulls back, and I want to scream. Instead, I whimper in disappointment.

A thick finger enters me, and I hear his breathing shift. Is he watching what he does to me? Another finger joins the first, and my hips rock against the drag of his digits. In and out. Slicing into my center. Carving a niche in my heart. He owns me at this moment, and I'd give him everything—*all of me*—as long as he doesn't stop touching me.

"You respond so easily to me," he groans, and the tension builds again, creeping, crawling. My toes twitch, and then he removes his fingers.

Son of a bitch.

I hear shuffling once again and sense him standing before me. "Lean forward," he demands. "Grip the armrests if you need to, but don't touch me." I lower my arms and rest my hands just above my spread thighs. I lean forward until something touches my lips. Smooth. Tight. Skin.

He doesn't need to ask. I open for him, and he enters my willing mouth. My tongue swirls, and my cheeks hollow as I suck him deep. He sets the pace, slowly rocking forward, and desire rips through me. I need the release. I reach for myself, knowing I'm exposed to him in this contorted position. My fingers find a mix of cool flesh and wet heat. I stroke until he notices. He draws back from my mouth, a pop sound following the release. However, my mouth follows the retreat, salivating for more of him. I might have growled, gnashing my teeth. I want him.

"You little cheater," he hisses. The ottoman drags across the carpet as if he had shoved it away from him. His hands swat at mine, and I return them over my head, gripping the back of the chair. His hands grasp my inner thighs, holding me open and on display. The only sound between us is ragged breathing and tense anticipation. I'm ready to beg him to take me when the moist tip of his dick slides through my weeping folds. My head thrashes on the back on the chair while the smooth skin drags over my sensitive spot.

"Dolores," he growls. "Let me in." His voice rings with more than he says. "I'll pull out. Just a little…Just once." He can't complete his thought as he separates me and slides through the tender folds once again. I'm coating him—skin on skin—and I can't remember the last time I was with a man without a barrier.

"Trust me," he begs.

"When was the last time you were like that with a woman?" I have to ask. He freezes, the hard length of him resting against my entrance.

"A long, long time ago, Dolores." My lips twist as he hesitates, hovers. "Please don't bring anyone else into this right now. It's never been like this for me, Dolores. I want you."

There's something in his voice. The plea. The honesty. The raw truth that I might be different. My leg curls around his hip, and I nudge him with the heel of my ruby red shoe.

Welcome home, Tin Man, I whisper internally as he takes the hint and presses his tip to my entrance.

"Fuck," he growls almost unintelligibly as he slowly slips into me and halts. His fingertips dig into my thighs. Bruises might occur, but I don't care. He can mark me. He already has. My heart will be scarred forever after this.

He drags me to the edge of the short cushion and lifts one leg to his shoulder. I'm so full, so open to him, and completely at his mercy. Open-mouthed kisses trail down my ankle and calf. Then he lowers the leg to the armrest. One hand remains near the opposite leg. He rolls his hips, adjusting himself inside me.

My God that felt good.

"Dolores," he calls out like a prayer. "Hold on, sweetheart." He shifts his body so both hands are braced on the chair, and he lifts to delve into me deeper, harder, faster. I curl under him, legs spread wide, fingers clutching the back of the chair. He's hitting something inside me I didn't know existed, and the orgasm will surely rip me in two. It races from my toes and rushes down my chest, barreling toward the center to crash and explode in the most decadent release I've ever experienced. My knees close on his hips as my back arches, and I scream.

"Dolores," he pants, our bodies jostling with each intense thrust. I can't help myself. My voice dominates me as I warn, "Don't you dare leave me."

Red heels connect around the back of his thighs, trapping him from pulling back.

"I'll. Pull. Out. But…" His stuttering voice breaks—a sign he's on the edge.

I don't speak. I don't want him to come on me. *Not Rusty*, whispers through my thoughts at the most inopportune time.

"Dolores," he strains, warning me with a desperate plea before he stills. His back stiffens as he halts his jagged thrusting and commences to pulse inside me, filling me with his hot seed. My heels unlock, sliding over his hips until my body sags. He awkwardly folds down over me, wrapping his arms around my back and dragging me against his chest.

"That wasn't very responsible," he mutters into my shoulder before kissing it. Our breathing matches, ragged and spent. His heart beats against my chest, the rapid rhythm keeping time with mine.

"Please don't say you regret it," I whisper. The moment of euphoria pulls back from me, receding too quickly. His fingers fumble as he tugs the blindfold to my forehead. Sharp light brown eyes sparkle like candlelight at me.

"I regret absolutely nothing I've done with you, Dolores. My only regret might be that I can't do this every day of my life with you."

My heart crashes. So intense. *He's lost in the moment*, I think, as am I. I kick off my ruby red shoes and take his lips, deciding to stay in Oz just a little bit longer.

chapter 20

Condom Sense

[Garrett]

Please don't say you regret it.

Is she kidding me? There's nothing I regret less in my life than entering her as I did.

Was it responsible? No.

Was it incredible? Yes.

I haven't felt something like this in...I don't even know. Can I remember as far back as the late eighties, being a reckless teen, and sleeping with my high school sweetheart in the back seat of my mom's sedan...nope. Besides the fact I'm a man, compared to my teenage body and hormones of thirtysomething years ago, so to my dick, this is unique, indescribable, and truly special.

It's the same for other parts of me.

Tap, tap goes something in my chest.

We collapse on the bed after a quick shower of suds and scrubbing but nothing further. I need a few minutes to recover, so Dolores curls into my side. It's nice—this cuddling thing—or maybe it's just her. I have this sense she isn't pretending with me. She doesn't have a hidden agenda. She doesn't want to know the bottom line of my bank account. She doesn't care about any of my things. So while she strokes her fingertips over my chest, combing through the fine hairs making a vee between my pecs, I close my eyes and just breathe her in.

At some point, we drift off to sleep, but I awake to another fulfilling fantasy of her mouth on me, savoring and salivating over my rock-hard erection. *God, her mouth*. It's heaven.

What is she doing to me?

I've asked myself this question a thousand times in the past few weeks. Is it really that she's doing something to me, or am I just opening up to her? It's been strange being here, bringing up the memory of asking Kate to marry me. The look on Dolores's face when she finally asked me why here and why her. I can't explain myself. I trust her. I trust her to be honest and not to leave me.

It's a deep-rooted fear. One steeped in little boy leftovers from a father who dumped us, and the foolish heart of a young man throwing it all on the line for a woman not free to accept my offer. Somewhere inside me wants to cling to Dolores while another part of me tells me not to hold too tight. She doesn't need another person to take care of in her life. She's told me about her mother, her grandmother, the diner, and all the things she does for others.

Who does things for her?

I haven't asked because the answer's in her eyes. She's alone, like me.

Is she lonely?

I wouldn't say I was, but now that I've spent so much time with her—the nightly dinners, the dance lessons, a weekend away—Dolores will be someone I miss greatly if she leaves. Loneliness is the haunting emotion I'd feel if she went away.

I like her. A lot.

Do I love her?

I was joking when I said it earlier. *You know you love me.* A slip of the tongue, so to speak, but the question is, could she love me? Could I love again, love her specifically? My hollow heart beats. Not so hollow anymore, methinks.

I sit up and tug her from my slick length.

"I wasn't finished," she murmurs, drowsy still, maybe drunk on me. God, I want her to be.

"Come here," I say, guiding her up and over me. We took this position last night, but something slipped in her eyes when I told her to ride me. I flip her once we align, and she spreads her thighs to accommodate my legs. "Are you sore?"

I went a little rough on her in the chair. My dick jolts with the memory. My heart skips with a new feeling.

Dolores shakes her head on the pillow. "But maybe we could slow down at first."

I lean over her, reaching for the nightstand where I stowed the condoms I should have used earlier. She doesn't question me as I kneel back and sheath myself. There's no urgency like an hour ago, and my heart races. She's looking at me like she sees my soul.

Do you know how I feel about you?

Can you hear my heart beating for the first time in a long time?

Does the rhythm of yours match mine?

Her mouth curls as if she's read my thoughts, and I shift my eyes from hers. Bracing myself on one arm, I guide my dick to her entrance. I swipe a finger upward, finding her primed and ready for me. I wish I was bare once again as I'm slick as well from her mouth. Slowly, I enter her, waiting for a whimper of pain. When there's no response, I glance up to find those blue beams focused on me. She's watching my face, not how our bodies join. The look is intense. A gleam in the deep sea I haven't seen before. My heart races faster while I ease into her.

Lowering to my elbows, I still and brush back hair near her cheek. Our eyes hold. Our hips move.

What is she doing to me?

I have my answer. It's buried deep within, under painful childhood memories and broken teenage dreams and scars from a woman who was never mine.

Dammit. This can't be…but that internal organ disagrees, as does my body moving in sync with hers. Our eyes connect almost more fastidious than our lower region. If I were a child, we'd be locked in a staring contest. Yet I sense neither of us wants to look away first and break the spell. Our eyes link in more ways than our bodies.

"Dolores," I whisper, taking my time to glide back and plunge forward, feeling each ripple against my ridges.

"Shh," she soothes, reaching up to press a hand to my face, and then combing her fingers back through my short hair. My mouth lowers for hers. I've lost the game. She wins. She can take my body and my soul. She already owns my heart. The one I didn't think I had to give.

+ + +

With a new day, I have a different perspective, and I shake the intense emotions from the night before. Our second round of sex was too much, and I try to ward off the weirdness this morning with a quickie before I showered alone, attempting to distance myself from her.

My heart gallops within my chest with irritation.

I must stop these feelings of her, for her, wanting to be with her.

We leave the vineyard, and I decide to take her on a trip down Highway 1 along the coastal edge and redwood forests. I can't decide if the long drive is a way to clear my thoughts or prolong our time together. I'm a total contradiction at this point with distance desired yet the fear of separation. It will take us twice as long to get home on this path. *Home.* I'm starting to think of her as belonging in my place with me.

Knock it off, I scold.

We eventually stop at a visitor's center and walk along the designated path to view the trees. Neither of us has hiking boots for a trek through the woods, but I want her to experience the massive trunks up close.

"It's huge," she teases, wrapping her arms as far as she can around the mammoth base and tipping her head back to peer up the steep column.

"That's every man's favorite compliment and every woman's dream."

Her laughter blends with the quiet surroundings, and my heart speeds up once again.

Stop thinking of her, I scream, and then she looks at me. Her blue eyes in broad daylight are just as intense as last night in the dark. Her smile is slow like drizzled chocolate. How I've wanted to see that smile since the moment I met her, and here it is, aimed at me.

For some reason, irritation and attraction mix, and I rush the few steps to come up behind her. She huffs as my body slams against hers, forcing her into the sharp bark.

"Garrett?" she questions, and my head takes over. *Must stop feeling for her.* I paw at her shoulder, tug back her sweater and nip her hard at her neck. The bite bucks her hips, making it worse for me as her backside slams into my rising dick.

"Fuck, I want you." How do I mean the words? Do I want all of her or just her up against this tree?

Tap, tap goes my heart. *You know the answer*, it whispers. My hands move of their own accord and slip under her sweater, searching for the button on her jeans.

"Garrett," she hisses. "Someone will see us."

"Only the trees," I tell her, still nipping harshly at her neck while fumbling with her pants. Unbutton. Unzip. And my hand slips in. She pops back against me again, and a finger delves in while I use the force of my hips to press her forward. With my hand trapped in her jeans, I grind against her backside. This is going to get messy.

I add a second finger, pressing at the waist of her pants with my free hand to loosen the material. She releases the tree and struggles blindly behind her to unbuckle my belt. I help. Within seconds, she's cupping me while I feverishly finger her. I haven't gotten off on a hand job other than my own in years, but I pump into her fist while my digits curl inside her.

"Give it to me," I growl, frustrated with myself. Why am I acting like this? I question at the same time I curse her for making me want her so much.

Don't leave me.

Dolores muffles her scream against the tree, stilling to clench my fingers, and I jet off over her palm. Our ragged breathing echoes around us, and I lift my head, conscious for the first time that someone could have seen us. My forehead lowers to her neck.

What have I done?

"Dolores?" I question. *Don't hate me.* "I'm sorry."

"You okay?" she asks, her voice trembles, and she shakes against my chest. I withdraw my fingers and fumble with redressing her. She gently pushes my hand away and straightens herself. I step back. I have nothing for her hand, and I shrug out of my coat and flannel, then offer the shirt to her. She doesn't look up at me, and I sense I've accomplished what I set out to do.

Distance. *She's too close, Tin Man.* But my newly restored heart sinks to my belly. I reach for her cheeks, forcing her to peer up at me.

"I'm sorry. I don't know what came over me."

She nods once, rolling her lips. She doesn't speak, and her eyes have that lost look again.

Dammit. I did this. I tug her to me, holding her tight to my chest with a hand at the back of her head and another around her waist.

"You…you do things to me, make me feel things, and I don't know how to handle myself."

"S'okay," she slurs into my cotton tee, but I press her back. My eyes search her face, and I see it. The hurt.

"It's not."

She averts her eyes, fighting the hold my hand has on her head. My stomach roils. I don't like her not looking at me, struggling to look away from me.

She's going to leave.

Isn't this what you want? My eyes find hers, and I will her to know that I'd never hurt her. And no. No, I don't want her to go home, back to Georgia.

"I'm sorry," I whisper, and her head lowers for my shoulder. *Look at me*, I scream internally, but I did this to her, to us. My arms slip around her, and I tug her tightly to my chest. She doesn't hold me back.

"Sweetheart?" She slips her arms up my back, pressing into my shoulder blades, sensing I need her to hold me in return. "Did I hurt you?" Is it physical? Was I too rough?

"Just my heart, Garrett." Her voice is so low I'm not certain I hear her correctly. My heart hurts for her as well. It aches for her. How do I explain I'm protecting myself, but it's a lost cause. I'm going to follow her down any path she leads me—yellow brick or not.

chapter 21

He has a headache

[Dolores]

Sometime after noon on Monday, Garrett cancels our dinner plans.

I have the worst headache.

I haven't heard this excuse before, though I've used it myself on Rusty. He would be pissed instead of sympathetic, and he'd keep his distance for a week to punish me for something I couldn't prevent.

Is there anything I can do? Bring you something or make you soup later.

I don't know how soup would help a headache, but I want to offer him comfort.

I get these sometimes. I just need to sleep.

I understand.

Something happened to us yesterday afternoon on our way back. Actually, it happened Saturday evening when it felt like he was making love to me. His eyes, so intense, gazing down at me as he moved with slow, deliberate pulses, filling me and treasuring me. The connection was deep, and I'd never felt like I did at that moment. Not with James. Not with Rusty. Not with a few men between them. The moment was powerful and disturbing, and Garrett tried to distance himself the next morning. *I think.* There was the morning sex. The finger fucking against a tree. But between those rash, rapid couplings, he still held my hand and spoke sweetly to me. He's a complete contradiction, and my heart can't keep up.

Then we returned home. His place. Denton's place.

"I…I think I need some sleep, tomorrow being Monday." It was such a strange thing to say, but I didn't argue. We hadn't spent overnights together other than this weekend and my Thanksgiving self-imploding. I didn't want to feel like I was getting a brush-off, but let's call a spade a spade. I was.

"Okay. Well, thanks for the weekend. I really enjoyed myself." I tried not to smile too big, no hint of how I was feeling, no coyish recall of the amazing things we did together.

You do things to me, he said.

He did things to me too. Things I was afraid to feel and admit. I'd been down this road before.

Keep it to yourself, Dolores.

"I'll see you tomorrow?" I hated the question in my voice as I toyed with the handle of my bag. He wasn't going to walk me into Denton's. He wasn't going to hold me again. We awkwardly stood in the space between—the no-man's-land of his place or mine.

"Yeah, how about dinner?" He didn't sound enthusiastic about it, and my heart sank, but I let it be.

"Sure." I paused a beat. "Good night."

He reached for the back of his neck and scrubbed. Tipping his chin to me, he said, "Thanks for coming with me." I bit my inner cheek. There wasn't a hint of sexual innuendo, which was so unlike him. Or maybe this was him. I was getting a dismiss-slip from the player next door.

I decided to call my brother to distract me after Garrett's text. Maybe a familiar voice from home would ground me, remind me I don't belong here anyway.

This is Oz. Home is calling.

"What was that?" I ask as I hear a crash before Denton even says hello.

"Oh, nothing. Just a little work on Magnolia's." He pauses, and then says to me, "Hang on."

Denton finally agreed with me about moving our grandmother, Magnolia. It is not a good idea. She has lived in her post-Civil War home most of her life, and after losing our mother, I didn't think another change for her would be in her best interest. Denton wanted to sell the family farmstead, but we learned we couldn't. The house is tied to the land which loops back to land entitlement. It could only be inherited, never sold.

I'm relieved, as I had hoped, one day, I'd own the house. I don't have the financial means to fix it up, but one day, it might be mine. Of Magnolia's two children, one is deceased and the other lives in Texas. Aunt Rosalyn doesn't wish to ever return to Blue Ridge. There are only three grandchildren living: Tommy Carrigan, our cousin; Denton, and myself. None of us have children, though our deceased cousin, Kit, has two. We are a rather small, sad lot as far as family goes.

Magnolia always told me we were a maternal line, meaning the house went from her grandmother to her mother, who was an only child; to herself, who was an only child; who had two girls. I am the next in line female not to mention the one who has taken care of my grandmother—and her house—for years.

Another crash occurs as I wait for Denton to finish speaking to someone. Then it goes quiet around him.

"Hey."

"Hey, yourself. What is happening over there?"

"A little home improvement. How is California?"

Denton does this often—deflects topics—when he doesn't want to give me details. However, after my weekend away, I find I want a little more information.

"California is great. I want to know what improvements you are making to Magnolia's."

"Magnolia's?" He hesitates as if her house isn't the place he's improving.

"Got some other place to improve?" Denton newly returned to Blue Ridge for the love of his life. He didn't move into her home for several reasons. After a long talk with Magnolia, our grandmother agreed Denton could temporarily stay with her.

"No, Magnolia's, of course. Most of it has been structural. Supports for the foundation. Roof. Window measurements. Boring stuff."

Actually, it sounds exciting to me. I'd love to see Magnolia's house restored to grandeur. It would make a nice bed and breakfast. The thought surprises me because I've never thought such a thing before.

"Do you have plans for other improvements?" A list filters through my head. New kitchen. Refinished floors. Update bathrooms.

"Just taking it one step at a time. Structural seems most immediate. So California? I miss my ocean. How's it been?"

"I went to Napa this weekend." The sound of joy rings in my tone despite Garrett blowing me off. *It's just a headache.*

"Napa? That's awesome. I'm so glad you're getting out and traveling."

"Yeah, Garett wanted—"

"Garrett?" he interrupts. "What does Garrett have to do with Napa?"

"As I was trying to explain," I began in my big sister voice, "he wanted to see a place and asked me to go with him."

"Garrett," he repeats as if he hasn't heard the rest of what I said. I realize I also haven't been overly forthcoming with the fact Garrett and I spend time together.

"Yes, your neighbor. The one who took me to a spa and shopping because you asked him to."

"I didn't..." His voice drifts. "Dolores, I like Garrett as a businessman. He's ruthless, and he gets what he wants. He's been a decent friend to me. But as a guy, he can be an asshole. Don't get wrapped up with him."

Too late, I think, but then I remember his dinner cancellation. *It's nothing, Dolores. He has a headache.*

"I'm fine," I say, words I recall speaking too often in my life. I'm not fine. I'm falling in love with a man who lives across the country from my life.

"How's Mati?" It's my turn to change the subject.

He sighs, and I can almost hear his happiness. "She's good."

"That's it." He normally jabbers on and on about her, her volleyball team, and her new grandson. *Blah, blah, blah.*

"What else can I say? Life is good."

I weakly grin. *Lucky him.*

+ + +

Close to four in the afternoon, Garrett sends me another text.

Can I ask you a huge favor?

Soup, I think, a little too hopeful.

Can you walk Wally for me?

Sure. Of course. Wally. Something doesn't settle well with me, but I meet him at his door when he gets home.

"You look terrible." Actually, he looks hot as hell in his business suit of sharp blue with a crisp white shirt, and I want to undress him right here in the hallway.

"Thanks." He chuckles, and then he winces. He presses two fingers on his temple.

"Poor baby," I say, and his eyes leap to mine. He unlocks his place, and I call out for Wally. Garrett winces again.

"I'm just going to shower. I'll leave the place unlocked so you can bring him in when he's finished." He steps into his condo, drops his keys on the counter, and continues down the hall to his bedroom.

Alrighty then.

Wally easily follows me, and we saunter down to the beach. It's getting colder, and I consider what Denton asked. *How's my ocean?* I stare out at the waves, crashing into each other. The seas are rough this evening. Just the concept of beach living is so opposite my mountaintop town. Denton isn't really a wealth of information. I should have asked him about the diner, but I didn't. I haven't asked in a month, but something niggles at me. Hollilyn Abernathy, my sort-of manager, had her baby a week before Thanksgiving. I should have asked who was in charge, but I know why I didn't. I don't want to hear someone else is handling things better than me. Ignorance is bliss, *they say*. I can understand why sometimes.

If nothing else, I should call Hollilyn and congratulate her. During the week of Thanksgiving, I had my meltdown, and then Garrett and I celebrated the holiday. It wasn't until the weekend when I learned Hollilyn had her baby, and her boyfriend-baby daddy proposed.

Death. Birth. Proposals. *Life is everchanging*, I think as I watch Wally chase a sea gull.

Who knew my life would bring me here?

How long will you stay? a voice inside my head whispers to me. It's the one question Denton doesn't ask. He keeps telling me to take all the time I need. I've taken enough time, though. I'm feeling the itch to do something again. If nothing else, I can't spend my days waiting on Garrett to get home and entertain me.

I sigh as I call out for Wally, who surprisingly listens to me. He slows as he nears me and walks at my side while we take our time to return to Garrett's.

When I enter his place, I decide I'll make him dinner anyway. Simple chicken with seasoned rice. Something quick and easy. As I struggle with the pots and pans, Garrett enters his kitchen, scrubbing at the back of his neck.

"What the hell are you doing?" His eyes pinch as he speaks.

"I was going to make you dinner. Something you can reheat when you feel better."

His eyes close a second, and he breathes deep. His tone is sharp when he says, "I don't need food." I stop what I'm doing, leave the pans where they sit on the counter, and turn for the door. I'm making him worse.

"Wait," he snaps, and I stop short of exiting, my back to him. He's suddenly behind me. Not touching me, but breathing me in with only a sliver of space between us. "I'm sorry."

His arms wrap around me, and he tugs me against him. His nose dips into the juncture of my neck and shoulder.

"You don't have to be sorry. I can see you're in pain. I'll just leave you be."

"Don't go," he whispers, and something in his tone keeps me in place.

"You said you get these sometimes. What happened?" Concern fills my voice.

"Maybe it's like a caffeine headache? You know when you don't drink enough. It's a sex-deprivation headache instead." He chuckles, but then he winces against my skin.

"Would sex help you feel better?" I tease. He groans. There's no way he could concentrate or perform with the pain I sense he's in.

"You're ridiculous," I mutter.

"My dick you want to lick?" he teases, still speaking into my neck, and I laugh. At least he sounds more like him than he did last night at the door.

"Incredible," I say.

"Insatiable, you mean." We had sex seven times in forty-eight hours. Seven! That's a week in two days. He can't possibly feel deprived.

He walks us backward until he hits the edge of the couch.

"Stay with me," he mutters, and I can't deny him with the strain in his voice. I sit on his cushions, and he lies down with his head in my lap. He turns on the television with low volume, and I comb through his hair with my fingertips, rubbing gently over his scalp. After a few minutes, he shifts so his face presses into my stomach.

"The light's bothering me," he explains.

"I can turn it off." I'm not really watching the movie anyway.

"No." His voice sounds garbled as he presses his nose to my belly and then wraps an arm around my lower back. I continue to stroke over his head, watching him. His eyes close. His brows pinch. He's so vulnerable in this position—anchoring himself to me—as if he's afraid I might drift away.

"I'm not going anywhere, baby," I say softly, leaning toward his ear.

"I like you calling me that," he says, his voice sleepy as he snuggles into me, pressing tighter at my back.

"Sleep, baby." *Sweet dreams, Garrett.* I hope they are filled with me.

chapter 22

Santa's List

[Garrett]

I wake to a tender snore above my head and a kink in my neck. I roll to discover I'm still positioned on Dolores's lap, and I glance up at her. Her head lies at an awkward angle against the back of my couch. One hand must have been on my hip, but when I shifted, it slipped to my front, which bulges as I was having the most lucid dream about her. Us. Together.

She was laughing as she ran between grapevines in bloom, and I was chasing her. Her skirt billowed out behind her, and her laughter called back to me. She wanted me to follow her. I eventually caught up to her, wrapping an arm around her from behind, and we tumbled to the ground. Under the broad blue sky and bright sunshine, we made love, and warmth from both the day and her body surrounded me. The heat is one reason I woke. I'm burning up.

I sit up gingerly and startle Dolores who gave one hearty, deep snort before lunging her head forward.

"Goodness," she mutters in a groggy voice. "Did I wake you?" Her fingers swipe at the corner of her mouth.

"No." I reach out to cup the back of her neck and just stare at her. We have this uncanny way of looking at one another for longer than should be comfortable. Her looking back at me is like she can see deep beneath the surface of me.

Can you see inside my hollow chest?

I didn't mean to hurt her yesterday. I was a total dick. I didn't mean to be short with her earlier about the pots and pans. When I have one of

151

these headaches, it hurts like hell, and I'm sensitive to noise. I also don't like bright light. I'm still a little foggy. With a nudge at my hip from Wally, I break the hold I have on Dolores.

"He needs to go out again," she says. "I can take him."

I turn toward the windows to discover it's already dark. I don't want her walking on the beach this late at night.

"I'll just take him down to the grass by the lot and be right back," I say, rolling off the couch and walking to the front door. I turn to look back at her, her sleepy gaze watching me as she crosses her arms on the back of the couch and rests her chin on her hands. An achy panic fills my chest, and I rub at the place near my heart. "You'll stay, right?"

"I thought you'd want me to go home."

"I don't. I'd like you to stay."

Dolores's brows furrow while she gives me a dreamy grin. "I'm not going anywhere."

The pounding in my chest increases. "I'll meet you in bed in ten."

"Sex deprivation," she teases as her grin increases.

"I'll sleep better if you're next to me," I admit, not wanting to seem like a sex-starved teenager who only wants one thing from her. I want so much more from her, and the realization hit me hard today.

I missed her.

Have I kissed her yet tonight? I need to kiss her. I need to apologize.

Since I took Dolores to the vineyard, my investment vision has become clearer in my head, and I spent the greater part of the day working on details. I have a plan, and for me, that means I want immediate gratification. I told myself it was the reason for my headache, but in reality, it's all the overthinking I've been doing since leaving Dolores yesterday evening. I need to tell her what happened in Atlanta. What Denton suggested. I think that's what brought on much of today's headache. My thoughts weighed heavy on me all morning, and I'd worked myself up. I should have told her this weekend. I should have kissed her last night. I should have asked her to stay with me. She consumes me, and my chest aches with this need I feel for her.

After Wally does his business, I return to the condo and climb into my bed. It's a bit surreal to see Dolores under my sheets, waiting for me. I mean, we've slept here before together, but this time, it feels different. I crawl in next to her but remain on my back, staring up at the ceiling.

"I need to apologize," I say and turn my head to face her. She's sitting up in bed, and an image of us in this position in the future filters through my head like the dream of chasing her through a vineyard. A silly dream.

"For what?" She gives no hint to her feelings, but she was hurt yesterday with my behavior in the forest. I didn't give her an explanation, and then I just left her at Denton's door last night.

"Yesterday, I…I don't know why I acted the way I did. I don't know why I sent you home."

Dolores stares over at me. "It's okay," she whispers much like she did into my chest while we stood in the forest. Why hadn't I told her then how I felt or at least tried to describe this feeling inside me? Her brows pinch. It's not okay how I acted, and I have an idea. A way to make it up to her.

"I have something to ask you." I broach the subject, chewing on my lip as Dolores stiffens beside me. I softly chuckle. That came out a tad dramatic. Then again, asking Dolores to attend the *WomenFirst* Christmas gala is big for me. This year the event is especially important, and making her my date is an unprecedented move on my part. "I have this thing to attend, and I was wondering if you would go with me."

Her forehead furrows as if she's trying to find an angle. "What kind of thing?"

"It's a Christmas thing." I don't know why I'm minimizing the gala. The organization raises money for women and children of domestic abuse. It's a good cause and one dear to me as my father left our mother with four small children and a broken heart under a few crushed ribs.

"Like a Christmas party?" Her voice lowers as if she has forgotten we are upon the season.

"It's a fundraiser for charity with a Christmas theme."

"A Christmas theme," she scoffs as she stares at me. "So a Christmas party. Do I need to get dressed up?" Her wardrobe isn't always her top concern, and from the purchases she's made, it's clear most of her clothing is casual and practical. The dress for our dance lessons won't be enough this time. She's going to need something a bit fancier for the party.

"Why don't you let me take care of it?" I suggest. She needs something elegant and long and black to set off her eyes and her hair. Her head tilts, questioning me.

"You aren't going to make me wear an elf costume or anything ridiculous like that, are you?"

I chuckle. The pain in my head has subsided considerably. Instead, my thoughts fill with her wearing a naughty elf outfit and me playing sexy Santa. She could sit on my lap and tell me all the ways she's been a bad girl this year.

"Actually, it's a bit more formal than a costume party."

Her eyes narrow, suspicious once again. "How formal?"

"Can you just trust me?" I tease, suddenly wanting to surprise her with a beautiful dress and a fancy night out. It's the perfect evening to tell her everything.

"I do trust you." The way she says it sounds like something more, something deeper, and suddenly, my chest pinches again. An echo, like a singular drum, thumps behind my ribs. I sit up and lean toward her, kiss her like I should have done last night, and this morning, and when I came home. I missed her mouth all day.

"How is your headache?" she asks after a long latching to one another. Our bodies shift closer and begin to entwine.

"You cured me," I tease.

"I'm not a doctor." She giggles under the kisses I place on her neck.

"No, but I think you're a miracle worker." She's definitely more powerful than a cardiologist if she's resuscitating my heart.

"You're sweet," she murmurs, returning to my lips. Her mouth moves tenderly over mine, drawing my lower lip between hers. Then she nips me.

"And you're naughty," I tell her while her eyes gleam in the dim light of my room. My headache forgotten, I press my back to the headboard while Dolores's eyes track my bare chest, fully on display for her. I push down the sheet to reveal red boxer briefs and pat my lap. "You've been very naughty, and Santa wants to hear all about it."

She laughs outright until I reach around her back and awkwardly drag her over me.

"I'm going to crush your legs," she jokes, but I'll have no body shaming here. I set her fine ass up close to the firm bulge straining behind the cotton material. With her back to my chest, I force her legs to straddle mine as she faces away from me. She's wearing a T-shirt of mine, and my hands work up her inner thighs as I speak.

"Now, tell Santa all the ways you've been a bad girl."

"I think I'm supposed to tell Santa how I've been a good girl," she corrects me until I reach the cotton over her sex. My fingers rest against the damp heat.

"Such a good girl," I moan and then dip a finger under the seam and into her. She bucks back, her hands flailing for purchase somewhere. "Lean forward." With her thighs splayed open, her hands fall to my knees, which I bend to force her legs to spread even wider. We're a mix of angled legs as I add another finger to her center.

"On second thought, lean back," I mutter, wanting the weight of her body against my chest. With my free hand, I move her hair over one shoulder and nibble at her neck while I tease her sex. "Good girl."

She purrs, and the sound spurs me to add a third finger. Dolores stretches and draws me into her, and a drop of moisture gathers on my briefs. I work her with three digits before my dick gets his turn. Releasing her, I hold my fingers up, and Dolores reaches for my wrist. She tugs my fingers to her mouth and opens to suck them.

"Sweet fuck," I mutter, pressing at her back to shift her forward. I wrestle with my briefs until Dolores releases my fingers and adjusts herself to tug the material down the remainder of my legs. She shifts herself to remove her underwear. The separation between us is brief, and I quickly scoop her under her armpits again, dragging her back to reposition her how she sat before. The seam of her ass splits and surrounds my dick.

"Fuck," I hiss. This woman. *What is she doing to me?* We need lube for her to slip up and down my length in this position, and while I'd love to experiment with her ass and some play, I want my Santa fantasy. I tip her hips, and she leans forward, bracing her hands between my thighs, which are holding hers open wide once again. She reaches under her and guides me to slick folds and then falls back to draw me into her.

A string of *fucks* murmurs from my lips. She's in the reverse cowgirl position, taking the lead to ride me, and my eyes might cross with the pleasure this angle gives.

"So naughty. So stunning," I gasp through ragged breaths as she bounces up and down my dick. With her ass between us, I watch it lift and lower while she swallows me into her. My hand slides down her spine until my palm flattens at the base. I stretch my thumb to rest at another entrance. She stiffens but continues to rock over me. "Ever have anyone back here?"

"Not my thing," she stutters as she draws up and then plunges back down. Her pace increases. I won't push her, but my thumb applies pressure to the puckered opening. Her breath hitches before she speaks in a strangled tone. "What are you doing?"

"Do you like this?" My voice lowers, watching her ass move and clench as her body jostles up and over me.

"I…I don't know."

I simply hold my position, teasing but not forcing. The increase in her rhythm tells me she might like the hint at her back door—a little excitement from the unfamiliar—but I lose my concentration when she touches herself while she rides me and comes undone in record time.

"Santa's not done with you yet," I warn, tossing her forward so she lands on her front. I crawl over her and lift her hips. Instantly missing her warm wetness, I slam into her. Another litany of curses scrolls through my head, mixing with audible grunts and skin-slapping thrusts as I lose myself in her again and again and again.

"One more, stunner," I demand, slipping my fingers to her front, tugging and flicking at the nub to set her off. She presses back at me, hinting she's there, and then she stills, curling her back like a stretching cat. *Fuck.* I come so hard I see stars dancing over her body. My dick pulses and pitches and jets an unending release.

"God, I needed that," I mumble into her back, my forehead resting on her shoulder. She chuckles with me inside her.

"Me too." The air turns serious, heavy with the weight of more to be said. Then I realize I'm bare inside her.

"Dolores," I groan. "I wasn't wearing a condom. Again." The comment should crush our moment, but Dolores simply collapses to the mattress, and I follow as I can't seem to pull myself free of her yet.

"Well, Santa, it seems you've been a bad boy yourself. How does Santa punish himself for misbehaving?" She giggles into the mattress under her head, and I quickly pull out of her. I smack her plump backside, and she lifts the upper half of her body to look at me over her shoulder.

Dear Santa, please let me keep her. Keep me on the bad boy list if this woman will continue to look at me like she is at this moment. Satiated. Complete. Happy.

How would I live without her if she decided to leave?

"Santa's always good," I mock, and her eyes sparkle as she stares back at me. Her hair drapes over her head like a freshly fucked sex kitten.

"So good," she purrs, and I'll take lumps of coal in my stocking forever to hear this sound from her again.

chapter 23

My Fair Lady

[Dolores]

The next day, a car picks me up and takes me to Le Couturier, a quaint, high-end dress shop off Rodeo Drive. Michel, which sounds like Michelle, is the woman I'm to meet, and I wonder if she's another someone who might have slept with Garrett. He certainly is well acquainted with personal shoppers and salon stylists. With a kiss to each cheek, Michel leads me into a back room where I stand on a circular platform.

"Mr. Fox has asked me to dress you." Her accent is as rich as her name, and I'm beginning to feel a little outside myself just as I did the day I was pampered at the salon. I don't know who I am in these fancy places, and I'm not used to being handled by others. Hair. Makeup. Dressmaker. It's all foreign to me.

"Hair down or up?" she questions, and I look at myself in the mirror. It's down today, but I don't know how I'll wear my hair the day of the Christmas-themed event, as Garrett called it. *Just call a spade a spade and say Christmas party.* But something tells me, with the type of dress required, this is more than some holiday office get-together. Garrett will be arranging hair and makeup appointments for me at Denton's place on Saturday afternoon. I'm certain that costs a pretty penny.

He's done so much for me. A bit of *My Fair Lady* meets *Pretty Woman*. A new me. A real lady. The clothes. The dance lessons. The weekend wine tasting. My thoughts drift to the diner and how much I miss the place and the woman I was. Not the tired, strung-too-thin, be-responsible-for-it-all person, but the woman in charge of her own business. The independent woman who took care of herself. It's been nice to have someone else meet my needs, and Garrett certainly does that in the bedroom department, but what am I doing *for him*?

I stare at my too-wide eyes as the designer decides for herself that my hair should be half up and half down. She gives it a messy look with a hairclip on top of my head and then steps back for the clothing rod holding three sample dresses. The first is long, black, and glittery with spaghetti straps and a slit up the side. It's form-fitting and elegant, but I don't feel quite right in it. It screams red carpet and trophy wife, which I'm clearly not. The second comes to my neck in a halter cut with nude fabric to the top of my breasts. It emphasizes my arms, which shouldn't be the focus as I don't have any definition in them. It isn't flattering. When the final dress is removed from the bag, I can't get a sense of it. It's lace from waist to neck with a nude inlay bodice. I'm thinking I'm too busty for the thing, not to mention the full skirt that cuts across the simple black silk with a rather revealing stretch of the fabric. It's more than a subtle slit up the side panel but a fully exposed left leg.

"This is my favorite," Michel mutters as she helps me into the dress. With my back to the mirror, I don't get the full effect until I turn. In the reflection is someone I don't recognize. The bodice clings to my midsection, accentuating my breasts yet keeping them contained. Lace wraps from neck to wrist with large cutouts of exposed skin. The waist hugs my true waist and flows A-line to the floor. The large swatch of fabric opening the skirt does what I expect—exposes my left leg almost to my hip.

"You won't be able to wear thigh-highs with that," a rough male voice says behind me, and I twist to find Garrett in the room. Suddenly, the place seems too small for three people and this dress. Michel walks over to him—dressed impeccably in a charcoal gray suit with a vest— and gives him the two-cheek kiss. She mumbles something to him, but he isn't looking at her. His eyes are trained on me. He chuckles softly and then asks her if we can have a moment alone.

Garrett steps up on the circular platform and runs his hands down my sides, under my arms, outlining my hips. He's examining the material like he's a connoisseur of female clothing. His head lifts, and he meets my eyes in the mirror. His hands pause at my waist.

"This isn't the one I envisioned, but now I don't think I can see you in anything else." His voice is chalky, deep, and low. We stare at one another in the mirror. "You are so beautiful."

A blush creeps up my skin, tainting it pink, and Garrett's hand slips to the revealing slit. His mouth presses below my ear. "Shimmy out of your panties."

"What?" I choke, trying to find his eyes in the mirror, but he faces the side of my head, his eyes close as his lips press under my ear again. I reach within the skirt and tug until the material slips over my hips and falls to my feet. I step left, revealing the deep cut, leaving my underwear wrapped around my right ankle. Garrett faces forward once again and watches his hand disappear under the black silk. Without a word, his fingers plunge into me, and my mouth falls open with the intrusion.

"Watch yourself," he whispers. "See what I see when you come apart."

"Garrett," I warn. "The dress?"

"It's already yours, and I want to watch you fall to pieces in it." His fingers slide in and out, curling in a manner I hadn't felt before with him. He's demanding and delving, and the rush comes quickly. I watch myself as my breathing accelerates, and my chest heaves. Garrett's bright eyes don't leave the mirror. His fingers are hidden under the skirt, but I don't need to see them. I feel them. Every fiber of my being feels his fingertips and the edge of his knuckles and the hair on the backs as he takes me with those firm digits.

"Garrett," I whisper, warning him again. It's going to be fast, and it's going to be huge. A scream rumbles in my chest. My eyes widen in the mirror, but Garrett doesn't break his expression. His concentration on bringing me to my knees remains intact as we both watch me explode. I need something to hold as my legs shake, so I reach back for his neck, curling my arm behind me to hold on to him. His fingers on my hip tighten, and I close my eyes.

"Watch," he commands, an edge to his voice as if any moment he's going to tip over instead of me. When I open my eyes and witness our position, I come undone. I bite my lip to hold in the scream burning up my throat. I moan and curse him in my head until he starts swearing at me.

"Fuck, you're fucking beautiful, and I want to fucking fuck you right here in this fucking gorgeous dress and watch you drip all over me."

Whoa. The words set off a second detonation, and this time, I choke on his name, fighting the rebel yell inside me.

"Garrett," I hiss, dragging out his name.

"Fuck yes, again," he barks. His lips press against my skin as he watches me fold in the mirror. My fingers clutch at his wrist where his hand has disappeared within the dress. I groan, almost in torture as a second orgasm rips me in two. I want him inside me like I've never wanted anything in my life. Right here. Right now.

But he kisses my shoulder and slowly withdraws his fingers. Within seconds, he's back under the dress with a cloth wiping me.

"What's that?" I don't recognize my voice as I ask. My legs tremble, and I'm still on edge, wanting him to fill me.

"A handkerchief." He removes the material and folds it with one hand, tucking it back into his suit pants pocket. I chuckle with the thought of this modern man carrying such an antiquated piece of fabric. He pats his pocket after securing it.

"You can't walk around with that in your pocket," I mock in horror.

"It's the closest I can get you to my dick right now. I'll feel it against my thigh all day, torturing myself until I can get home to you tonight." *Home.* To me. He kisses my shoulder again and then tips my chin to face him. "It won't be fair to the other ladies that you'll be the most beautiful woman at the event."

"You said it was a party," I bite, my voice breaking on what the word *event* might mean.

"Po-tay-to, Pa-tah-to." He quickly kisses me and steps down from the platform. "Change and I'll take you to lunch."

Lunch? Sure, he's all cool as a cucumber after what he just did, and right now, the only thing I want to eat is him.

+ + +

The week passes in a blur of casual dinners and sexy time with Garrett, and I should be happy. I am happy. I can't remember ever being so content in all my life, but a sliver of me is missing.

It's colder in California than I expected in early December, but I quickly find my destination as I walk the streets.

On the Go Diner.

I climb the stairs as if I'm entering another era when I enter the diner car. The theme is the mid-1950s, so loud and bright and white. The space practically gleams from the chrome accents. The music croons, and the heat cranks. It isn't exactly my taste, but I like the premise behind the place. True to their branding, soft drinks are served in shapely glasses, and fries come on paper plates. The women wear bright uniforms in pink, turquoise, and yellow. I wonder for a moment how a themed diner might work in Blue Ridge. I'd want something more sophisticated, a little older looking, more classic. *Think black and white movies*, my brain says. Ideas begin to pour into me. Lush booths. Dim lighting. Candles. It doesn't exactly fit the image of the current diner, which is more your typical greasy spoon. A one-stop shop for coffee and breakfast, but it's time for a change. Could Blue Ridge handle it?

The community has already been rather accepting of Blue Ridge Microbrewery and Pub up the street. Billy Harrington didn't open the place to hurt me; he did it to revive the downtown strip as well as attract tourists. He had his own personal reasons for mixing things up, and I admit it's helped our little town. The locals love Dolores's Diner, but does Dolores? I sigh as I question myself and sip the coffee placed before me. We don't have a Starbuck's in Blue Ridge like every other American town, but maybe what we need is a coffee shop and a diner. I fall back in the booth and look out the window at the quiet side street.

How can I guess what Blue Ridge needs if I don't even know what I want?

I've been skipping out on life for nearly eight weeks. Two months. This isn't me. I don't run away. I don't avoid. Then I consider Rusty. It's what I've been doing the whole ten years I've been with him—avoiding my emotions just to have sex with him.

And after sex with Garrett Fox, how could I ever return to a man like Rusty Miller?

You can't, my heart says. *And you don't want to,* my girlie parts cheer.

I reach forward and cup my hands around the thick ceramic mug. What about Garrett? He enjoys playing dress-up-Dolores, but how does he feel about me? We're ignoring the elephant in the room, which includes the fact I don't live here. Could I stay? I've enjoyed California, but I'm still in vacation mode and disassociated from the day-to-day living. What would I do here? Garrett's the only person I know in the area, which is dangerous. It makes me dependent, and I don't want to be. Then there's the matter of not having a job. How do I explain myself? I own a business, but I walked away.

You can take the girl out of the diner, but can you really remove the diner in the girl?

I should call Denton. I should call Hollilyn and see how the diner is managing without me. I should get my shit together. My phone pings, and I notice a text from Garrett.

Home soon.

I smile weakly, but I'm no longer certain where that is anymore.

chapter 24

It's A Party Thing

[Dolores]

"Have I told you how stunning you look?" Garrett says to me, leaning toward me in the back seat of the hired car. This car is a little different from the others I've been in with Garrett. More plush. More legroom. I could kneel before him and give him a blow job if I wanted to, or he could lay me across the seat and make me silly, but I'm too on edge to think of sex. Then again, sex might be just the thing I need to take the edge off.

"Yes," I say softly, squeezing his hand in reply. My palm is sweaty against his, and I'm surprised he hasn't complained. He's told me at least six times that I look beautiful, starting with the moment he walked into Denton's place and found me fully dressed and waiting for him. Of course, he looks beautiful as well in a black tuxedo with a vest. I've seen men wear them at weddings over the years, and I can honestly say no one wears one as well as Garrett. He's comfortable in his own skin and equally comfortable in the formal attire. He looks ravishing if that were a word still used today.

When we pull up to the hotel where the party will be held, my nerves hijack me. The place is alight with bright lights and a line of cars. People crowd what looks like a red carpet and cameras flash. I notice the couple before us getting out of their vehicle. The man helps the woman exit the car, and they pose for a second. She's a vision of gold with dark hair piled on her head. Slim. Young. Confident.

"What am I doing here?" I mutter.

"You're with me," Garrett states, leaning into me once again and kissing my neck. The hairstylist decided my hair should be up, emphasizing the textures of ink and chrome within it. I didn't realize I'd spoken out loud, and I'm too late to reply as the driver stops. Our turn to exit. "Just hold my hand," Garrett suggests, scanning my face before telling me one more time I look beautiful.

Garrett exits first and then holds out his hand for me, like the gentleman in the car before us. The second I exit the vehicle, I'm blinded.

"Don't look at any one light," he warns too late. Thankfully, we pause for a moment so I can at least get my bearings on the red carpet leading into the hotel. "Keep your head up, sweetheart."

I'm thankful for the coaching, though I'm beside myself. A little warning would have been nice. This is anything but a party. It's a full-on event, and I feel like royalty without the tiara as Garrett leads me down the path to the entrance. A blonde in a formal gown greets Garrett before he gives his name, and then Garrett hands over an envelope.

"We don't have your guest's name on the list, Mr. Fox," the woman sweetly says to him.

"Candi, you know I called and added Ms. Dolores Chance to my ticket." The woman—Candi—scrolls down her iPad while she sweetly blushes from Garrett addressing her by name. My arm rests loosely within his, and he tugs it tightly against his side, casually keeping his hand in his pocket. He's poised. Prepared. As though he's done this a hundred times, and I imagine he has.

"Oh, here she is," Candi states, all sticky sweet like her name.

"Thank you, Candi."

"Anything for you, Mr. Fox," she replies coyly, and Garrett leads us forward.

"Anything for you, Mr. Fox," I mock once we are out of earshot of the waif of a woman.

"Hmm, I have so many ways I could address that request from you," he teases me as we wait in another line. He explains the receiving line leads to the fundraising hostess, a world-famous woman who advocates for women's rights and assists those domestically abused to get back on their feet. She has locations in New York, California, and Chicago. Ingrid Tintagel is a stunning woman, roughly my age. Her hair is an interesting shade of rust, and her eyes sparkle bright green when she sees Garrett. She's obviously familiar with him as her face pinkens like the young thing who took our ticket information.

"Garrett," she drones. "How wonderful to see you again. I can't wait to hear your speech."

What?!

"And who must this be?" she questions, reaching out a hand for me. I wait a second too long before reaching for hers, remembering too late my hand is clammy. It doesn't matter as she only grips my fingers in an I'm-holding-a-dead-fish handshake.

"Ingrid, this is Dolores Chance." Ingrid's pleasant smile responds to his introduction.

"What a lovely dress. I'm so happy to see Garrett attend one of these events with a date." Her teeth nearly clench as she says date as though she's crunching on sour candy. I turn to Garrett, surprised by her comment. "I hope you enjoy the evening. Garrett, honey, Candi will find you during the evening and let you know the particulars."

Garrett smiles, and I continue to marvel at this woman's familiarity with him. He leads us forward, smiling and nodding at people as we cross the room.

"What the hell?" I mutter through my own clenched teeth. "A speech?"

"It's no big deal. I'm the keynote speaker. I just give a little address before dinner."

I tug at his arm to stop us from walking, forcing him to spin and face me.

"This sounds like a much bigger deal than some Christmas-themed office party."

"It isn't," he says, nodding in the direction of someone off to my left, and then leans forward to briefly kiss me. I don't think our lips even met, and I don't like it. It's unfeeling and cold, and reminds me I don't fit in with these people.

"Garrett, you could have warned me. You could have told me."

Looking me in the eyes, he smiles, and says, "Dolores, I need to give a speech before dinner. I hope you like prime rib. That's the main course."

"Garrett," I groan until his arm wraps around my waist, and he tugs me against him. He leans toward my ear, and whispers, "Have I told you how beautiful you look?"

"Oh my God, you're complimenting me to avoid the subject."

"I'm complimenting you because it's true. Relax. Let's have some wine." Taking my hand, he leads me to a crowded bar where he knows many of the people, or at least those people know him. He shakes more hands than I can count and introduces me to so many I'll never remember.

When we finally sit for dinner, Garrett is introduced. I'd like to say I paid attention to every word he spoke, but I'm too impressed by his public speaking to a room full of people to fully listen to his words. He's calm, cool, and collected. The audience chuckles, and I miss the joke. He thanks the organization for their work with women, and then Ingrid Tintagel moves to stand next to him. She kisses him on the cheek and holds his arm a second to address the crowd.

"Your generosity this evening will keep doors open for women in need and provide them with much-needed opportunities to get back on their feet. I don't need to remind you all of this night's purpose, but I would like to honor Mr. Fox for, once again, being one of our top gift givers. Tonight's donations from him were made in the name of his lovely date, Ms. Dolores Chance." Ingrid scans the front row of round tables where we've been seated until her eyes fall in my direction. "Thank you for inspiring this man."

The audience applauds as Candi walks up on the raised platform and holds up a giant check with five zeroes to display Garrett's contribution. Cameras flash. People stand and clap. I remain seated, staring at the man I don't know on the stage.

When Garrett returns to his seat, I lean over, cup his cheek, and kiss him sweetly. During the time it took him to return to me, I remind myself the money is for a good cause.

"I think I'm supposed to say thank you. That was very generous, though unnecessary to do it in my name."

Garrett's cheeks pinken. "Yeah, I didn't know they were going to do that. I'm by no means the largest contributor to their fundraising efforts, but I think she did it because I was the speaker."

"Your speech was wonderful." *Although I didn't hear it.* He beams with pride and reaches for his drink. He's on his third one, and I realize for the first time he might have been anxious to speak to all these people. It makes me wish I had paid better attention to what he said, but I was too distracted by how good he looks and his commanding presence over the crowd.

Before dinner is served, I excuse myself for the restroom. Garrett offers to walk with me, but I need a moment. While I'm taking care of business, I hear women chattering outside the door, oblivious to the others within the restroom. It reminds me that I don't have any girlfriends here. I hardly have any at home either. Occasionally, I went out with Mati and Cora Conrad, but the times were rare. I worked too much, and I was tired most late nights. Then there was Rusty.

I exit the fancy stall, which was more like a private toilet closet, then wash my hands and head for the lounge separating the sink area from the main door to the washroom.

"I heard he found her on the street. She's a survivor of domestic abuse." I don't know why the statement stops me, but I step back and reach for another hand towel as if I'm drying my hands. I can't quantify them as paper because they are too soft, but they are disposable.

"No, she's some woman who was staying in his building. He set her up in Denton's apartment. Funny that woman has the same last name," a second woman states. Same last name as Denton? *We're siblings, you idiot*, I want to interject.

"I didn't think Denton had any family," the first adds sadly, and I imagine her pouty little lips like she feels sorry for my younger brother.

The famous musician certainly didn't mention his family in interviews, and now I understand. "The last time I was at Garrett's, he told me Denton had gone home because his mother died."

My breath catches, processing the timing of such a statement.

"She's a special project for him," the second speaks again. "He's always been like that."

"That's not true, honey," the first pipes in. "I wasn't a project of his."

They both giggle. "No, he's been a project of yours."

My brow pinches, and I stare at myself in the mirror. A young blonde woman looks at her reflection and applies a new layer of lipstick to lips which don't need more. She smiles softly at me through the glass as the women continue.

"Well, I'm sure once *whoever she is* is gone, he'll come back to me. He always does. He never holds on to them for very long. You know how he is. Let's get a drink."

Silence falls after this statement, and I meet the eyes of the woman three sinks down again. We both hear the roar of the party as if a door opens and then the silencing of the noise after the door closes.

"That's Alicia Graystone. I'm told she's wanted to hook her claws into Garrett for years. She's jaded and bitter because he's 'friend-zoned' her." The woman air quotes into the reflection. "The other woman is Hunny Cumerford. They think they know everyone, but they don't. And they're both social climbers."

She slips her lipstick back in her clutch and comes closer to me.

"Denton Chance. Are you really his sister?"

"I am." My brows pinch surprised she's making a connection.

"I'm Ivy Everly. Denton played in the band with my mother, Kit Carrigan." She cocks her hip and eyes me a moment. "They were cousins, which means…"

"Oh my God." I stare at the young woman before me. My best guess is she's under thirty, and the resemblance becomes clear. "I'm your cousin. Second cousins as you're my cousin's daughter."

The thin woman steps forward and reaches out to hug me. I'm not a random hugger, so the connection throws me off, but after hearing those women speak about me, her comfort and the sense she's family make me feel better. Tears well in my eyes for some reason.

"Is Tommy here?" Tommy and I spoke at my mother's funeral, catching up on old times, and seeing him tonight might settle my nerves even more. A familiar face would be nice in this crowd. My heart pumps with the possibility as I pull back, keeping my hands on her shoulders. I can't seem to let her go now that she's hugged me. She's so beautiful and holding her seems to ground me at the moment.

"He's not. But he'll be tickled I met you. How long have you been in town? Have you seen him since you've been in California? We need to have you come to dinner."

"I've actually been here a few weeks, but I need to get back home before Christmas." It's the first time I've said such a thing, and I realize in saying it that it's true. I need to go home by the holiday. Guilt riddles me that I hadn't called my cousin in these two months. We weren't particularly close as adults, but he's still family. "I'm sorry I haven't called him." My voice lowers. Ivy's cool hands have remained on my lace-covered arms, keeping us tethered together.

"No worries, but maybe before you go home," she suggests. "I'd love to get to know more about you." The words are spoken genuinely, and I smile despite how my insides feel. "May I introduce you to my husband?"

I nod and follow Ivy's lead out of the bathroom.

chapter 25

Dance With Me

[Garrett]

Dolores has been in the bathroom a considerable time, and I'm beginning to grow concerned. I'm about to go in search of her when she finally re-enters the ballroom. I'm once again astounded by how gorgeous she looks in that dress, and my breath catches as I remember what I did to her when she first wore it. She's so wound up tonight I can't wait to strip her out of it and remove what weighs on her.

Not to mention, you have something important to say to her.

She's with a younger woman, and the two talk animatedly as if old friends. Instead of coming for me, I see the woman direct her to a man with chin-length hair and thick scruff on his face. The man hugs Dolores easily, and my blood boils. Excusing myself, I step away from a dull conversation about birds and head in the direction of Dolores. As I approach, she looks at me, her face blooming. I can't help but smile back at her, and our eyes hold.

The young man's head turns in my direction as well, and I need a second as he looks familiar, but I can't place him.

"Garrett," Dolores addresses me, leaning forward for my hand. "This is Ivy Everly. She's the daughter of my cousin, and her husband, Gage."

Gage Everly. As in Gage Everly of Collision?

"Hey man, it's nice to meet you," I say, offering a hand. He shakes mine firmly, and I reach for his wife's.

"You smile just like Dolores." Their mouths match, and Dolores smiles broader. I've never seen her beam so much. Her hand rubs up the back of the girl with familiarity.

"I didn't know you had other family here," I mention.

"Neither did I," Dolores replies just as surprised. She quickly explains the connection with Denton, whom I knew had been part of Chrome Teardrops, and their cousins, Lawson Colt, aka Tommy, and his sister, Kit Carrigan. "It's a bit surreal, and I'm sorry again that I haven't reached out."

"That's okay," Ivy says. "I'm sorry again about your mother. I understand." A knowing look passes between the two women. "But before you go, you promise, right? Dinner."

"Go where?" I ask, my third drink suddenly not settling well in my stomach.

"Dolores said she's going home for Christmas, but we still have a few weeks."

Dolores licks her lips as Ivy explains. *A few weeks*.

"Well, that sounds like a good plan. Getting together before you go." My eyes bore into Dolores, and her cheery expression fades. Gage's head volleys between me and Dolores, and he reaches between us for his wife.

"We should keep making the rounds so we can get out of here," he says to Ivy, clearly interpreting the sudden awkward tension between Dolores and me. She's wringing her fingers as she looks up at Ivy.

"It was so good to see you," Dolores says, and Ivy steps into her for a hug. When the younger woman pulls back, her hands grip Dolores's upper arms.

"Try the cupcakes. The owner is a good family friend of ours. And fuck those women in the bathroom. Don't listen to them." She giggles when Gage's mouth falls open, and then she follows her husband's lead to circle the room. I want to get out of here as well, but I promised Ingrid I'd dance one dance with her before whisking Dolores up to a room. She doesn't know I booked us one. I wanted to make the night enchanting for her, but all of a sudden, I'm questioning everything.

"You're leaving," I say, stepping up to her.

"I haven't decided. It just came out, but I think I should probably go home in time for Christmas, and you should too. You missed Thanksgiving because of me."

"You don't want to spend Christmas with me?" I'm shocked I'm questioning her, and even more shocked that I want to spend another holiday with her. I haven't made any plans to head home although my mother won't appreciate another bailed holiday.

"It's not that…" Her voice drifts.

"Then explain it to me."

"I don't belong here, Garrett. It's like I'm playing dress up or make-believe. This isn't me." She tugs at the skirt of her dress, almost revealing both her legs. One is already on display, and I had a hand on it under the table all evening, imagining what I could do to her. I've been hard since the moment I saw her in the dress again, and touching her warm skin had me on fire throughout dinner. I want to get us out of here and up to our room.

"You look beautiful. The dress suits you."

"Garrett, you're not listening. It isn't the dress. It's me. Those women think I'm some special project of yours."

"What women?"

"The ones in the bathroom. Alicia something and someone named Hunny." She chokes on the second name as if it must be a joke. It is a joke. Both women are.

"They're nobodies."

"Well, they seemed pretty familiar with your body, especially Alicia. She says she can't wait until I leave so you'll go back to her."

"What? I would never…" But I stop abruptly. I've already cut Alicia off, but that doesn't stop the stalking. An occasional text. A suggestive message.

"I see," Dolores mutters.

"No, you don't. I'm not here with Alicia. I'm here with you. You heard Ingrid. I never bring dates to these things."

Dolores eyes me a moment. "You don't bring one so you can go home with someone random."

The statement stings although she isn't wrong.

"I thought we weren't going to do this. Bring up past mistakes like Alicia." It isn't true, actually. We haven't discussed what we would or wouldn't reveal to each other. Most things have just come naturally between us. I told her about Kate. She told me about Rusty. That's all we need to know. Neither of us is attached to another, but then again, we haven't confirmed we're attached to each other. I didn't think we needed to define things. We're nearly living together, spending every day and night with one another.

"Listen. Alicia is…"

Suddenly, music flares to life, and the lights of the ballroom dim. A microphone squeaks, and Ingrid chuckles over the loudspeaker.

"Ladies and gentlemen, please enjoy this evening's entertainment. And Garrett Fox, you owe me a dance." Being called out at this most inopportune moment doesn't make me happy. Dolores smiles weakly as her eyes flit over my shoulder. Before seeing her, I sense Ingrid on the path for me.

"One dance, and then we are out of here," I warn Dolores. She nods as Ingrid approaches, and I put on my best face to greet the matron of this fundraiser. Escorting her to the dance floor, we begin to move, but I keep my eyes trained on Dolores with every turn.

"She's very beautiful although not who I would expect you to date."

"Ingrid." I chuckle cautiously. "You shouldn't pretend to know my type."

"I was your type once," she mutters, reminding me of another night of poor judgment. Ingrid is roughly the same age as Dolores and a beautiful woman in her own right, although she's had some work done since our night together. It's wrong of me to be dancing with her, but I'm putting on a social face for the charity.

"Well, she is my type," I say in defense of Dolores. "She's everything I've ever needed." It's all true. She's funny, a bit awkward, sexy as hell, and smart. Ingrid's brow lifts, surprise on her sculptured face.

"She's a lucky woman."

"No, I'm a lucky man."

The tempo changes, and a sultry song begins. Ingrid steps back from me, and I bow as if I'm grateful for the dance. The music drifts, sounding like a modern tango. I decide I'd like one dance with Dolores before we head upstairs, and I'm crossing the dance floor, on a mission for her, when Alicia intercedes me.

"Garrett, I've been looking for you all night."

"Really?" I snap. "Stalking much."

Alicia smirks, pressing at my chest. She dips her head and smiles upward like she's flirting with me, but her eyes say she's a cat ready to pounce, claws only hidden within her paws. We stand on the edge of the dance floor but still within the realm of the overhead spotlight. I don't wish to make a scene, but I'm about to cause one if she doesn't move out of my way.

"Let's dance," she mutters, pressing me backward, under the stream of brighter lights, and I know I'm fucked.

chapter 26

Cinderella And The Fall

[Dolores]

My mouth falls open as I watch Garrett take a step backward, returning to the dance floor. I've held my breath the entire time he danced with Ingrid. They'd make a striking couple as she holds herself like a queen. She's old money from New York, Garrett explained, and it's a concept I can't wrap my head around.

But this…this betrayal of him dancing with a second woman. I need some air.

I turn and nearly smack into Ingrid.

"I always thought they'd make a beautiful couple," she says, positioning herself to face the dance floor, watching Garrett. A false smile graces her smooth cheeks. Her eyes are too tight for someone close to my age. "Then again, I thought he and I would do the same. But I was wrong." She slightly turns, her eyes drifting over me. "The way he's been looking at you. He can't take his eyes off you."

I look up to see Garrett looking in the general direction of where we stand, but we are shadowed by the dimness, all lighting focused on the dance floor. I don't know how to respond to Ingrid, and suddenly, I feel myself slipping into Rusty-mode, accepting that my man might be sleeping with others and not doing a damn thing about it. I confronted Rusty a few times at the beginning of our loosely termed *relationship*, but over time, I fell into a rut of keeping my emotions in check if I wanted to sleep with him. I hate myself for the thought.

I should storm the dance floor and make a claim on Garrett, but I won't. I don't know that I have a claim on him.

"Who is she?"

"Alicia Graystone. They've been friends for years."

I know the code for friends—friends with benefits. She's probably been his plus-one to events, although Ingrid mentioned Garrett hasn't brought someone to this gala in the past. As I watch them dance, I see the familiarity they have with one another's body. The grace as they spin in unison, and my breath hitches. The dance lessons I took with Garrett flash before my eyes. Garrett was so practiced in his moves, and now I see why. He's done it before.

She's a project to him.

Oh my God, my brain screams.

"Ingrid, will you excuse me?"

Her pinched eyes narrow as she nods, and I walk in the direction of the restroom, but once I enter the hallway, I know there's no turning back.

My fingers fumble in my clutch, trembling as I reach for my phone. I press the Uber app Garrett helped me install and type in my request. I almost fall down the stairs in my four-inch heels with a thin strap at the ankle. I hold my phone while I descend, and it rings in my palm. Thinking it's Uber, I answer out of breath.

"Hello?"

"Dolores?"

"Mati?" I haven't spoken to Mati in almost two months, and the twang of her Georgia accent brings tears to my eyes. "What's wrong?" She never calls me, and especially knowing I'm not in Georgia, something bad had to have happened to warrant a call.

"Nothing's wrong. Are you okay? You sound out of breath."

"I'm fine." The familiar phrase tastes bitter on my tongue.

"You don't sound fine."

"Mati," I huff. "What did you call for? Did something happen to Magnolia? What about Denton?" My chest pinches as I haven't been faithful about calling my grandmother. Denton and I did a brief Monday call check-in, and he assured me earlier this week that she was hanging in there despite my mother's death.

"Everything's fine. I just…Dolores, when will you be coming home?"

"I don't know. Why? Mati, if something happened, you have to tell me. I'll be there tomorrow."

"No, no. Don't rush. It's just…I probably shouldn't be making this call, but I think you should come home."

I pause as I step out into the cold California evening. I don't even know how to properly identify an Uber, and with my luck, I'll get into the wrong car, be kidnapped, and dumped on the side of the road. My mind races as my nerves ping-pong from this call. Something is not settling well in my stomach. If Mati says it isn't Magnolia or Denton, what could it be?

"Is it Hollilyn? Did she burn down the diner?" I laugh without humor until I don't hear any response. "Mati, what is it you aren't saying?"

"I don't want to upset Denton, but I just thought, woman to woman, you might want to know…you should probably be here, and soon."

"It's the diner, isn't it?" Mati doesn't say anything, and I have my answer.

"Did it burn to the ground?" My blood freezes in the cool California night as a car slows at the curb, and I read the plates. This is my ride.

"Nothing that extreme," she mutters unconvincingly. "Don't be mad, okay? He had good intentions. I just…I thought you'd want to know."

"Mati, this is killing me." I fall into the back seat of the sedan. I don't need to speak to the driver as he already has my destination.

"Don't worry. Please. I don't want you to cut your time short if you aren't ready to come back. I understand. I do." And I know she does. When Mati lost her husband Chris, she folded into herself for a while.

"Hang on," I say to Mati and then address the driver. "Can I change my destination to the airport?"

The Uber driver lifts a brow in the mirror and smiles. More money for him, I think. He tells me to cancel my ride and reschedule the airport. He'll claim the job.

"Mati, I'm heading to the airport now."

"Are you sure?" But she exhales a sigh of relief.

"I think it's time I come home." After this evening, there's no place I'd rather be.

chapter 27

The Chase

[Dolores]

"What the hell is going on?" I bellow in stunned surprise as I stand inside my diner. Inside what used to be my diner. Inside my ripped apart diner. The booths are gone. The checkered tile floor torn apart. The ceiling dangles with wires. Griffin Duncan stills with a power tool in his hand.

"Dolores?" He questions like he doesn't recognize me. Griffin Duncan and his brothers own a construction company. Their other brother, Kent, owns the local hardware store. Somehow, they are distance cousins, and it reminds me of the connection to Ivy Everly. I shake my head. I don't have time to think about the past twenty-four hours. I took a midnight flight to Atlanta and hardly slept on the plane. Once I got home, I removed my dress and changed into my old, familiar clothing which feels scratchy and uncomfortable against my skin compared to what I wore in LA. I glare back at the burly man with a thick beard before me. If we weren't distantly related, I might be attracted to him, but that's what gets small-town people those backward ass reputations about inbreeding.

"What do you think?" he asks cheerfully, almost with pride, taking in my demolished diner.

"I think I want a fucking explanation." The tone of my voice lets Griffin know I have no idea what is going on. My nerves are shot. My emotions frayed. I'm exhausted. His face falls.

"Denton wanted to surprise you," he says sheepishly, nervous eyes darting everywhere they can but to look at me.

"And what does Denton know about a diner?"

Silence falls between us.

"Exactly."

I'm lifting my phone to call said brother when russet locks and patchy facial hair catches my attention. Rusty Miller never could grow a full beard or develop the sexy scruff popular nowadays. He has tufts of stubble here and there, blending with acne scars. Because of those marks, he isn't able to grow hair on his jaw. The hair on his head, however, is thick, and wild, giving him his nickname. Russell is his real name.

"Rusty?" I swallow as I take in his appearance, shocked to see him working an honest job. He's a member of Devil's Edge, the local MC where James Harrington is now second in command. Rusty mainly works for them, or so I thought. I've never asked what he did for the MC, as he'd never tell me anyway. But working with Griffin seems on the up-and-up despite the fact my brother hasn't informed me he's destroying my diner.

"Dolores?" His voice rings in question like Griffin's, as if the man I've slept with for ten years doesn't know me. Then I remember my hair. My fingers swipe over the smoothness. It took a while to wash out all the spray, and my scalp still aches in parts from the hairpins from the previous night's updo. I ignore the pain in my head and my heart.

I shouldn't have run away.

"You look different," Rusty says, still taking in my hair and then roaming my body. I shiver under his appraisal and not in a good way. I can't believe I slept with this man. I can't believe I gave ten years of my life to him while holding my emotions in check and ignoring his carousing with others. I have no emotion for him. "You look older."

My breath hitches, and my gut clenches like I've been socked. I shouldn't care what he thinks. I don't care, actually. His opinion of me no longer matters. I shudder with irritation, and then I feel it.

A presence behind me.

My eyes close.

I must be imagining him.

"She looks fucking stunning," an angry, rough male voice speaks.

"Who the fuck are you?" Rusty asks, dropping the electrical circuit tester in his hand and stalking closer to me.

"None of your business," Garrett states, and then his hand presses against my lower back. Rusty's eyes fall to the motion, and I want to lean into Garrett. I want to melt against him and beg him to forgive me, but I'm too awed and extra raw at finding my diner in shambles.

Griffin steps in front of Rusty, holding him back with a large paw on his chest. "No trouble," Griffin warns Rusty, and then he glances over his shoulder at me. "I'll give Denton a call and let him know we're on hold." There's a question in his voice, and I look around the room.

On hold? We are long past holding on this mess.

As Griffin lifts his phone, he forces Rusty—who isn't taking his eyes off me—backward. They disappear into what I assume is still my kitchen, but anything is possible at this point. Still aware of Garret behind me, I spin for him. Without thinking, my arms wrap around his neck, and I hold him to me.

"I was so worried. How could you leave me like that?" he mutters into my neck, squeezing me like he never wants to let me go. I melt into this body, relishing the feel of it against mine. It has only been a few hours, but I missed him. I shouldn't have run.

The comment stops my thoughts, and I lean back, pushing him arm's length away from me.

"How did you know I was here?"

"I called Denton."

My head shakes. "You called my brother?"

"You sent me a text and then didn't answer any of mine."

I'm going home. I didn't say more. I didn't know what else to say. I'd turned my phone off the moment I purchased a plane ticket.

His eyes narrow. "Imagine my surprise when I looked over to see you talking to Ingrid and then notice you'd disappeared. Ingrid said you went to the restroom, but after ten minutes, I stormed the room myself. A maître d' at the hotel told me he saw a woman fitting your description leave while talking on the phone." He pauses, cupping my face. "Why did you leave?"

I simply shake my head, feeling off-kilter with him standing before me. One minute, this man looks amazing in a suit; another, he's impeccable in a tux. But he doesn't wear anything better than these jeans and a puffy winter jacket. He's casual, but something else is unusual about his outfit. The boots on his feet look like old work boots, scuffed and worn, and he wears only a white T-shirt under the open coat.

"I went back to the condo after you didn't answer your phone or text messages. I didn't think you'd be anywhere else. When you weren't at my place, I banged on the door of Denton's. At first, I thought you were just pissed off at me and punishing me for some reason by not answering. I waited half an hour before the neighbor below complained. Then I called your brother."

"I'm sorry I made you worry." Maybe leaving a quick note or sending a good-bye text would have been more appropriate.

"Mati…isn't that her name…answered Denton's phone," he continues, ignoring my apology. "She told me she spoke to you, and you were on your way home. *To Georgia.*"

Mati. That little busybody. I need to hug her after I throttle her for not telling me about this mess.

"Why are you here?" I question, still holding him by his biceps away from me.

"Because you promised me you wouldn't leave, and you did." His tone softens. "I trusted you."

"I'm sorry." The words fall from my mouth, vomiting on the floor at his feet. Guilt ripples through me for leaving in the manner I did, and I'm about to step into him when the rustle of miniblinds collide with an opening door as Denton walks into the diner.

"Dolores?" he says in the same questioning voice as Griffin and Rusty.

"Why the hell does everyone keep saying my name like they don't recognize me?"

"Because you look different," Denton clarifies. "You look good. Healthy." The final comment floats between us as if he's surprised.

"Well, despite the fact you look pissed off." My hands fall from Garrett's biceps, and Garrett shifts to stand next to me.

"Garrett?" Denton questions, stepping forward. "What are you doing here?" His eyes travel from Garrett to me and back. They widen, and a hint of panic fills them. "Are you here to sign the contracts?"

I experience a sensation of the world spinning into a vortex and sucking me down, down, down as I slowly twist to watch Garrett turn his face from my brother to me and then avoid my eyes.

"What contract?"

"I…" Denton closes his eyes and wipes a hand down his face. "I wanted to surprise you. I wanted to make things better. Make up for not being here."

I'm outside myself, floating around the demolition of the diner and dreaming all of this, I think. I don't understand what he's saying to me. It's as if I'm underwater, and nothing is clear. "What does this have to do with Garrett…" I pause a beat as my eyes shift to the man next to me, his head lowered. "…and contracts?"

Denton exhales, his eyes trying to hold mine. "I couldn't just gift you the money. I have the money, but the amount needed is too large. It would be a tax issue for both you and me. I spoke with Garrett, and he suggested a low-interest loan, one he could foot, to make it look like an investment instead of a gift. This works better for both of us."

"How is this better for me?" I snap, waving a hand at the demolition around me. Another thought occurs. "How are you covering Magnolia's renovations? Are you gifting her?"

The two men fall silent, and my head swivels from one to the other.

"He didn't tell you?" Denton asks, staring at Garrett in wonder, and out of the corner of my eye, I see Garrett scrub at the back of his neck.

"I was going to," Garrett mutters.

"Tell me what?" I snap, glaring at the side of Garrett's head. He inhales deeply and looks over at me, his eyes troubled as he speaks.

"A vineyard."

I don't understand. *What is happening?* I want to scream, but instead, I wait out his explanation.

"Your brother…" Garrett stops and shakes his head. "*I* met your brother when I came to Atlanta. We got to chatting about my idea, and he hinted at the land around your grandmother's house. I didn't give it a second thought, but then we went to Napa and…" The weekend rushes through my memory. The things he did to me. The talks we had about his future, his dream, his plan. He wants to own a vineyard, and he needs land.

My eyes jump to Denton, glaring at my younger brother. Hatred simmers beneath my skin. "What were you planning to do with Magnolia's?"

"I don't know yet." A bed and breakfast flits through my head, but that had been my idea. *For years from now!* "I just thought I would fix it up and make it nice for her. We could discuss its potential later." The hint of Magnolia's age and eventual death lingers in his words. Then again, he's lying. For twenty-seven years, I've hardly seen my brother, yet I know when he's lying as if we were seven and five again.

"We?" I snap at my younger brother, who suddenly looks like a sheepish child. "There is no *we* here, Denton." I flick my fingers between us. "You seem to be making all the decisions without consulting me." A pointed finger jabs at my own chest. I stammer, willing myself not to cry, steeling myself to be the woman I was before I left Blue Ridge. In hindsight, I hate that woman, and I deflect the emotion back on my brother.

"This is my diner, Denton, and Magnolia's house is my home." I wait for him to argue. I own a small house just outside of town, but Magnolia's house is my future. I'm in no rush for her to pass, but it's mine. A moment of fear ripples up my spine. "Where is Magnolia?"

So help me if he says he put her in a home like he wanted. I'll kill him with my bare hands.

"She's at the house. She loves the changes."

A small glimpse of gratitude fills me, but only the smallest of small sparks. I turn back to Garrett.

"I still don't understand what you have to do with this."

A vineyard. The land around your grandmother's.

My head turns back to Denton. "You can't sell Magnolia's land. It's landlocked."

Denton nods once. "But we can use the land for whatever purpose we want."

"How?" I bark, my heart racing, the pulse at my neck throbbing.

"With a silent investor, we could run our own business from the land like the farm it once was."

With an investor?

"You knew about this?" I turn on Garrett, my anger shifting to him instead of my brother. I can't wrap my head around what he's telling me. The plans he's made—*without me.*

Garrett opens his mouth, but there's nothing to defend.

"Did you play me? Was this part of the plan taking me to Napa? Did you…did we…" I can hardly find my voice. I can't catch my breath. "Was I a project like those women said?"

"No," Garrett cries out, turning to face me and gripping my arms.

At the same time, Denton steps forward, and questions, "Wait?" My brother stares wide-eyed between Garrett and me, taking in the position of his friend's hands and the hurt in my expression. "Did you fuck my sister?"

The crass question spit from Denton has Garrett rounding on him and blocking my body behind his. "Watch your fucking mouth."

I wrap my arms around my middle, uncertain how to feel or what to do.

"Dolores," Denton begs over Garrett's shoulder, "tell me you did not sleep with him."

I can't answer him. In fact, I don't even want to look at my brother. I don't want to look at Garrett either. They're equally part of this betrayal. Garrett knew I owned a diner before I told him, and he knew my brother was demolishing it. *He knew.* And now, he's somehow involved in wanting Magnolia's land? I can't think.

"You bastard," Denton snarls at Garrett, but I've had enough.

"Both of you, get out."

"What?" they say in unison, focusing their attention on me.

"This is my diner, and I want you both out." My voice shakes, but I try to stand taller despite the arms wrapped around my center.

"Dolores," Denton begins, stepping closer to me. "I wanted to surprise you. I wanted it to be nice for you."

"You have not been here in twenty-seven years, Denton. Twenty-seven! I'm the one who took care of everything. Me, Denton. You know nothing about what I want. You don't get to waltz back in here and make decisions for me *about my business*." Tears well, hot, agitated drops of liquid that sizzle down my cheeks in my anger. I hate that I'm crying in front of him. "Leave my diner alone. Get. Out."

Denton's expression widens in surprise and then slowly collapses. It's a low blow, but he deserves it at the moment. Garrett reaches for my back, but I twist my body away from him before he can touch me.

"And you," I say quietly, hissing through clenched teeth. "You wasted a trip to Kansas."

"Georgia," he corrects until his eyes meet mine and understanding blossoms.

"Go home, Tin Man. The fantasy is over."

"No," he demands, stepping into my space, but I hug myself tighter, stepping away from him. "You said you wouldn't leave."

"Why do you care? I'm sure Alicia is next in line." The words sting, his expression crestfallen while his eyes harden.

"Why would you say such a thing? I care about you."

"You care about an investment."

"Screw the investment. I'll just gift you the money."

"I don't want your money," I spit. "I've never wanted that from you." More burning tears spill as my eyes shift to my brother, who is keeping audience over our argument. I never wanted his money either. I just wanted my brother back. I just wanted Garrett to feel the way I feel about him.

You're such a fucking idiot, Dolores.

"Go home, Denton. I'll call you later." I can't deal with both men collectively.

Garrett keeps his eyes on me as I watch my brother spin and walk out the door. When the diner door clicks shut, Garrett speaks again.

"Sweetheart, not wanting my money is one of the reasons I like you so much. You're refreshing and unassuming."

"I'm naïve and stupid." So stupid to think he slept with me because he was attracted to me when it sounds like all he wanted was a business arrangement…with my brother. My stomach roils. "Was *I* a part of the contract?"

"Stop it," he barks in my face, and I flinch. "Stop right there." His tone sharpens, and he reaches for my cheeks, pressing me until my back hits a wall where a booth used to be. His voice begs, "Don't do this."

"I'm not doing anything," I growl. "That's my problem. I let things happen around me, over me." This is the story of my life. "I've been doing nothing for nearly two months, and now I've got the fucking mess of a lifetime on my hands." The reality of the diner socks me in the stomach, and my body trembles like a shock victim. The truth slowly sinks in. I don't have the financial means to fix this mess, and this mess means I don't have finances period. I sob once and then suck back the sound, blinking away the blur of Garrett's face before me. I force the pain inward, caging in my heart. I'm good at this. It's who I am. My heart races within my chest as a lump clogs my throat. The old me is back, and she's choking me inside.

"Let me help," Garrett says, his head lowering to mine as if he's going to kiss me.

"Don't kiss me." I don't trust my emotions. His lips on mine will shatter me. I'll be a wreck like the diner.

"What?" He freezes midway to my lips.

"Stop using sex to distract me." My skin prickles with thoughts of him touching me, licking me, making love to me. *Was it all a game?*

Take me against this wall and make me believe it was real and not a dream.

I shake the thought.

"I am *not* using sex to distract you. Don't make me into him." His finger points in the general direction of my kitchen where Rusty and

Griffin have mysteriously disappeared and not returned. "I want to connect with you. I need to be close to you." His voice grows deeper with each word he speaks, sounding desperate and hurt and confused, which are all the ways I'm feeling.

Images flash in my head.

His mouth on mine. His hands in my hair. His body joined with mine. He'd look me in the eyes, and I could feel him peering into my soul, stealing my heart with his.

His heart. He said he didn't have one, yet at every turn, there it was, or so I thought.

"I am not him," Garrett growls, drawing me out of my memories. He's right. He's not. I thought he was so much more, and I was wrong.

"I need you to leave." I eye the decimated room around us. I'm at a breaking point, and Garrett must sense the destruction within me because he backs away.

"You promised you wouldn't leave," he whispers like a petulant child not getting his way. I rack my brain for a retort—some promise he made me—but I come up short. He gave me everything, yet I took it all for more than it was.

The Wizard never assured Dorothy he'd take care of her, and Garrett has done the same thing to me.

chapter 28

There's No Place Like Home

[Dolores]

Within fifteen minutes of Garrett's silent exit, I'm on my way to Magnolia's. As I near her home, it looks like something from another dimension, and it's a similar sensation as when I entered my diner. I feel like I'm in some kind of *Twilight Zone* episode. Scaffolding on the outside of the three-story house proves work has been done on the roof and repairs are being made to the clapboard. All the shutters have been removed and stand propped along the side of the house. The front porch has been rebuilt with new, unpainted columns holding up a repaired overhang.

When I enter the house, brown paper covers the hardwood floors leading down the hallway to the kitchen. I pass the front two parlors, one on either side of the main hall, then the dining room and the grand staircase opposite it.

"Who's there?"

I don't answer as I enter what looks like the makings of a kitchen straight out of a home improvement magazine. A half wall has been taken down, opening the area and allowing for a better breakfast bar. The original cupboards have been removed, and white base cabinets stand in a new configuration to fill the space. A light gray wood flooring gives the old kitchen a fresh look. Countertops and modern appliances are missing, though.

"Magnolia?" Our grandmother has never allowed us to call her grandmother, and as I stand in the nonfunctioning space, I wonder where she is.

"Breakfast room."

I walk through the second entrance to the kitchen and into a little nook of a room with a green-painted built-in cabinet to my right and a small circular table situated near a bay window. Magnolia sits within the window area. Both Mati Rathstone, Denton's girl, and her best friend, Cora Conrad, are present.

Mati's a petite woman with an athletic build and a fiery spirit to match the lion-like red hair. Her bark-brown eyes give me a sympathetic look. Her new best friend, on the other hand, is a platinum blonde, thin and snarky as ever after all these years. Her temper has settled a little since her divorce, which is the connection between the unlikely pair. The death of Mati's husband and Cora's divorce drew the two single women together, though Mati isn't single anymore. She has Denton.

Mati stands to hug me, and I let her envelop me, though I don't return the embrace. I feel empty inside, and although her arms touch me, I can't feel the comfort she's trying to give me.

"Are you mad?" she asks, pulling back and searching my face.

"I don't think mad describes it."

Cora sets a mug of tea on the edge of the table near me, and I take in my surroundings. The breakfast room is a substitute kitchen with a Keurig machine on the table. A toaster oven sits on the built-in cabinet next to a single old-fashioned hot plate.

"What's going on here?" I ask, tired of all the topsy-turvy construction I had no say in. I step back from Mati, skip the offer of tea, and swipe my hand through my hair, holding a clump of it at my neck.

"Denton wanted to fix the place up a bit as he…*we*…live here."

"You live here?" I shriek, questioning Mati who had her own home near town. At least, when I left for California, she did.

"The university plans to rent me an apartment at the beginning of the semester, so I sold my house to Jaxson…" Her voice drifts, and she glances down at her feet. Mati has a new job. This I already knew, but I wait for more details about why her son bought her home. She doesn't explain. "A few changes have happened since you left."

"I can see that," I snap with sharp sarcasm, twisting my head to look around the breakfast room. I'm expecting Martians to walk in any minute and punk me. *Joke's on you, Dolores.* You've entered an alternate universe. I'm losing my mind.

"He had the best of intentions," Mati offers, interrupting my thoughts, and defending Denton. "But I think he got in over his head with two projects at once, and as the diner is yours… well, I no longer thought it was right for him to take over without you. I thought you might want a say in what happens."

"Ya think?" I bark again, dragging out my Southern drawl to match hers. Sarcasm mixes with the exhaustion catching up to me. "I just don't understand why you didn't call me sooner. Why no one thought to call me before anything ever happened?" I'm speaking to the air because neither Mati nor Cora are at the heart of my issues. Neither is my grandmother who addresses me.

"Girl, come give me a hug and take a load off those shoulders." This woman knows me. I'm ready to detonate all over this small room. "You look like you're gonna run away again."

I'd like to run again, only I have nowhere to go.

My grandmother's words bring fresh tears to my eyes. I haven't been very faithful to her as I left without a word and only spoke with her a handful of times in my absence. I round the table and reach down for the matron of my family. This woman is my everything. She saw my father for who he was and always found ways to go around his back. And she did it with grand gestures like gifting me the diner when he didn't want to send me to college and giving Denton a guitar and letting him practice at her home because she knew he needed a way out of this town. Remiss in my behavior, I step over to her and wrap gentle arms around her frail figure.

When I pull back, her pop bottle-shaped glasses magnify her eyes, which seem extra wide and concerned behind her lenses.

"Missed you, girl." The words break me again, and I swipe at loose tears leaking down my cheeks. She cups my face like she did when I was a child, and her eyes scan my face. "Take a seat."

I sit where Mati was, and Mati sits next to me.

"Tell me all about California," Magnolia says with hesitant encouragement as if I've been on an adventure. She's trying to distract me, but I don't want to think about California, or Denton's apartment, or the man who lived across the hall. He was my adventure, not the destination of where I was. I won't know where to begin on my journey of self-discovery without spilling all the glory and guts of being with him.

Garrett.

He looked so broken standing in the diner.

But I'm broken as well by his withholding the truth and Denton's lies.

Are you here for the contracts? I need more answers.

"There isn't much to tell," I lie to myself. "I can't think of California right now. I need to think about my diner."

"I want to know more about the hunky man at my hotel," Cora teases, wiggling her brows as she tries a second attempt to draw me away from the issues at hand. "He's a dream on two legs. Denton's friend, correct? Where do I find more friends like him?" Cora eyes Mati, and Mati weakly smiles. Cora is another woman over forty in Blue Ridge, and the pickings for available men are slim. We saw a few of Denton's old band members this October, but they are all married. Of course, there are all the Farrington brothers, but I don't think those boys want a thing to do with Corabelle Conrad.

"I don't know that I'd trust Denton's judgment," I snark, ignoring Cora's description of Garrett, willing myself not to think of the too-attractive man and what he might be doing checking into her lodge. *Why is he here?* "His name is Garrett Fox."

"And what's he doing in Georgia?" Cora begs.

"He's here on business." The words spilled from my lips, tasting bitter on my tongue.

"He's here for Dolores," a male voice states, and we all turn to see my brother standing in the doorway between the breakfast room and the dining room.

"He is not," I snark before noting a *tap, tap, tap* on the brown paper in the hallway like nails drumming on a desk.

"No man travels from Los Angeles to Blue Ridge, Georgia, unless it's about a woman." Denton's expression softens, and he gazes down at Mati who blushes. My stomach feels sick as I witness their love.

"He's here for business," I throw out at my brother, reminding him of what I just learned.

Denton shakes his head. "Speaking of being here, can you tell me why you didn't call to mention you were coming home?"

"Surprise," I jest without humor, mockingly waving jazz hands at him. Only, I'm the one surprised by everything. The *tap, tap, tap* grows louder with a gentle *thump, thump* intermixing. The sound becomes clear as a chocolate lab rushes into the breakfast nook.

"Wally?" I choke as the dog trots. His tail wags weakly as he saunters to me with his eyes lowered and his ears back. I practically fall from the chair, folding to my knees to draw him into me. He allows me to curl around him, and I nuzzle my face into his neck. For the first time in my life, I take comfort from an animal.

"How did you get here?" I ask him as if the dog can answer for himself.

"I take it you recognize this pup?" Magnolia teases.

"He belongs to…" How do I describe my relationship with the owner? We don't seem to have one. "Denton's neighbor from California."

"The one who crossed a country to see you," Denton adds.

"I like your new hair," Cora interjects, feeling the rising family tension in the room and attempting to deflect it again. "Very chic. You look amazing." Cora's undergone a change herself since her divorce. She's the first person to act like my transformation isn't peculiar. Once again, I have Garrett to credit for the change in me. My ribs hurt, and suddenly, I feel short of breath as I recall the salon and shopping. "Thank you. I have some new clothes, too, but I left them all in California."

"Actually, they're out in my truck," Denton interjects.

"What?"

"Garrett packed you a suitcase and brought it with him. He called me to meet him at the lodge. It's how I have Wally. He thought the dog would bring you comfort."

I huff.

I hate dogs.

But as my hands scratch behind Wally's ears, and he looks up at me with his strange blue eyes, tears blur my vision again. I don't hate Wally. I hate Garrett. He thinks of everything. And I really, really hate him.

Don't lie to yourself, Dolores, my heart says.

I want to ask why Garrett didn't bring Wally here himself, but then again, he parted from the diner with the final word.

In my head, I see Garrett's stricken face as we stare at one another.

Eyes that typically search for the other's soul can't handle the intensity of Garrett's glare. I'm the first to pull away. When I do, I hear Garrett's resolve in an exasperated sigh. He reaches for my cheek, and I don't flinch away. My eyes close when he leans in for a kiss at the corner of my mouth.

"I'm leaving you, then," he whispers, before pulling back and walking out of the diner.

"He really checked into the Lodge?" I ask even though Cora has already clarified this information, and Wally at my feet confirms it.

"Says he'll be staying a while. We didn't get into too many particulars. He told me to come check on you."

Garrett.

"I'm fine," I lie, and Mati's eyes bore into the side of my head. Magnolia pats my hand either in sympathy or as if she knows better—*I'm not fine*. I'm dying inside with thoughts of my demolished diner, the improvements to Magnolia's, and Garrett's presence in Georgia.

"This guy looks like he needs something to eat," Magnolia addresses Wally, who she reaches to give a tender pat, and he obliges her hand by moving toward her. *Traitor.* His tail begins to *flop, flop, flop* at the excitement in Magnolia's voice. She stands on shaky legs, and my brow pinches. Has she always been so deliberate in her movements? She steadies herself with a hand on the table before shuffling toward the kitchen with the aid of her cane. Wally follows her like a trusty guard dog, sticking to her side with her slower pace.

"Is she okay?" I turn to Denton, worried the dramatic changes have taken a toll on her.

"She's fine. She loves the improvements and has been a part of every decision we've made."

"We?" I snort. "Well, at least she's been offered the courtesy."

Denton sighs. "I'll set up a meeting with Griffin, and he can show you the plans for the diner. They've only done structural work. Updating plumbing and electricity so far."

"How about if *I* call Griffin and take over from here?" My blood begins to boil again. I don't need Denton giving me a rundown of what's been done. What's done is done. I need to salvage my diner.

"I only wanted to surprise you," Denton says, his voice dropping as his arms cross over his chest. "If you had stayed in California a little longer, it would have all been finished."

"And it wouldn't have been mine," I snap. "It would have been all your ideas. What you thought best, not me." I have my own ideas for my restaurant. How I want it to look. What brand I want it to have. Where I want it to go next. Denton stares at me, and I feel the weight of Mati's and Cora's eyes at my back. "I know I should be grateful somehow, but I can't find gratitude at the moment. You must see this is more than a surprise. This is a shock. Gross negligence of what *I'd* want. You didn't consult me on anything."

A tiny bit of guilt sparks inside. Magnolia gave me the diner. Not both of us. Me alone.

A woman's place is in the kitchen as long as she owns it.

I fought the guilt for years until Denton made his millions, traveled the world, and did things I'd never do because I was the one with the diner, not him. I let the guilt go and owned my destiny: Dolores's Diner. Which is all the more reason I'm angry. It's mine, not his.

"I just wanted to offer you a little breathing room." His voice remains apologetic, and I appreciate the thought. I do. But I can't get over my irritation. It's too much at once, and I can't even consider the house and Magnolia's land yet.

I'm suddenly tired, so very tired.

"Why don't you go upstairs and lie down?" Cora suggests like she lives here and is part of the family. Mati and she have been visiting Magnolia regularly, and then my sick mother for the past year, so in many ways, Cora has blended in with us.

"I'm afraid what I'll find upstairs." I glare at Denton. We each have a room in the seven-bedroom home, albeit antiquated in many ways. Our mother moved in with her mother when our father died years ago. She returned to her childhood bedroom with minor updates and lived the remainder of her days in this house. I assumed I'd live my final days in this house as well, but Denton's takeover has me questioning everything.

"Nothing upstairs has been touched yet," Denton says, though I find his words less than reassuring.

"I think I'll head upstairs for a while then." I nod, dismissing my brother. We have nothing more to say at the moment, and when I exit the room, I find Wally at Magnolia's feet as she sits in her corner chair in the front room. She waves a hand, swiping upward, directing me to my room, and I'm happy to oblige. I'm relieved to be at Magnolia's because I don't think I can face a night alone in my house. When I snuck in this morning for a quick shower, I already felt the familiar loneliness of living there. Being in Magnolia's for a few days as I re-acclimate to Blue Ridge is just what I need.

I dismiss the yearning for someone else I might need.

Welcome back to Kansas, Dorothy.

chapter 29

Best Friend's Older Sister

[Garrett]

I give Dolores the night, but the next day, I find the infamous Magnolia McIntyre homestead, thanks to the help of a nosy busybody named Cora Conrad, the owner of Conrad Lodge where I booked a room.

"No," Denton says, rushing off what looks like a newly built front porch. He holds both his hands up to me as I approach, and I stop in the path. It snowed overnight, and I'm thankful I looked at the weather before I hopped a plane for the other side of the country. I shove my hands into my puffy jacket and huff out a steamy breath as Denton storms toward me. "She doesn't need you here."

I glare at Denton. "Are we fucking sixteen? As I told you yesterday, she's a big girl, Denton, and can make her own decisions. Which, I might add, you took from her."

When Denton came to pick up Wally from me, we didn't say more than a few words to one another. Everyone needed a minute to cool down, but today is a new day, and I want to see my girl. Denton stops, his breath coming out in a mist of warm air in the cold morning. He glares back at me. "I thought you told her about the contract."

"Why would I tell her? I didn't realize it involved her." I'm lying to myself, though. We'd talked often about our grandparents, and then I took her to Napa where she had all these ideas about a vineyard. I could see it all in my head, and while Denton's suggestion had been in jest, the plans took off for me. Instant gratification man. I'd called him on Monday after our weekend away to solidify the contracts for review. He promised he'd allow me to use the land for profit in exchange for the quote-unquote investment loan I'd given him. I'd planned to tell Dolores everything after the gala event. I had big plans for that night as well.

Dreams. Silly pipe dreams. Again.

Denton turns his head, and I follow the line of his vision. The flat land goes on for miles. The house is the only thing standing, along with a protective surrounding of trees. Rehabbing the home is underway, and I knew this when I saw him in Atlanta. He wanted to do something nice for his grandmother. After all, she's the one who bought him a guitar and allowed him to practice at her home, giving him a dream like my granddad gave me. He told me he hoped to make it into a bed and breakfast one day but was in no rush. The tourism industry in the small community was on an upward trajectory, which gave me another reason that a winery here would be a sound investment.

"This is so fucked up," Denton mutters, running a hand over his salt and pepper hair. "She's so angry with me."

"Do you blame her? You took her business and tore it apart."

"I planned to put it back together."

"Without her input?" My defense of Dolores doesn't surprise me, but it surprises Denton. His eyes narrow as he looks at me.

"You care about her." There's a question in his voice, but I'm not explaining myself to Denton before I talk to Dolores. It's more than caring.

"Is Dolores here?" The informative Cora assured me Dolores was staying at her grandmother's for a few days, so I can only hope I'm not too late. For a few short minutes, I worried she would go back to that schmuck Rusty.

"She's inside," Denton offers with defeat in his voice. He twists and waves a hand for me to continue for the house. Denton follows and then reaches around me to open the front door. Instantly, I notice the potential of the house. A parlor off each side of an extra-wide hallway hosts an abundance of seating. A dining room to the right after one parlor holds a large table. A grand staircase to the left will be stunning with some new stain. Eventually, we enter a kitchen in the process of being refinished. Denton leads me around a corner into a breakfast room. Here I see a frail woman with sharply cut gray bangs and glasses that look like the bottom of two soda bottles perched on her nose. They magnify her blue eyes, which I imagine matched Dolores's decades ago.

"And who might you be?" she questions, dipping her head to roam up my body. She's not checking me out but inspecting me.

"This is Garrett Fox, Magnolia. The man Dolores mentioned."

"The neighbor who crossed the country for her?" My head flinches back at the direct question. How could she know such a thing? It's a reminder Dolores ran away from me. She's hiding out here in Georgia to avoid me.

Then why are you here? my heart asks, but I know the answer is hope. I'm hoping I'm wrong about Dolores. I'm hoping she feels the same way about me as I do about her. I love her.

"Magnolia," Denton warns, and I chuckle softly to lessen the awkward moment.

"Well, what do you want with her?" She addresses me.

"I'd like to apologize," I begin. First things first. Dolores needs the truth from me.

"Should have brought flowers. In my day, men were gentlemen, and flowers worked while groveling."

"Yes, ma'am. I should have." I realize I don't even know what Dolores's favorite flower is, or if she even likes flowers. Then I think of the things I do know. Dolores loves classics. Black and white movies. Tango dances. She'd want roses.

I lean forward as if I'm going to share a secret with Dolores's grandmother. She leans toward me, elbows resting on the table that separates us. "I'm also hoping to woo her."

Denton swears under his breath. Magnolia sits upright and nods once. "Thank God. That Crusty Rusty wasn't worth the dirt under her feet. You still need flowers, though."

"Magnolia," Dolores admonishes, and I turn to see her standing just inside the kitchen. My breath hitches. She looks tired with red-rimmed eyes and a splotchy face. *Has she been crying?* Dolores is one of the strongest women I know, but that doesn't mean she doesn't break down when she's alone. I don't want her to be alone. I don't want her to cry. And I especially don't want her to cry over me.

I take a deep breath and give her a weak grin. She watches me, biting the corner of her lip. Lips I miss.

"I thought I'd take Wally for a walk. I don't want him to be a burden to you."

She nods and pushes a section of hair behind her ear. "You know I don't mind him." I hear the scrape of his nails on the paper covering the entry hall floor, and then I see my chocolate-colored dog. He saunters up to me, and I squat to give him a good rub behind the ears. I focus on him, uncertain of what to say next. Tension slowly fills the breakfast nook.

"I couldn't get a meeting with Griffin until tomorrow morning." Denton addresses his sister, frustration ringing in his voice. "I swear these small-town workers hardly work."

"I said I'd handle it," Dolores snips at her brother, still keeping up her guard with him.

"I know, but I wanted to follow through on one last thing." His voice rings with hurt and apology. I imagine Dolores has heard *I'm sorry* too often in the past twenty-four hours.

"Yeah, well, they better get to work. I need a diner back in business by Christmas," Dolores snaps. That's in two weeks. Her demands might be a bit unreasonable, but when I look up at her, I see she's all business. She means it. She needs a Christmas miracle.

Slowly, I stand, reminding everyone I'm in the room. "I guess I'll just get Wally's leash," I say, although I have no idea where the item is. Dolores tips her head for me to follow her. She's wearing a pair of her skinny jeans and thick socks, but she's back to an oversized sweatshirt. She rubs at her arms as she crosses through the kitchen and enters the hallway. Pausing at the bottom of the grand staircase, she spins to face me, and I brace myself for the wrath I saw her throw at her brother. Instead, her eyes soften.

"I could come with you. To walk Wally," she offers, and a pinch of hope spikes inside my chest.

"I'd like that."

"Be right down," she says, turning and racing up the staircase to a landing. I watch her backside as she jogs the steps, and when she spins for the second set of stairs, she catches me. "Were you checking out my ass?"

"I wouldn't dream of looking anywhere else."

"You're unbelievable." She huffs a chuckle as she disappears up the second stairwell before I can respond.

"Too bad I want you to believe me," I mutter as I wait.

"You break her heart, and I'll kill you." The threat comes from a little old lady I didn't hear approaching even though she uses a cane to stand inside the kitchen.

"If I hurt her, I give you permission to give it your best shot."

"I own a 1965 Remington .22 I keep in good condition, and I'm not afraid to use it."

Yikes. Although, if I recall my first experience shooting a gun with my granddad, a .22 isn't going to take down a human, but her point is made.

"Understood," I say, rolling my lips to prevent a chuckle and give her a humble nod.

"Don't be trying to use your good looks on me, young man. I've got Denton and Tommy Carrigan as grandsons. Pretty eyes and a sly smile don't work on me."

I bite my lip, trying not to laugh. This woman has spunk, and I know exactly where Dolores gets hers from.

"No, ma'am," I say, attempting to act more contrite. Dolores returns down the stairs with a beanie cap on her head and a long puffy jacket with a thick furry collar on the hood. She's the vision of a snow bunny, and I want to hunt her down.

"I just need boots." She nods toward the kitchen, and I follow again. There's a mudroom off the side of the kitchen and a second staircase leading a few steps down to an exterior door. Dolores slips into a pair of snow boots with fur matching her collar and leads me out the back of the house. She calls for Wally, and the traitor that my dog has turned comes at the command of her voice. He's a Californian through and through, though, and doesn't know how to respond to the snow under the pads of his feet.

"You baby." She insults Wally like she does with that exaggerated tone, and he looks up at her with all the trust in the world. She pulls a tennis ball from her pocket—a fresh one—and tosses it out toward the field. We follow Wally as he races for the object. After several long minutes of only the snow crunching under our feet and Wally's grunts, I speak.

"It's so quiet here. Peaceful." The silence is eerie but also refreshing, completely the opposite of the constant noise of LA. It reminds me a little bit of the area around River City. The wind whistles, and the cold stings, but if this is the only way to be near Dolores, I'll take it.

Dolores looks up, squinting into the cloudy day as she watches Wally run. "I never thought I'd leave here. Never considered whether I wanted to or not. I had the diner and my grandmother and my mother. It was enough.

"I'd never been to California. I didn't hate it, but I knew I'd never make it my permanent residence. I was restless there, though I enjoyed my visit." She glances at me while we walk next to one another, each of us with our hands buried in our coat pockets. I don't look over at her but forward at Wally, feeling like a teenager on the verge of a breakup. You know it's going to happen before it happens, yet you're still blindsided by it. Then again, I was more often the one to do the breaking up until Kate.

"I need to be here, Garrett. I need to fix this."

I understand. I do. Her brother has made a mess of things.

"Can we back up a bit?" I question, my heart racing as I need some answers. "Can you tell me why you ran off without telling me?"

She takes a deep breath. "I'm sorry about that. I am. Ingrid was telling me how she thought you and Alicia would make a nice couple, and Alicia had just called me a special project. And then Ingrid mentioned how at one point she wanted to be with you. And you were dancing with Alicia like you'd done it a hundred times before." She pauses. "You didn't have to lie about the tango lessons."

"I didn't lie. I'd never danced like that until you. And fuck Alicia and Ingrid." My tone is sharp, and Dolores flinches, but I'm pissed. "Why didn't you come to me before you ran off? I was there with you. *You.*"

"You looked rather practiced on the dance floor." She's snarky, and I want to retort but don't want to fight.

"I attend a lot of events," I huff, scratching at the back of my neck. "You already know this about me."

"I do, and it's a reminder I don't fit in your world." She glances up at Wally racing down the lane. "I was headed home to Denton's condo when Mati called me. She didn't say what was wrong, but the urgency in her voice told me it was time to come home. To Georgia."

"And you couldn't have called me? You sent me a text, but it didn't explain anything." I stop walking, and she steps in front of me and turns to face me. "I would have come with you."

"Why?"

"Dolores, come on," I mutter. She can't be this dense, but she stares at me, waiting for an answer. "The other night, I had everything planned. I wanted it to be perfect. I…" I realize I'm admitting too much. Dolores's brows pinch, and she takes a step toward me, questioning me with the expression on her face.

"What did you have planned?"

"It doesn't matter now." I huff, scrubbing my hands down my face. I was an idiot to think she felt the same way as I did, but I'm not fool enough to admit it. Now that she's told me she won't return to California, I'm getting the impression she wants nothing to do with me.

"Look, I'm sorry I didn't tell you about the contracts." I need to change the subject, and Dolores tips back her head and then turns her body to continue walking. Wally is quite a bit ahead of us, and I whistle for him to come back. As he races toward us, I explain myself. "Denton mentioned the land. It was just a suggestion. More like a joke, but after our visit to Napa, I got to thinking…maybe it wasn't such a bad idea." I can't add how I hoped she'd be on board with me. How I hoped she'd want to be a part of the vineyard with me.

"I'll cancel the contracts, though, and just gift you the money. I don't fucking care about the money, or the contracts, or any of it."

"You can't give me the money," she huffs, looking deflated.

"Dolores." I pause, reaching out for her arm to stop her. "I want to do this for you." Does she hear what I'm saying? She's staring at me, wheels spinning inside her head. "I have an idea." I bite my lip and glance left, drawing courage from where we stand.

"You know I want a vineyard. A place that's all mine for retirement someday. This is the perfect spot." Dolores doesn't blink. She makes no motion whatsoever. "Let me use the land. It isn't being used, and it's perfect."

"What do you know about starting a vineyard? I thought you wanted to buy one already established."

"I changed my mind." I didn't realize I'd changed my mind until I started a budget and an outline of my business plan. Magnolia's is large enough to get a good start. I don't need the house, so the building is neither here nor there to me. "Magnolia can stay in the house for as long as she likes. Denton suggested the property as collateral on the loan for the diner."

"It's my diner. And my inheritance," she states, her voice falling small.

"And I don't want you to give it up. I want to borrow it, and I'll amend the contract."

"What about your money?"

"Dammit, Dolores. You're more precious to me than money." The cold nips at my cheeks, but I don't feel the sting. The heaving of our breaths and warm air leaking from our nostrils fills the space between us instead.

"We can work something out," I begin, hesitating with hope. "Keep the money to improve the diner. Let me have the land to build a vineyard. It's a win-win."

"Why?" Dolores questions, her face still pinched in misunderstanding.

Because I don't want to be away from you.

Because I want to do this with you.

Because I want to be where you are.

"Because it's just sitting here, waiting to be used, and I want my plan to begin. My future. Here."

Her breathing becomes more ragged. Her nostrils flaring in the cold. Her lips are pink. Her face rosy.

"I don't know," she says, and I step toward her, right up in her space, desperate to touch her face but holding back. She isn't looking up at me. "I should talk to Denton, though Lord knows he didn't offer me the same courtesy."

"We can talk to him together. I'll explain my vision to him. He doesn't want to keep the place. Not for any purpose. He just understands it needs to stay within your family."

"But…" Dolores opens her mouth and then clamps her lips shut, rolling them inward.

"What?"

She shakes her head, unwilling to explain her thoughts. *Dammit.* She's killing me here. Deflated, I suggest we turn back.

"We should head back to the house. Wally's California feet don't know how deadly this snow can be." I chuckle without humor. I'm distraught. She doesn't want to hear my plan and doesn't want to be part of it, a part of my future.

I whistle for Wally again, taking the tennis ball that's been in my pocket and toss it toward the house. We walk in silence again, my thoughts filling with ideas that will never come to fruition for this place.

"What did you have planned?" she asks, surprising me with a more cheer in her voice. "You said you wanted the other night to be perfect. What did you have in mind?" She hesitates in asking, and I exhale deeply in frustration.

"I don't think it matters now." The irritation of losing both the girl and a vision in the same twenty-four hours suddenly weighs down on me.

"I'd still like to know."

"Dolores." I stop. "I've been on my own for a long time, and I thought I was fine with it that way. Especially after the scandal with Kate. I've kept my heart in check. Tin Man, remember?" I knock on my puffy coat over my left pec for emphasis. "And then I met you, and I shared things with you I haven't shared with anyone else, like owning a vineyard someday. So forgive me if I hesitate in giving you the last part of my soul when you're standing here rejecting me."

She blinks and blinks again, liquid filling her eyes. *Shit.* Don't cry, I think. However, this might be the first time waterworks won't work on me. Raw and restless, like I'm standing naked in this flat field on this cold mountaintop, I can't take any more disappointment.

"Pretend I'm the Scarecrow. My brain is curious." I don't want her brain to be curious. I want her heart to be open. She's smiling, but it isn't reaching her eyes. It isn't filling her face like I know it can.

"Fine," I huff. "I booked us a room. I wanted to take you upstairs and make love to you. You looked so beautiful in that dress. That gorgeous, fucking, stunning dress. I just wanted you to feel special, and I wanted you to know how much I love you."

I'm breathing like I'm running a marathon. I'm not winning the race, but I'm sprinting like my life depends on it.

"You what?" she whispers, her eyes wide and glistening as a single tear drops. I close my eyes. I can't watch her cry. It will break me, and I'm already broken.

"I love you," I say, turning away, preparing for her to rally against my emotions. Instead, she steps up to me, her coat brushing mine. Gloved hands cover my cheeks, and she forces me to turn in her direction.

"I love you, too," she says softly. "It's been there for a while now, and when I saw you with all those elegant women at a fancy gala, I just didn't think I belonged with you. I wouldn't be enough for—"

My mouth stops the rest of her words. Her cold lips turn warm underneath mine as I press against her, drawing her to me. My heart fills. The heart I didn't have, which she returned inside me, swells and swells as I take her lips. Without words, I tell her in this kiss how much I love her, how I'll do anything for her, anything she asks. I just want us together. I pull back abruptly.

"I wanted to ask you to be my partner…on the vineyard. Work with me to selfishly make my dreams come true."

Her breath hitches, and she blinks in confusion. Maybe it's too much to ask. She's been through a lot the past two days, and this might be the final straw for her.

"Don't ever leave me like that again." I breathe out against her red lips, my forehead pressing to hers. "My heart can't take it."

"I'm sorry, Garrett. I'm so sorry." She tips up and takes my mouth with hers, speaking back to me with her sorrow and her fears. I want to believe she's telling me she wants me to be with her. She needs me. When she slowly pulls back, she tugs my lower lip with hers. "We'll figure it out, right? Together."

My lips press into her forehead as I confirm, "Together, sweetheart."

chapter 30

Puppy Love

[Dolores]

We remain kissing in the cold field, our mouths keeping us warm until a brick of body thuds into the side of us. Garrett stumbles, and my legs tangle with his, and in the bulking winter clothing, we go down to the hard, snow-covered ground.

"Oof," he says, landing in such a way so he takes most of my weight. Wally dances around us, yipping and yelping, and a déjà vu happens although this time it isn't sand.

"Are you okay?" I stare down at Garrett under me as he rolls his eyes and turns his head.

"I just need a minute," he grunts, and I slip off him.

"Wally," I ground out. "You stupid, bad dog," I say in that voice he loves, wagging his tail harder as he races around us. Garrett twists his head as he chuckles at his pet.

"I think he's trying to tell us something, like get out of the cold, dumbasses."

I huff in response and stand slowly, holding out my hands for Garrett so I can pull him up. He pushes off the ground with one hand, the other placed in mine. Swiping at his backside, he knocks the snow off his jeans.

"I'm wet," he states.

"I think that's my line."

He stills for the briefest of seconds and then his cold hands cup my face, and he's kissing me again. I don't mind the sting of his cool fingers as his mouth is warm and tender. He's swallowing my tease, and I want to be closer to him, connect like he said. But sex isn't our only connection. Garrett has this crazy idea about a vineyard—here—at Magnolia's, and he wants me to be a part of it. For a moment, I can see it. Us together. And my heart races with the thrill of it.

I pull back and slip my arm around his waist. "Let's go inside."

He nods and wraps an arm over my shoulders.

We still aren't close enough. I accused Garrett of wanting to distract me with sex, but right now, I want the distraction. I want to believe it's all real. What he says. What he wants.

I love you.

My heart cartwheels in my chest. For the past forty-seven years, I've rarely heard those words. Never heard them from a man unless he was using them to reel me into bed.

But this man? He wants more than just me in bed. He wants a freaking vineyard. And me.

We enter the back door and hang up our coats. Wally shakes himself before heading up the short number of steps to the first floor.

"Dolores?" Magnolia calls out.

"Magnolia," I respond, my voice carrying. Who else is going to walk in her back door?

"Still got that man with you?"

"Still here, Magnolia," I shout back as Garrett wraps his arms around me from behind and kisses under my ear.

"Take me upstairs," he whispers, and I still.

"What? Here?"

He murmurs into my neck, "I need to be inside you."

The words race through my body, instantly heating me. Reaching for his hand, I tug him forward, up the stairs and down the hall until I find Magnolia in the front room knitting. Wally lies at her feet. Her hands shake, but she still works the needles. Slowly.

"Hey, we fell in the snow, and I'm taking Garrett upstairs so we can change."

"Uh-huh." She nods, not looking up from her yarn work. She doesn't believe me, but I don't have time to argue. "Just remember those old beds make a lot of noise, and your room is above this one." She peers through her magnifying glasses in the direction of Garrett.

Oh. My. God.

"Magnolia!" I shriek in shock—and guilt. She knows exactly what I intend to do, but she's warning Garrett.

"Then we won't use the bed, ma'am." Garrett winks at her, but his face is serious, and I spin to bury mine in his chest. I can't believe he just told my grandmother he's going to have sex with me. Without another word to Magnolia, Garrett turns us for the hall, and with both arms around me, he tugs me down it to the stairs. There we break apart, and I reach down for his hand. I take one step up, and Garrett stills me, his eyes on mine as he clears his throat.

"Magnolia," he calls out. She doesn't answer, but I've no doubt she's listening. "I'd like to take Dolores upstairs with your permission." He pauses. "See, I just told her I love her, but I think she needs some further convincing. I have a proposal for her, and then I have a proposition for you." He winks at me.

Proposal? He can't be serious.

"I'm not into anything kinky," she bellows back, and I want to die on the stairs. My mouth falls open, and Garrett laughs, his face pinking under his two-day-old scruff. "That's not to say you aren't nice looking, though."

"Is your grandmother flirting with me?" Garrett whispers, his face even more flush. I'm biting my lip, fighting the laughter at his embarrassment and this conversation. A giggle escapes, and I tug at his hand to encourage him to follow me up the stairs. We practically race, and the bedroom door echoes when we close it harder than we intend.

"Oops," he says as I fall against the wall beside the door. Instantly, he's on me. Hands in hair. Lips on lips. My hips buck forward, and he presses me back, sliding his hands down the curve of my body. "I've missed you so much."

Realistically, it's only been two days, but I know what he means. I didn't like sleeping without him, being without him. We remove each other's clothes in a frenzy of sweaters and socks and jeans. Once naked,

I remain against the wall, shivering with the chill in the room and the anticipation of Garrett. His mouth returns to mine, his hands cupping the sides of my neck and then skimming over my shoulders. He drops one to my thigh and curls around it, lifting my leg to hitch high against his hip. Then he slips into me without foreplay. I don't need it. He's taller than me and needs to bend at the knees. His head lowers for a breast, sucking at my nipple. His hips aren't moving, and I tip mine forward for friction. A firm hand halts my hip.

"I need a second," he mutters into the skin he's covering in kisses. Perched on one leg with my back against the wall, my body vibrates for balance. I quiver in his arms, and he releases my thigh and slips out of me. "Down on the floor."

I fall to my hands and knees, and he thumps down behind me. I lower to my elbows, pressing my forehead to the rug. Garrett spreads my knees by placing both of his between mine and slams into me, sending me forward. With a rapid-fire, pummeling action, he repeats the motion, quick and sharp, and I meet him thrust for thrust, arching back against him, taking what suddenly feels like a punishment.

"Don't." He huffs. "Ever." He puffs. "Leave me." His voice fills with anguish with each slapping movement. The hammering motion emphasizes each word and his need, his fear.

"I'm sorry," I grunt, taking my penance and loving it. He slips out of me, and I whimper from the loss. A hand at my hip curls around my belly, and he flips me. I land softly on my back, the short fibers of the rug scratchy under my skin. Garrett hardly misses a beat, and he's inside me again. My knees draw upward until Garrett finds my shins. Pressing at my legs, he forces them to my chest. I'm open for him, and he drills deeper, deeper, deeper. The thrusts come hard and quick, but the orgasm races faster, slamming into me within seconds of this new position. I bite my tongue, holding back a scream as the thought of Magnolia the floor below flashes through my head.

"Dorothy," he hisses, drawing me back to him instantly. With a strained voice, he speaks. "There's no place like home. And this is mine." I want to laugh. The giggle rolls up my belly, and my mouth pops open, but then he covers mine with his and stills. Pulsing commences. Once. Twice. Three times. He fills me while a strangled growl crawls into my throat. His arms wrap around me, and he holds me, awkwardly arching my back and pressing me to him as if he doesn't want to let me go. My fingers slide up his back and delve into his hair, holding his head as he releases my mouth and dips his face into the crook of my neck. We remain on the floor, a tangle of limbs, racing hearts, and clutching arms until I hear Garrett sniff.

"Babe," I whisper, tugging at his short hair, hoping to see his face. He shakes his head, holding me tighter, squeezing me. Another inch and I'm not going to be able to breathe. He wipes his face against my shoulder and then draws up, going for my lips again, but I stop him with hands on his cheeks. "Garrett?"

His eyes remain closed, his forehead coming to mine. "I love you." Three simple words yet so much emotion is tied up in them. "I love you, Dolores."

He sounds surprised, questioning—hesitant even—and then he pulls back, his eyes liquid fire, and repeats them again. Confident. Definite. Honest. His mouth comes to mine, and this time, I allow the kiss, a soft, tender meeting of our lips.

"I love you, too," I whisper against his mouth as he slowly releases mine.

"I'm so tired," he says, not letting me go as he slips out of me, followed by a surge of fluid.

"Why don't you rest?"

"Come with me," he mutters. I should. I'm tired too. The emotional stress has caught up to me. The diner. Garrett being here. His declaration. I need a minute, or my thoughts will haunt me, preventing me from sleep.

"You climb into bed. I'll be up in a bit. I should check on Magnolia."

Garrett stares down at me, his brows pinched, but he doesn't argue. His knees crack as he kneels back and tugs me to sit. Then he stands and helps me up. Naked and sweaty, he climbs into the full bed and looks at me over his shoulder.

"You'll come back." There are a question and a warning in his voice. "A rainbow isn't going to keep me away from you."

A rainbow? And then it hits me again. He really is a Wizard.

+ + +

I slip back into my leggings and the oversized sweatshirt and steal down the stairs to the breakfast nook, which is acting as the kitchen. I use the Keurig to make two cups of tea, taking one to Magnolia. Of her two front rooms, one receives more sunlight than the other. It has bookshelves and two antique couches in need of repair. Magnolia prefers the other parlor, which is darker on this gloomy afternoon. It opens to a screened-in porch, which looks sad and lonely on a winter day. Magnolia sits in a chair, staring out the window with Wally at her feet. I take a chair opposite her.

"I brought you some tea."

She nods in gratitude, and a small smile graces her thin lips. I love this woman more than anything, and I've done her wrong by running off like I did. She took me back easily when I showed up yesterday morning and left me alone as I rolled restlessly in my bed most of the night. We haven't been alone since I arrived.

"I'm sorry, Magnolia," I say, offering so much more than the apology.

"Whatever for, girl?"

"For running away." For leaving her when she needed me most after my mother's death, after her child's death. For escaping across the country and hardly having any contact for weeks. For not telling her how overwhelmed I felt.

"Honey, you think I didn't want to run away from life on more than one occasion?"

Actually, I didn't ever think that. A pillar of strength, my grandmother owned her own business before women did such a thing, and without a man by her side as he had died young, leaving her with two small girls. They were spoiled and unappreciative of their mother—one running after a preacher man and the other marrying the future town mayor. She lived through the Great Depression, wars, and controversy in this town, supporting most of it with her businesses.

"There's nothing wrong with taking a break. We all deserve one. And we all need one once in a while if we are going to survive life in general."

I sigh. She's right. I've just never known how to slow down. I don't know how to relax. There was always the diner. My mother. Her. Rusty. Everything else came first.

"I heard about the diner although I haven't seen it. I don't think Denton was in the right, but his heart was. He's trying to make up for things beyond his control. At least you came back." She chuckles, and I find the humor in her words, though she isn't joking. When Denton left, he never looked back. Not for twenty-some-odd years, leaving me with our horrid father and our sick mother. Leaving me to hold things together while he followed a dream and saw the world. I didn't dream outside my own backyard, so I couldn't fault him for the wanderlust of a rock band, but that doesn't mean I didn't want to get out of Blue Ridge once in a while and live a little.

"It's a huge mess," I say, running fingers over my hair, which I pulled into a knot on top of my head. I hold the steaming mug of tea in my other hand.

"Messes are what men make, and that's why God created women. To clean them up." She leans forward and pats my knee.

"I don't really know where to start with this one." I lightly chuckle with nerves.

"How about the one upstairs?"

It takes me a moment to realize what she means—or rather who?

"Oh, he's not a mess." I chuckle, this time with more humor. Garrett's one of the most pulled together people I know, but then I think of his face buried in my neck as we lay on the floor of my room. Did he shed a tear?

"That man's all kinds of messed up over you," Magnolia states, her head lowering, and she glares at me through those pop-bottle glasses. "He flew across the country, chasing you."

Chasing you. It's like an echo in my head. No man has ever chased me, yet Garrett did.

"I don't know what he wants from me."

Land, whispers through my thoughts, but so does the word, *together.*

"Your heart," Magnolia says softly. "And it's about time someone does." She never liked Rusty Miller, though he hardly came around here, and she knows all about my heartbreak over James Harrington.

"I guess I don't understand why," I return quietly, thinking of the diner and the project before me. Garrett is a successful businessman in his own right. He lives in California. *And he wants a vineyard here with you.* "Nothing makes sense lately."

"Nothing ever does when you love someone. You'll do things you never thought you'd do and say things you never meant to say. You'll feel heartache like you've never felt before and joy like your heart might burst. And you'll never make sense of any of it. That's the great thing about love. It doesn't need to make sense. It just happens."

My grandmother has been alone for almost six decades. I've never known a man in her life, yet she speaks like her husband, who died so long ago, still lives as the love of her life.

"How'd you get so smart, Magnolia?" I tease, never finding it strange to call her by her first name as I became an adult. This woman is one of my best friends, and I have the honor to call her family as well.

"Always have been," she teases. "I listened to both here"—she taps her temple—"and here." She pats her chest near her heart. "Sometimes one wins over the other, but it all evens out eventually."

I chuckle, and she reaches down to pat Wally snoozing over her feet.

"He's a good dog," she says without the mocking tone I use, and Wally wags once as if he agrees.

+ + +

I excuse myself from Magnolia and head back upstairs. Garrett is still crashed under the ancient quilt and two blankets on the bed. His California blood runs thin, and he looks peaceful tucked under the old bed coverings. I kiss his temple and mutter that I'm going to take a bath. I decide a soak will help me relax. He murmurs in his sleep, and I leave the room.

The bathroom is down the hall, and something Denton should consider if he's going to renovate the whole house. My mother's room was the back bedroom, and I always thought it would make a beautiful master bedroom with a view overlooking the fields beyond. My room is a front room, and the one next door has a boarded-up window. Even though the tandem door between the rooms remains closed and a towel rests at the seam on the floor, the room stays chilly.

Once the tub is filled, I sink into the claw foot porcelain, resting under an etched glass window. The draft doesn't deter me as the heat of the water fills the room. I lay my head back and close my eyes.

Garrett wants to own a vineyard. *Here.* The idea plays on repeat in my head. What does that even mean? I let my thoughts drift until I hear the quiet click of the latch on the door. Turning my head, I see Garrett entering with a ratty bathrobe of mine over his body.

"Well, you're a vision," I joke. His hair stands up a little, and he chuckles as he runs his hands through it. "My jeans are still wet, even though I set them over the radiator." He peers down at me in the tub. There aren't any bubbles in the water, so he can see all of me.

"Whatcha thinking about in that pretty head of yours?" he asks, perching his backside against the single sink on chrome legs. He crosses his feet at the ankles like wearing an old dingy-white terrycloth robe with a giant daisy stitched over the left breast isn't unusual. It's a far cry from his three-piece suits.

"So much," I mutter as I observe him. He's contemplative as well with his arms crossed over his chest and his fingers on his lip. He nods once and then removes the robe. Holding the edges of the tub, he steps in, facing me, forcing my legs over his thighs. I always considered this tub large until he settled in with me. He can't be comfortable with the faucet at his back, but he sits forward, stroking my thighs under the water.

"Tell me what you're worried about."

"Everything," I sigh. "The diner. The vineyard. You."

He nods again. "I find it's always best to start at the top of the list. Number one. The diner. Concerns." He's serious—like business-mode serious—and I want to giggle, but then I realize...*he's serious.*

"I don't even know where to start."

"You meet with Griffin. That's his name, right?" Garrett's brow pinches in recollection. "I say don't think about the diner until then. Look at the plans, see where they are in the renovation, and then take action. Make the changes you want."

It sounds so simple, and in his authoritative voice, I wonder what he's like in his boardroom. I eye his bare chest, glistening from the steamy water. I'd totally want him to do me on his desk if I worked for him. His lips crook, and his eyes narrow as if he's reading my mind.

"Focus." He chuckles. "Next. The vineyard." He breathes out, turning toward the window which casts a glow in the room but doesn't allow him to see outside. "I'd like to talk to Magnolia. It's her property, correct? Denton doesn't have any power of attorney over it."

I smile sheepishly as I shake my head. "I do, actually. She wrote it off to me when my mother was sick. She worried she'd die, so she reworked her legal documents." It's sad to consider but also a reality as my elders grow older. She needed peace of mind, needed to know how she would be handled if she became incapacitated.

"I still want to speak to her. Then with your permission, I'd like to talk negotiations with you. We can set it up with lawyers so they can explain everything in detail. How land sharing would work in your favor and mine." He pauses, his hands stilled on my thighs, but he squeezes so I understand him. "This is business unless we want to get to item three on the list. Me. What concerns you?"

"You don't live here. How will you manage a vineyard from California? How would I see you? Would you visit from time to time, and how does that work with me and—"

Wet fingertips cover my lips as his other hand wraps around my hips and he tugs me to straddle his lap.

"Slow down. First of all, I love you, so I want this to work for both of us. Together. My business is in California, but I travel all over for it. I can have my home base from anywhere, which means I can travel *back* to California whenever I need to. If I'm starting this project here, I'd like to stay here." He pauses, his eyes lowering to my chest. "I was hoping I could stay with you."

"I don't live here. I have my own house."

"At your house, then. Wherever you are is where I want to be."

I stare at him. Is he real? Am I imagining him?

"So you'd still keep your place in California and travel back there?"

"Only when I have to, and you can come with me." He tips his head. "And you're not answering my question."

I smile slowly, stroking through the damp hair on the back of his head, focusing on my fingers. "I didn't realize there was a question in there."

"I'd like us to live together." My head pops up, and my eyes focus on his. "Does it seem too quick? Because I can't think of anything I'd like to happen faster. I don't want to be separated from you."

"I'm not going anywhere," I assure him, sensing his fear once again. "I'll be right here." I lower a finger for his chest and draw a heart over his moist skin.

"I love you," he whispers, and I lean forward to kiss him. There's another space on him I'd like to be, and his dick springs against my inner thigh. I press against him as he unfurls, deepening the kiss with my arms and legs wrapped around him. I want to make love to him in this tub, but there really isn't enough space to move.

He pulls back, holding me by my lower back and stares. "Is our checklist complete? Can we stop worrying for just a little bit?"

"The list will be unending. I've just thought of another thing to add to the to-do list."

His smile quirks up at the corner. "It'd better be me."

I press against his generously hard length and giggle against his lips. "You can read my mind, so you really are a Wizard."

chapter 31

Property

[Garrett]

The next day, Dolores directs me as I drive us to her house. The place is small, looking almost like a cabin with a single window next to the front door. We enter a cool room that's neat and comfy but tiny.

"I hadn't turned on the heat as I wasn't here," she explains. An overstuffed couch sits on top of an area rug facing a television on a low table. There's a hall off to the side of the TV stand. Her kitchen to the right.

"It's not as nice as your condo," she mutters, and I turn on her as we stand behind her couch.

"Don't do this," I plead. I don't want her comparing things. I came from a home that didn't look too different from this one. Tidy, orderly but small. I'm not judging her, especially as it's a small town, and she's been a single woman. The thought gives me pause.

"What I want to know is if you slept with him here?" The idea of her with that red-haired grease monkey makes my blood boil, and I've tried not to think of it since yesterday when I saw him briefly in the diner. She didn't need to introduce us for me to know who he was. Wild orange hair lay limp over his ears with a patch of facial hair here and there. His eyes devoured Dolores even though his words sliced her up. He called her old, and I felt her bristle before me. She hadn't heard me enter the diner, too lost in the mess around her, but I wanted to throttle him for insulting her. Only, I sensed her instability. She couldn't handle a pissing match, and I didn't need one either. There was no comparison between him and me, especially after her reaction when I touched her back. If she had flinched, I knew I'd lost her, but she didn't. She leaned back, pressing into the comfort of my hand, and then when she turned to hug me, I didn't worry. But standing in her home, I envision him everywhere with her.

"I thought we said we weren't doing this."

"I need to know." I don't want to share all our indiscretions, but there was something about the way he looked at her. She wasn't as casual to him as she led me to believe. Or she didn't see the way he peered at her as though he owned her, possessed her. Giving her up isn't going to be easy for him, even if she fooled herself into thinking he didn't care about her. His evil glare said he did, at least on an ownership level. I shiver with the thought. *She's mine*, I seethe.

Her silence is my answer.

Without looking up, she corrects herself, "Well, not everywhere." She eyes the floor and shifts toward the kitchen. I'm on her in a second, lifting her to cradle my hips and carrying her into her kitchen. I lay her out on her table, devouring her neck and her jaw, struggling to get all the layers back off her body. I'm a madman, come to stake my claim.

"Garrett," she murmurs between kisses. "Not here. It's too cold." She's kissing me, but she's telling me to stop, and I do, pulling back as I feel the weight of my crazy.

"How he looked at you makes me insane."

Her head tips in question when she weakly grins up at me while sitting on the table.

"We can't stay here," I whisper, knowing I'll hurt her feelings after I told her I wanted us to live together.

"Why?" she whispers, touching my cheeks.

"I'll see him everywhere with you." I close my eyes at my own weakness. Jealous and petty and wanting her all for me. Soft lips brush mine.

"I agree. It's too lonely when I think of being here."

"But I'm here now," I teasingly assure her, tugging at her hips. I might have to swallow my pride in this case.

"I'll sell. I can use the money to manage the damage to the diner."

"The diner isn't damaged; it's being renovated, and you'll have all the money you need." I lower my eyes, scratching at the back of my neck because I know I have to tread lightly. "But I wouldn't mind you selling this place if you want. We can stay at the Lodge for a while until we figure something out."

"Magnolia would never forgive me. Plus, she has all that room. We can stay there."

I'm pleased to hear this solution as I'd prefer to be at the heart of the operation where the vineyard begins and so does our adventure.

"I need about an hour to pack up some things. Why don't you head to the Lodge and check out? There's also a hardware store in town. Duncan's. You might be able to get a dog bed for Wally. I'll call Denton, and he can meet us here with his truck." I love how she's thinking of things. Planning is a sign of accepting. She hasn't said yes to anything, but after our checklist discussion, she seems calmer.

Note to self: negotiate in the bathtub more often.

+ + +

After I check out of the Lodge, I find a dog bed for Wally and a grocery store for some necessities, then head back to Magnolia's. Dolores called me to say Denton can meet us in an hour and a half at her place.

As I arrive at Magnolia's, I knock, not wanting to let myself into her home. There are so many things to discuss, and I don't want to have any conversations until Dolores and I can talk to her grandmother together. Magnolia has other plans, though.

"What are your intentions?" she says after I've set the groceries on the cabinet with a makeshift counter of plywood over the top. She has an old refrigerator for now, but I'm assuming something industrial and flashy is coming based on the space provided. I pause while placing things in the fridge, debating if I should speak candidly to the matron of the Chance family.

"My intentions? I'd like to marry her." I shouldn't be telling Magnolia before anyone else, but I figure she's the one to ask if I'm going to do this properly.

"What do you want from her?"

"Her heart." I'm honest and direct with this woman who looks like she'd accept nothing less from me. I meet her stare. Her shrunken figure with large glasses and a sturdy cane does nothing to dissuade me from recognizing she's a force, and I need her blessing.

She nods once, lips pursed but pleased.

"Actually, I'd like something from you as well. Shall we discuss it now?"

"Be useful and make me some tea in that fancy machine, and then we can talk."

I chuckle as I finish setting things in the fridge and follow Magnolia to the breakfast room. The fancy machine she references is the Keurig.

"I'm told it's easy to use, but I can never figure out the buttons." She nods at the contraption while I press the appropriate button, and the heater roars to life. Tea dispenses shortly afterward, and I set the cup on the table. For a moment, I feel like a college kid again, fresh out of business school and ready to take charge of the world, one project at a time. A renewed sense of enterprise fills me, and I'm reminded of old-world deals where people discussed things in barrooms and shook hands to seal agreements.

I explain what I want. The land. The vineyard. The use of the property but not a purchase of it. I explain profits and sharing with Magnolia. She was the original business entrepreneur of this family, making a diner in her grandmother's name and selling fried chicken and fresh eggs to travelers on the scenic train route through the mountains. She explains to me how she got her start.

"It always starts with an idea." She winks. "Then it turns into a dream."

This was my dream. Strange that while I explained everything to Magnolia, I thought of my granddad as if he were in the room with me.

Hopefully, he's proud of me fulfilling his dream, even if he wasn't here to see it come to fruition.

"This all sounds good to me. It's always broken my heart that the land went to waste. Neither of my girls wanted what my grandparents worked hard to maintain. Then that no-good Kip Chance stole a portion of the land for a subdivision, thinking he could blackmail my daughter and gain the rest of the land to build up a city."

I sit back in my chair. I hadn't heard this story yet. Magnolia waves a dismissive hand.

"I'll let Denton explain. He's the one who discovered everything. As for this proposal, you write it all up legal and fancy, and I'll have Denton and Dolores take it to the lawyer to read. We use Charlie Harrington in town. He's the mayor."

The mayor is a lawyer? I chuckle softly. *Small town*, I remind myself.

"How are things going here? The renovations?"

"Why? Is the next thing you're going to ask to purchase this old place?"

"No, ma'am, but your granddaughter suggested we live here for a bit." *Shit*. That was a slip, and scratch at the back of my neck. I might be overstepping here.

"Oh, she did, did she? What other promises did she make you?"

"None yet, really."

"She know you want to marry her?"

"Not exactly."

"But you love her?" If Magnolia hadn't been a business owner with the diner, her second calling could have been police interrogation. I'm under a firing squad of questions, and sweat trickles down my back.

"Yes, ma'am, I do."

"Huh," she says, sitting back in her wooden chair.

"Why huh?"

"She thinks she doesn't deserve you, but I told her she was wrong. She deserves everything and more in this world for all she's put up with. Her father being the king of horrible. Her brother leaving like he did.

And that no-good motorcycle thug. You're a sharp looker, but I'm reminding you of my gun. She's been surrounded by poor men, and I'm not talking about money. You better be a good one and be good to her."

"Understood." I chuckle. "I plan to be the best man…because of her."

"Smart answer," she whispers, leaning forward and giving me a wink from behind those thick lenses.

chapter 32

Baggage

[Dolores]

I've got a suitcase full of clothes and a pile of things to donate. My favorite blankets are folded and stacked over a box of books and necessities. I'll also take the television and an antique rocking chair from my bedroom. I mentally mark the bed, the couch, and kitchen table for storage, which I'll need to figure out.

All these things run through my head as I wait for Denton and Garrett. When there's a knock on the door, I don't give it a second thought and open it. In an instant, Rusty enters and has me backed against the wall. His mouth on my neck physically repulses me. With strength I didn't know I had, I shove him off me.

"What the hell do you think you are doing?" I shout, staring at him with his wild eyes, disheveled hair, and a heaving chest.

"You're my woman."

I bitterly chuckle. "Don't be a Neanderthal. I'm not your woman."

Rusty steps up to me, forcing me flat against the wall with his proximity.

"You're mine if I say you're mine, and everyone in this town knows you belong to me." While this might have once been true—the town thought of me as his girl by his association with Devil's Edge—there is no basis to a relationship.

"We had sex, Rusty. Like you did with half a dozen other women in the county. That doesn't make me yours."

"You belong to me. Club rules."

"I'm not a member of your club, and I'm sure James would stand by that ruling." When I first started spending time at The Ridged Edge, a biker bar about fifteen minutes outside of town, James stated in no uncertain terms that I was not to become a member. He signed his fate to them, but he wasn't allowing me.

For old times' sake, I remember snapping at him.

Because you're like family to me. The comment made me shudder. As if all those years of fucking him meant he was sleeping with a sister.

As a superior to Rusty in the club, James would fight an affiliation between me and the bikers. I might be considered Rusty's girl by half the town out of fear, but I wasn't an official member of the MC.

"Don't throw James at me," Rusty snarls, his love-hate relationship with the second in command not a secret. Brotherhood forces them to have each other's back. Jealousy causes Rusty to despise James.

"Don't threaten me," I retort. Rusty's hand comes to my throat, and while I've never been afraid of him, fear ripples through my belly.

"What's he got? Money? Shiny toys? He'll throw you to the side once he uses you up, Lores." Rusty hated my old lady name and wanted me to change it. Lores sounded badass, but I've never felt like a Lores, even after all the times he's called me it. It's as if he wanted me to be someone other than who I am.

"It's Dolores," I hiss. "And he isn't going to throw me away."

Rusty chuckles, still holding my throat, stroking my skin and making it crawl under his thick thumb. "What'd he do, say he loves you? Played right into those fucking words you want to hear?" Rusty steps closer, his breath assaulting me like a slap. My nostrils flare, filling with the scent of alcohol. He's drunk. "But does he make you feel as good as I do?"

"He's better," I snap, tempting my fate. Rusty pulls back, the palm of his hand coming for my face. I turn my head, preparing for the contact when another knock hammers on my door. Rusty pauses mid-swing, halting his hand prepped to slap me. The door is beside us, and keeping his eyes on me, he yanks it open, changing course as if he expects someone else on the other side. *Please don't let it be Garrett.*

"Ranger," Rusty croaks, calling James by his MC name. He holds the door open, trapping me behind it.

"Heard Dolores was back. Wanted to check in on her." Here's the thing, James Harrington never speaks to me. He might have said I was family, but he's acted like I'm a pariah ever since Evie. He would never randomly check on me. Tall and lean but with solid muscle, he's not as broad as his older brother, Giant, but his strength is unmeasured. The typical Harrington eyes are soft brown, but James is the only one with blue. They aren't teasing like most of his siblings, but hard, cursed by life, and mean. James could look at you and melt you with a glare.

"I'm here," I mutter, the door muffling my plea. I need James, and I've never been so thankful for this surprise visit. He steps forward, the hard thunk of his motorcycle boots hitting the squares of tile marking my entryway. His entrance forces Rusty deeper into my living room. As the door tugs forward, James's eyes narrow, looking behind it and catching my eyes.

"You doing okay, Dolores?" I don't shift my eyes to Rusty but keep them focused on James. I slowly shake my head once. No. With that simple look, James rounds on Rusty and sends him to the floor with a blow to the face.

"You fucker," Rusty nasally garbles. His hand covers from nose to chin, and when he pulls it back, it's coated in red.

"I warned you," James states, glaring down at Rusty who doesn't look up at his biker brother. I don't understand his meaning, but James turns to me. "You okay?"

"Better now," I whisper. James looks around the room, noting my bags and the box.

"Moving?"

"I'm staying at Magnolia's for a bit. I'm selling this place." It's the first time I've said it out loud other than to Garrett. The moment I walked into my little house, I knew I couldn't stay here with him. While I have no doubt Garrett would be larger than life in this small space, there were too many other memories haunting these walls, and I didn't want Garrett tarnished by them. I didn't want us in the middle of them. Being at Magnolia's would be better.

"Heard you were away. Come back with some guy," James states. Rusty spits behind James, and James rounds on him. "You're going to clean that up."

James turns back to me, and I'm taken aback again by his knowledge of my whereabouts. He doesn't seem like one for town gossip since he was once the center of it. The moment strikes me as unreal as James speaks to me like we've been best friends since second grade, which we had been.

"I did. I was. I mean, yes. I was in California, and I met someone. Someone special." I chance a glance at Rusty, who slowly stands from the wood floor behind my couch. "We're together."

Rusty huffs, and James tips his head to the side, but only his eyes shift to Rusty. "Duly noted." He's making a statement to Rusty, warning him to stay away from me. "We'll miss you at the club." Rusty's head shoots up, glaring daggers at the back of James's head while I absorb the lie James tells. James will never miss me. He hasn't missed me in years, but he's also offering me this protection.

"Need some help here?" he asks, nodding at the bags, although I don't know how James could help me on a bike. I'm about to explain how Denton is coming in his truck when Garrett barges in the door with a concerned Denton behind him.

"What's going on here?" Garrett questions, taking one step toward me and gripping both my shoulders. James steps back, strategically placing himself between Garrett and Rusty. Denton enters farther into the space between my couch and front door, which is clearly too small for five adults.

"James?" Denton questions next, ignoring the presence of Rusty behind a seething biker.

"Long time, no see," James says. He offers Denton his hand, and a silent conversation seems to ensue between two men who were friends long ago.

"What happened?" Garrett murmurs, not letting me go, and I draw my focus back to him. I lift my arms for his neck and step into him, closing my eyes against the glare coming from Rusty behind James's back. "You're trembling."

"It's nothing," I lie, not realizing the level of my fear until I'm in Garrett's arms. He moves as if to release me, wanting another look at me, but I don't want to let him go, so he spins with me still clutching him. One hand removes from my back, and he shakes hands with James.

"Garrett Fox. Want to tell me what the fuck is going on here?"

"We were just leaving," James's roughened voice speaks. "Just checking in on our girl, but I see she's in good hands now." There's more to James' words. He's releasing me to Garrett. Not that James has any hold on me, but the intention is clear. He's going to keep Rusty away from us.

"You should stop by sometime. See your sister," Denton interjects, and I slip in Garrett's hold to rest my cheek against his chest. I avoid looking at Rusty but watch James as his expression hardens.

"I'll consider it," he mutters, but there's no conviction to what he said. He won't be visiting his sister anytime soon.

A silent nod of understanding takes place between James and Denton, and then James spins to tilt his head at Rusty as a signal to move. Without a glance back at me, Rusty passes his superior, anger still vibrating off him as he exits my house. James follows right behind him and tugs the front door shut.

With only three of us in my tiny entry space, it's still too close quartered, but Denton doesn't move.

"What happened here?"

I give an abbreviated version of Rusty's surprise visit and James's even more surprising appearance. Garrett holds me tighter to his chest, his lips lingering at my hairline. Denton stares at me, silently assessing me.

"I'm okay," I whisper to both men.

With a short nod, Denton questions, "So where are we taking your stuff?" His voice is a little too high when he asks, and I'm a little shocked Garrett hasn't already told him.

"I'm moving into Magnolia's."

Denton's been rubbing his hands together, either to warm them or to signal let's get busy, but the scrubbing palms come to an abrupt halt.

Then I add, "With Garrett."

chapter 33

Contracts and Deals

[Garrett]

Dolores and Denton remain eerily quiet after she drops the bomb about us moving into Magnolia's together. I feel like we should air everything out before we move a single object, but brother and sister circle one another, spacing out their movements like only siblings can, and begin to pack Denton's truck.

Denton handles the rocking chair while Dolores and I tuck her boxes in the back of the truck. When we arrive back at Magnolia's, the silence is thicker than a yellow brick. Denton and I tackle the boxes, television and rocking chair, carrying everything to the second floor and leaving it in the hallway after Dolores told me we could rearrange everything in the morning.

I slip into the bathroom for a moment and then pad in stocking feet to the staircase. From the top, I can hear raised voices. I travel down the two flights until I see Mati sitting at the base of the steps. Her head bowed, she holds a beer in her hand.

"What's going on?" I ask, still hearing voices from the kitchen.

"I'm letting the pot steam for a bit before I intervene," she mutters.

"Don't you think we should have discussed you moving in here as Mati and I already live here?" Denton asks, and Mati winces next to me.

"I didn't think to ask as you hadn't asked me about renovations on the diner," Dolores rebuts. I complete the descent down the wooden stairs and take a seat next to Mati.

"Did they always fight like this?"

"Denton spent more time fighting with his father than his sister. They were typical older sister, younger brother. She liked to play mother. He liked to annoy her. But when he left, the dynamics changed. I think they're trying to find their way around each other. So many years have passed," she mutters, taking a sip from her beer.

"How long was he gone?" I knew Denton was estranged from his family. His sister was the only person he mentioned and only on rare occasions.

"Twenty-seven years." She sighs, letting the time lapse linger. *Sweet Jesus.* I could never stay away from my family for that long. Then again, I didn't have the history Denton had with his dad. Mine was just gone.

"I didn't want to worry you," Denton snaps in the background.

"What are they arguing about?" I question, thinking I better make myself comfortable on the stairs.

"She wants to know why he didn't tell her about the diner or the house. He's trying to defend how she's handled everything for years. He wanted to give her a break."

I'd surmised as much from Dolores and then when Denton asked me to look after her. When I saw him in Atlanta, he told me how his sister had handled everything back in their small town.

I just want to do something nice for her. For both of them. He referenced his grandmother, as well.

"She's pissed he made a deal with you without discussing it with her." *Right.* "And he doesn't have a good rebuttal for that." Mati smirks.

I'm not certain I do either as I didn't know then the scope of Dolores's involvement in Magnolia's property. But I sigh, content that we'll have lots of time to figure everything out—together. While Dolores told me she has no intention of leaving me again, I assured her equally that I wasn't going anywhere. I understand she needs to be here for her grandmother and her diner. It's who she is, and I wouldn't change a thing.

"My brothers fought constantly, never good at a true argument. It's a wonder Charlie became a lawyer."

"I heard he's the mayor."

"Yep. That too." She doesn't say more, and I remember Dolores telling me her father had been mayor.

"Did you know their dad?"

"Unfortunately," she mutters. She doesn't offer anything else. We hear a *tap, tap, tap* coming from our right and turn in unison to see Magnolia struggling down the hall from the front of the house.

"How long we gonna let them yap at each other?" Magnolia asks.

"I figure they're almost done. Nothing's resolved, but most of the accusations are out," Mati states, smiling up at Magnolia.

"Well, I've about had enough of it." She slowly moves past us, *tap, tap, tapping*. I stand, stepping off the final stair to follow Magnolia through the kitchen and around to the breakfast room. Dolores and Denton stand on opposite sides of the table, glaring at one another.

"Don't do this," Denton asks, his voice falling. Dolores crosses her arms and turns her head toward the window. Snow covers the ground, but the room has fallen colder than the outdoors.

"Sit," Magnolia snaps, and the two turn to look at their grandmother. "Don't make me make you two hold hands and say you love each other like you had to do as children." Denton slowly smiles at the mention of their childhood punishments while Dolores huffs, and I have an impression of her as a kid. Stubborn. Strong-willed. She tugs at a chair and sits. Denton grips the back of a chair and remains standing over it. I pull out a seat for Magnolia, who thanks me and sits.

"Here's how I see it," she begins. "My house. My rules." Denton's face shifts, fear edging his jaw. Dolores looks up in surprise. "Denton already began the renovations with the help of a designer affiliated with Duncan Construction. I like what I'm seeing, but Dolores can have input as it seems she'll be living here, too." Denton's head shoots upward.

"This house has six bedrooms upstairs," Magnolia reminds them. Her room is off the kitchen, and I have yet to see it. I don't need to see it. It's her private place. "Each of you pick a room." She sighs. "I'm a modern woman. I can accept that you'll each be keeping your significant others here as well."

My head shoots up to Dolores who still glares at her brother, and then I glance at Mati. Her brow rises.

"Roommates?" I chuckle.

"You can work that out in a minute," Magnolia interjects, not finding the humor in the situation. "He"—she points to me over her shoulder—"wants the land."

It's Dolores's turn to shoot her head up, her eyes landing on me, and Denton stands to his full height, crossing his arms. "What?"

I swallow hard at the accusation in Dolores's eyes. I've done it again. Made arrangements without telling her.

"I asked Magnolia for permission to use the land for a vineyard. I'll have lawyers draw up everything. She told me Charlie is your attorney. You'll keep everything but let me use the land for this project."

Denton's gaze falls to his sister, who lowers hers, and then he looks back at me.

"From now on, I do nothing without talking to Dolores first," I clarify. He and I were the ones joking about their grandmother's land as a possibility, and all this miscommunication has led to hurt feelings.

"You do realize this was a chicken farm. Birds for eating. And eggs for…whatever the fuck at first," Denton reminds me.

"Watch your language, young man," Magnolia interjects.

"A vineyard is rare here, so it's an open market. You have all this land not being used for something productive, and I…I want to do this." I completely understand we'd be starting from scratch, but that's what I want. From the ground up, literally.

"What about Fox Investors?" Denton questions, still trying to figure out my angle. His brows twitch.

"I'll still own my company, but this is for me. For the future." I sigh, looking over at Dolores. "For us." I smile weakly, but she isn't looking at me. Does she no longer want this? It's been another whirlwind twenty-four hours of emotional declarations and business explanations and discussions about the future. We're moving at the speed of a tornado.

"You really gonna stick this out here, man? This isn't LA. It's a small town." There's a poke at the community in his words, and Mati's breath hitches.

"I grew up in a town not much bigger than this. I think I can handle it. In fact, I'm ready for a change." I peer over at Dolores again, who still isn't looking up at me. I glare back at Denton. What's he getting at? He came here. He should understand. He gave it all up for a woman…and happily, I might add.

"What about the diner?" he asks, peeking over at his sister.

Although I should let her speak, I interject for her because I want to be clear. "Dolores is keeping the diner."

"And the loan on that?" I notice Dolores has covered her face with both hands.

"We'll work it out. It will all be in the contract."

"I just wanted to give you something," Denton blurts out quietly, and Dolores finally glances up at her brother. He swipes fingers through his hair. "I know I wasn't good to you. It wasn't fair to leave you with him." For a moment, I think he means Rusty until Dolores begins rapidly blinking. "I suppose Mother wasn't much better. I'm sorry, Magnolia." He's insulting her child, and his eyes shift to their grandmother, who has remained quiet despite her initial demands.

"I know you understand my reasons for going, and I'm coming to terms with your reasons for staying, which is why I wanted to do this for you."

"It's been a lot to take in," Dolores softly replies. "The diner is a disaster. Then the house. It's not about the house, though, Denton. It's about steamrolling over me."

"I wanted to give you a break."

"I get that, but it's also breaking me. I'm used to being in charge. Making the decisions. Living my life on my terms. You're pulling the rug out from under me."

I understand how Dolores feels. If she's done it all on her own for so long, it's hard to relinquish the reins a little bit. She's having trouble delegating as she wasn't given the decision to delegate.

"I'm sorry," Denton whispers. "I'm sorry for all of it."

I'm uncomfortable with the heartbreak I hear in my friend, and my eyes meet Mati's. Maybe we shouldn't be present for this apology. Then I glance over at Dolores and know I can't walk away from her. She's been strong for so long, but she needs someone to be her strength.

A Tin Man is solid, even if he has a rusty heart.

Dolores doesn't answer her brother. She nods, and I hope this is her acceptance of his apology. Words aren't enough. She needs time.

"Maybe we need some time to process all of this. A few days. I'll have my lawyers draw up a contract and have Charlie look things over. Then we can discuss everything."

Dolores stands without a word and exits the breakfast room to the dining room.

"Stunner," I call after her, but Mati steps in my way.

"Let's let her be. Let her work this out for a second without being all in her face." Mati looks around the room, making a note of staring down Denton as well.

I nod, not knowing what to do next. Denton looks back at Mati and then stalks toward the kitchen. Mati shakes her head and takes a seat at the table. "Well, I certainly know how to clear a room, don't I?"

Magnolia chuckles, and I stare at these two, knowing I'll never understand the mysteries of women and their ways.

+ + +

Eventually, I make my way up to Dolores's bedroom. Her room has a constant chill seeping in from the room next door with a boarded window. This house needs new windows, and I plan to discuss all the particulars of the rehab with Denton first thing tomorrow.

Snuggling in, Dolores curls to her side, her back facing me. I stroke up her thigh, bare under the covers and massage up her tight back. Periodically, I lean forward and press a kiss to her shoulder. I shudder to think of what could have happened to her with Rusty. Thank goodness for small miracles like James Harrington. Dolores has told me all about their relationship in their teens and early twenties.

"Are you sure being here will be enough for you?" she mutters in a sleepy voice.

My hand coasts over her leg. "Being with you anywhere will be perfect."

She rolls to look at me over her shoulder. "I mean it. This is a small town, Garrett. Stuff like tonight is going to happen often." She means the impromptu party with Mati's children. Her grandchild. Her son's fiancée. Denton and Magnolia. It was a houseful and strangely made me very happy. I've been alone for a long time.

"I mean it too. I'm perfect as long as we are together."

Dolores eyes me from her odd angle. "You seem so afraid I'll leave you. Why?"

I duck to kiss her shoulder and speak into her skin. "My father left us as kids. It's silly, really. I'm an independent business owner, taking and giving as I please, yet I'm afraid to be left by the woman I love."

She rolls to face me. "I love you. I'm not going anywhere. But what if you decide this isn't enough, and you want to go…I'm the one afraid you'll leave me."

"Not a chance, Dorothy," I say, rubbing my nose against hers. "The Tin Man sticks once his heart begins to beat again." I kiss her nose and then roll her to her side with her back at my chest. She purrs as she nestles into me, her backside searching for my dick.

"You need to sleep, sweetheart."

She shakes her head in response, not speaking but continuing to wiggle against me.

"Dolores," I moan, knowing she needs rest, but suddenly rising to the occasion. Her back arches, her ass making contact. I slip my hands under the T-shirt she wears, using my wrists to lift the material as my palms caress up her spine.

"Feels so good," she mutters. She props up on one arm, allowing me to remove her shirt, and then collapses back to her side. My hands outline her body. The length of her arm. The curve of her hip. The dip of her waist. I lower behind her, pressing kisses along the curve of her spine. As I disappear under the tent of covers, I remove her underwear, dragging it over her knees to her ankles, where she kicks it off. My hands squeeze the firm globes of her backside, pressing them together and then spreading them wide. Her legs straighten, but I press at the back of her thighs, forcing them to bend and draw upward. With her backside in my face, I lower and lick across the seam of her.

"Garrett," she moans in warning as my thumb teases her puckered opening while my tongue lashes her sensitive folds. With a thumb testing at one entrance, my tongue slicks the other. She hisses again, remaining twisted on her side, with her knees clenched together, while I devour her in this position. Tongue lapping. Thumb flirting. My mouth salivates, and she whimpers as she nears release. Her legs stretch forward, kicking out from under the covers, to allow me to continue while she remains jackknifed on her side. My tongue delves forward, slicing into her, and she implodes, calling out my name on a strangled whisper. I lick her one final time. Then I suck on the firm skin of one cheek. I nip the other before I climb behind her.

"I'm feeling lazy, sweetheart," I mutter, keeping to my side, but holding myself positioned at her slick entrance. She opens her legs, but a hand on her thigh hints I want her to keep them closed. She'll be tight like this, and my dick pulses with anticipation. I clutch myself, dragging the tip along her soaked folds. She wiggles again, curling into herself to give me full access. "Hold on," I warn, and then I ram forward, the motion nearly blinding me as her tightness squeezes me in a way she hasn't before. I still, pulling my knees up behind hers. "Damn, you feel so good."

I pull back, maneuvering her hips to draw me in and then slide back to the edge. My eyes roll back again. It's slow and torturous and so fucking tight like this. We continue this languid, luscious dance for several minutes, both quiet as I fill her and tease her for a second release. The pressure builds at the base of my spine. My sac tightens, but suddenly, I need to see her face.

I pull out, and she cries, rolling to look at me over her shoulder.

"What's wrong?" she mutters, her eyes sleepy in the darkness of the room. I press upward and slip over her thigh, rolling her onto her back. I re-enter her before she's settled, and she huffs with the welcome intrusion. Balancing on my elbows, I peer into her eyes.

"Nothing's wrong," I say before pressing a kiss to her forehead. "Ask me again if I'll be happy here," I say, my voice rough with need, yet I hold back, keeping my eyes on her.

"Will this place be enough for you?" she whispers, her tone hushed and breathy. I slowly press forward.

"This. Right. Here," I say, pressing a hand to her thigh and then palming up her body, over the curve of her hip, the dip of her waist and resting on the side of her breast. "This is all I'll ever need."

I pull back, drawing out the building tension, and then slowly inch forward, filling her. My head lowers to watch myself disappear inside her.

"This is all I need." Repeating the measured movements, I realize I'm making love to her, giving her all of me, and taking all of her. "I love you, stunner."

"Love you too, Tin Man," she says on a sigh, her body following mine in a slow, steady rhythm. Her knee skates up my thigh, resting high at my hip. I wrap a hand over her ankle and press it upward once, twice. She lifts her arms above her head, gripping the wrought iron slats of the headboard. Her head tilts to the side, and I recognize her movement as something we learned in our tango lessons. I release her ankle, but she keeps it tight to my hip, and I relish the position she maintains as I lazily slip in and out of her. The heel of her opposite foot curls over my calf and drags up my inner leg. We continue this dance only as long as we can until she mutters, "Faster."

Our pattern continues—a drag and a draw—but the tempo picks up until we move as one. It isn't chaotic and quick like the previous times we've engaged in sex. It's practiced, planned, and predictable, but only because I know her body so well, and she follows my lead, allowing me to give her all the pleasure I can. She slips into a stillness. Her legs stiffening around mine as her head rolls back, and the familiar clench around me sets me off. I come in the depths of her, pressing as far as I can into her and holding her pinned to me by arms wrapped around her lower back. She sighs instead of screams, moaning words of *love you* and *stay forever* and *just like this*.

I collapse on top of her, breathing in her damp skin. Her arms release the bed and curl over my back, tickling her fingers up my spine.

"You are incredible," she mutters, and I chuckle.

"I'm so glad we finally agree."

chapter 34

Roommates and Socks

[Dolores]

I don't talk much over the next two days. I meet with Griffin Duncan as scheduled, and we discuss the renovations for the diner. Most of the updates currently in progress include items customers won't see. Electric. Plumbing. Gas lines. The questions remain on the interior of the place.

"What do you want it to look like? We can put everything back as it was with a few newer fixtures. But now would be the time for a change if you want to make it."

Time for a change. The answers come instantly. I tell Griffin my vision—classic dining car from a train mixed with the tradition of the diner—and he refers me to their interior designer.

"She's from At*lan*ta," Griffin drawls like this makes her sound important, or maybe he's just mocking her.

I chuckle because I can't even find the energy to laugh. I find myself slipping as if falling backward in time because I'm overwhelmed with everything. The diner. The house. Denton's betrayal…and Garrett's. He says he loves me, but I'm struggling. We didn't make love last night. He just held me, curled up behind me, nuzzling into my neck. He breathes me in like he's afraid I'm going to let him go. Let his dream disappear.

Hearts are on the line, I realize. Mine. His. I want to believe in him, but something niggles inside me, questioning if his love isn't tied up with his vision. His investment.

The next morning, I'm determined to get an honest answer, then I'll let my apprehension go. I find Garrett at the breakfast table, his laptop and phone on the circular surface along with a notepad. Glasses perch on his nose. He's wearing jeans with another sweater. The casual look suits him, but I wonder if he misses his fancy suits. I shake the thought. Wearing a T-shirt and undies under my old robe, I know it's not very seductive, but looking at him in my grandmother's worn out breakfast room, still the powerhouse man he is, I'm turned on in a way I haven't been in days.

"Good morning," he addresses me over the rim of his glasses, but I don't answer him. I straddle his lap instead. "Dolores?"

The corner of his lip crooks upward as he pushes the chair back from the table, keeping me on his thighs. Gripping the back of the chair, I start to roll my hips at the seam of his jeans. The robe billows around my legs, and I untie it, allowing it to drape open. His hands lower to my hips, slipping under the worn fabric.

"Whatcha doing?" he asks, his voice straining as I continue to rock over him, feeling the slow unfurl of his length under his zipper. Any minute, I'm expecting him to tell me to stop. To tell me he's busy. To tell me he has work to do. "Let's go upstairs." His voice is a whisper as he leans up to kiss me, but I pull back. My eyes narrow on his as I use the wood of the chair to balance and continue undulating on his lap. A thrill runs through me as he groans with my refusal to kiss him.

"Here," I say.

"Someone could walk in," he mutters, looking over my shoulder. I shake my head, my hips having a will of their own as they increase their dance. My sex moistens, clenching with need.

"I want you buried inside me."

Garrett swallows, fingers clenching the fabric of my shirt inside the robe. My eyes close, and my head lowers. The build is growing, crawling up my quivering thighs.

"What's this all about?" he mutters, his head tilting as I continue to ride him.

"Tell me I'm more important."

His brows lift, and his mouth pops open. His expression says he wants to say something, but he shifts. His eyes darkening. "You're more important than my work."

I'm rocking hard, the chair creaking under the weight of us. He shifts so I'm hugging the thick shaft bulging against the zipper of his jeans, and the pressure adds to my excitement. My panties are damp, and the friction settles right where I need.

"Tell me I'm more important than the vineyard."

"Dolores," he groans, his hand slipping to the base of my belly.

"Say it," I whisper, my voice throaty and deep.

"You're more important than the vineyard." He slips a finger under the elastic of my panties, then shoves it deep into me. The intrusion sets my legs trembling, and he thrusts his hips under the back of his hand.

"Is this what you need?" His voice has turned stronger, less pleading and more commanding. "Right here, right now, you want me to fuck you to prove myself to you."

My head falls forward as if I'm nodding, but he isn't wrong. Placing myself between him and his laptop, I want him to tell me I'm first. Not the vineyard. Not his business. Me.

For once, I want to be first to someone.

"You," Garrett growls, working his fingers harder, deeper into me. "You are the most important person to me." His mouth comes to my neck, nipping me as he works his fingers followed by the pump of his hips behind his hand. His thumb brushes my clit, and I explode, tightening my grip on the chair and clenching my hips over his. My head lowers to his forehead, resting against it as I gasp for air.

"Thank you," I whisper, my voice catching as tears burn in my eyes.

"I love when you take what you want from me," he says, pinning me with his stare. His mouth seeks mine, and I return the kiss with equal fervor, drinking in what he says, letting it fill me to the brim with happiness. I pull back slowly, tugging his lower lip with mine before releasing him. Shifting as if to move off him, he grips my hips to hold me a second longer. "You're my somebody, Dolores. *My*. Somebody."

"I love you," I tell him, and we kiss another moment, pouring into that kiss all the words, the fears, and the hope.

I won't leave you, I tell him with my lips on his.

I won't hurt you, he assures me.

We pull back, breathless once again. With a final peck, I slip off his lap and tighten my robe around my waist.

"Let's find some breakfast," I suggest. "I'll take care of that later," I tease as I point at the hard-on I've left him with. Garrett swats my backside as he stands to adjust himself and then follows me into the kitchen where we find Denton perched against the new island awaiting a countertop. His gaze is lowered as his arms cross over his chest, and his fingers draw over his lips.

"Denton," I say in the way of greeting. He doesn't look at me. His eyes leap to Garrett's.

"We need some ground rules," he states, keeping his focus over my shoulder to Garrett, who wraps an arm around my waist and tugs me back to him like a shield against my brother. "No sex in the common areas."

Garrett chuckles. "Roommate rules? Leave a sock on the door or something?" My brother shudders, uncrossing his arms and resting his hands on the uncovered top of the cabinets. He turns his head away from us.

"I was in a band for years. Too many close quarters. I'm too old for this shit." Mati enters the room, glancing among all of us. With clenched teeth, Denton repeats, "No common areas."

"I see the pot is calling the kettle black," she teases, walking up to him and slipping her arms around his waist. She tips up on her toes and presses a kiss just under his jaw. It's sweet, and the first time I've seen them truly affectionate with one another. My brother softens under her touch. She turns to face me, keeping her body against his. "It's only temporary."

"What is?" I ask, my eyes drifting to Denton. *Now what isn't he telling me?*

"We'd like to build a place of our own. On the property, if we can, but away from the main house a bit. We all need some space," Mati says, shifting her eyes from Garrett and me to Denton.

"When did you decide this?"

"We've been discussing it for a bit. Denton wanted to get Magnolia set up first. Fix this place for her. With you home, things are shifting, and rightfully so," Mati emphasizes, squeezing Denton who remains silent while she speaks. "You've always taken care of Magnolia, and we aren't giving the responsibility back to you. Fixing the house is for both of you…and I guess Garrett now too." Garrett's arms tighten around me.

"I want a place that doesn't hold so many memories. I want new memories," Denton adds, finally wrapping his arms around Mati to secure her to him. I understand. Mati sold the home she lived in with her husband for twenty-something years. Denton's only known Magnolia's as a place of refuge from our father. If he wants to build a new life here, he's going to need to start with a place of his own.

"Dolores?" Garrett deflects to me, kissing the top of my head. He's asking me to answer instead of speaking for me, and I appreciate the subtle context of his kiss. He's right behind me in any decision I make. *For us.*

"It sounds okay to me."

"So for the time being, it appears we're roommates," Mati confirms. "I didn't go away to college, so what's the sock thing?"

"It's when you hang a sock on the door because you're having sex in the room and don't want to be disturbed," Garrett clarifies.

"Warning your roommate that he might need bleach to clear his eyes of the vision of him doing something with…" Denton's voice drifts. He still can't look at me, and it makes me wonder how long he was listening to Garrett, me, and the creaking chair. Did he walk in on us, too? *Oh, God.*

"Anyway…" Mati draws out, and then we hear the tapping of Magnolia's cane. Her room is off the kitchen, keeping her safely on one level. Under her arm is a pile of something, cloth-like somethings, in a swirl of black and white. Magnolia dumps the pile on the kitchen floor and turns back for her room.

"Are those…?" I begin.

"Sweet Jesus," Mati mutters.

"Socks?" Denton croaks, his voice rising on the word, but Garrett laughs—a deep belly laugh. He stands behind me, in that way he has, surrounding me with his presence. His head lowers to mine, rolling against it as he continues to chuckle, and everything clicks into place. With Garrett at my back and the sound of his laughter—his happiness— in my ear, I know everything is all going to be okay.

I was his somebody, and he was mine.

epilogue

[Dolores]

We don't make the Christmas deadline I set for the diner. Many of the items we ordered were difficult to receive during the holiday season, like a new grill, which is kind of important for a diner. But before the year ends, and with a little team effort from some generous townsfolk, the diner gets a new life in time for the next year to begin. Deep maroon cushions make the booths comfy and intimate with a wood-grain table centering each space. A few four-tops have matching square tables with black wrought iron chairs for easy cleaning.

By day, it still feels like the diner, with breakfast and lunch menus, new and improved with some suggestions by Hollilyn Abernathy, soon-to-be Rathstone. Our chicken salad and egg salad remain the specialty, but we've done an overhaul on the dinner offerings. Dimming the lights and obtaining a liquor license for the future wine we intend to serve will make the space more romantic, more subdued, and everything I dreamed it could be. We've even recruited Apple Jane, Cora Conrad's daughter, for making us some specialty desserts from her genius with apples.

The biggest change will be the name. With a new theme, the diner needed a fresh title: Wine&Dine. I'm not trying to make the place into something it isn't. This place, however, is a new entity, and with a new year coming, it's going to be a great beginning.

Then there's Garrett. He's no longer the Tin Man to my lost Dorothy, but a true Wizard, making dreams a reality. Not with his money, which he certainly did contribute to making the diner shiny, but with his support and reassurance. I can do anything, he tells me, and he's got my back each step of the way.

"It really is everything," I say, glancing around the finished room. We open the day after New Year's. I take in the new coffee urn, silver and sparkling. The shiny stainless-steel top under the warming lights, which are dim and the only illumination in the space. The long low-top counter for single patrons with stationary stools. The deep booths.

"You're everything," he tells me, coming up behind me and wrapping his arms around my waist. He kisses my shoulder, and I lean back against him.

"It's so beautiful. I can't stop staring, though I can't focus on any one thing."

He spins me in his arms and cups my cheeks before briefly kissing me. "You're beautiful." Pulling away, he reaches for the remote on the table near us. He presses the black device, and the room swells with music—rich and sultry and very feminine.

"'Somewhere Over the Rainbow,'" I tease. The sound system was something he insisted I needed. While the old service piped in country music set on my iPad propped against a speaker in my office, the new system is remote, direct from a computer, and music can be changed with the touch of a finger.

"It's going to be all rainbows from now on," he retorts. Garrett lowers the volume but doesn't change the tune. He clutches me to him, startling me until his hand coasts up my arm. He grips my hand, and then he leads me up the narrow floor space between the booths and the tables. I giggle until he rubs his nose along my neck as we pause a beat. I fall into step, letting him lead as the music fills the room, cascading over us.

I'm not wearing heels, and he's not in dress pants, but his jeans and my chunky boots don't prohibit us from covering the floor as best we can until he dips me. He's lowered me to a table, pressing his body over mine. Our mouths find one another and begin a tango of their own with lips, tongues, and teeth.

"We need to christen this place," he mutters into my skin as his mouth travels down to my neck.

"Here? Now?" My voice cracks as I melt under the attention of his kisses. Each time he kisses me, it takes my breath away. Maybe it's because I love him, and I know he loves me in return.

He pops his head up, looking toward the locked front door and the lowered blinds. "Right here," he says, looking down at me. "There's no better time than the present."

"I think you mean, there's no place like home," I mutter as his fingers work the button of my jeans.

"That too." He chuckles. "You're my home, and there's nowhere better than in you."

"Now, you're just being cheesy," I tease, but I choke as he yanks my jeans to my ankles.

"You know I prefer incredible, insatiable, and unbelievable." He lowers his mouth between my thighs before I can respond, wasting no time to christen this room or prove to me he means what he speaks.

"The way I see it," he says after a long lap at my suddenly pulsing core, "I have eight booths and a few tables to service you on before I spread you out on that long counter." He nods his head, suggesting the single-seat counter.

"Oh, my," I whimper, but tremble with the anticipation of him taking me on every surface in this diner, claiming me as I claim him.

"All mine," he mutters, changing my words and returning to my center.

I'm a rag doll by the time he finally takes me on the expansive counter missionary style. He's already licked me, fingered me, and taken me from behind, wringing out three orgasms before slowing the pace to make love to me on the narrow surface. I can't give him any more of me, other than to let him fill me when he finally releases. Breathless, he lowers to me, covering me like a blanket, and we lie like this for a minute.

He chuckles softly into my neck. "We'll need to bleach the place."

"That's the first thing you think of?" I mock, teasing him as he props up on an elbow over me. His smile takes my breath away because I know it's all for me, and I'm so…happy.

"No, I was actually thinking of the first day I met you when Wally ran into you. You were all disheveled with sand in your hair, and—"

"A hot mess," I interject, not wishing to think of myself from months ago. I think of how much I've changed, and I owe so much of it to him. Dorothy freshened up in the Emerald City.

"I was going to say I knew you were different."

I do not like the sound of this, especially with him still connected to me. I shift, but he tenderly clutches my jaw, forcing me to focus on him.

"I didn't see it right away, and I'd find myself staring at you as if I knew there was something about you." He brushes back my hair, looking into my eyes in that way he does as though he wants to see inside me. I meet his stare, knowing I look at him the same way. "But I see it now. Your smarts." He taps my head. "And your heart." He pokes my chest. "And your courage."

The traits of the three friends in *The Wizard of Oz*.

"I was lost," I tell him, lowering my voice and rubbing a hand down his bare chest.

"You just needed some time off, sweetheart. A trip over the rainbow." I chuckle at the reference.

"California is something," I say, recalling the times we had there. It seems like another lifetime to me even though it's only been three weeks.

"You're home to me, Dolores, and I'll tell you again there's no place I'd rather be."

"I'm happy you're here with me," I tell him because it's true. He'll be returning to California shortly after I open to settle some business and set up a new routine of days there and weekends here. We formalized the contracts with Charlie as our mediator. Garrett gets use of the land while Magnolia still owns it. Garrett and I will live at Magnolia's. He has a soft spot for her, and if I know him, he's going to eventually wipe away the debt we owe him. I'll cross that bridge once we get there, though.

Home is where the heart is, the old saying goes, and my heart is with Garrett. He's all I need. And for now, I'll stick to my own backyard as long as Garrett lives in it with me. I'm excited about our future, and for once, I feel truly happy.

bonus scene

Over the Rainbow

[Garrett]

Starting a vineyard takes time which means patience, and as the saying goes patience is a virtue. Unfortunately, it's not one of mine. I'm more an instant gratification guy although I knew going into the wine business it would take years before production truly began. I'd wanted the vineyard as my retirement, even though there's no plan to retire anytime soon. I'm only fifty. I have years ahead of me, but when I'm ready to slow down, I want there to be something I enjoy, that's just for me. Or so I thought it'd be a party of one until I met Dolores.

I didn't intend to fall in love with her. I never imagined discovering her family owned property that was the perfect set up for me to begin my "future plan" dream. I certainly never expected those plans to include a wedding…mine.

I've been single most of my life, with a few near misses from my high school and college sweethearts and then the fiasco of Kate. Other than those relationships, nothing serious. I don't want to discuss Kate. She's a non-entity to me now that I have Dolores. Speaking of Dolores, I never realized all those missed relationships meant a better one was waiting for me in a small town in Georgia. As a man from LA, I suppose I imagined—if I ever got married—it might be a beach ceremony which seems cliché and appropriate to the California lifestyle. Maybe even a destination wedding to some place remote and tropical. But I can see it clear as day that Dolores and I will marry here, on her grandmother's farmland. That is, once I ask her to marry me.

I've already asked Magnolia's permission, being she's the matriarch of the family. I've even asked Denton, Dolores' brother, although I don't care as much about his blessing. He made it a competition to see who would propose first. (Denton beat me by asking Mati on Valentine's Day). But I plan to one up Denton's love letter proposal with a special something of my own.

Dolores and I haven't seen one another for ten days. It's too long but my business, Fox Investors, called me back to California in the end of May and with the grand re-opening of Dolores's diner and the start of tourist season, she didn't want to step away. She's dedicated and driven and determined to pay me back for the financial investment. I don't want her money, though, any more than she wants mine…but I digress.

I've cropped my bags at Magnolia's where Dolores stayed after deciding to make her small house just outside the downtown into a vacation rental property. It's tiny and neat plus the perfect walking distance from the main street. Dolores thinks I'm arriving tomorrow, but I was able to get out early and set my plans in place.

"I need a chicken Caesar wrap. One chicken salad croissant and a burger, medium, with everything." I wait until she calls out her order to her cooks, sneaking up behind her with a finger to my lips silencing Dolores's assistant manager Hollilyn. The buxom blonde winks at me and nods to her boss whose back remains to us. Dolores is pear-shaped in the best of ways. Curved hips. Ink at the base of her spine. Rich black and silver streaked hair that lands below her shoulders. I don't have to see the front of her to know her breasts sit high, tight and bursting in the white blouse she reserves for waitressing. She's abandoned the stereotypical diner uniform for something more casual.

I slip a hand around those smooth hips, startling her and she smacks at me at the same time she turns with a scowl, glaring over her shoulder. Then her mouth pops open and before she can speak, my lips crush hers. Sweet Lord, it's been too long since I've kissed this woman and the enthusiasm which she uses to return my kiss tells me she feels the same. Her arms snake around my neck, hitching her a little taller against me and I slip my palms down her back, cupping her backside to press her against me.

"Woo-wee," a female voice teases near us and Dolores breaks the kiss but not her hold on me. We both turn to see Hollilyn fanning her face with her order pad while she shakes her head.

"It's suddenly steaming six ways to Sunday in here." She continues to fan her face and nod at a customer, as if asking that customer to agree.

"Why, I never..." another feminine voice speaks, but Dolores interrupts.

"But you wish you had, Corabelle." Dolores chuckles after speaking and her eyes meet mine. We stare for a second, just breathing each other in, absorbing one another.

"I've missed you," she whispers.

"Same, sweetheart." Even though we've spoken every night on the phone, and multiple times throughout the day via text, there is nothing like holding her in my arms. Even better would be her wrapping her legs around me in private. "Office?"

Dolores's eyes sparkle as she nods. "Hollilyn, can you cover me for a few minutes?"

"A few minutes?" Hollilyn shrieks. "Is that all it's gonna take?" She winks at me, acknowledging her understanding. We're going to need more than a few minutes alone, however with the wood I'm sporting just pressing up against Dolores, I might not last more than a few seconds. My blood races as my heart hammers. I need inside this woman, and quickly.

Dolores takes my hand and I follow her to her new office off the kitchen. When the door shuts, it's like a pistol shot and the race to undress begins. I'd love to rip her shirt from her breasts, but she'll need to wear it to finish her shift. Still, my fingers nimbly hasten to remove the buttons while her fingers eagerly tug my shirt from my pants. Within seconds, my suit pants slip to my hips. Dolores's skirt is at her waist. Her panties are in shreds and I've slid into her.

"Home." I exhale as I speak, hitching her up to take two steps and set her on the edge of her desk. We've christened every surface in her diner. Tables. Chairs. Counter. And the top of this desk, but this time will be hard and fast. *No patience.*

"I missed you so much," she stammers between the punishing beat of me pistoning into her. She's slick and sweet as I waste no time reaching between us to stroke her clit while I move within her. "I'm not going to last."

Her breath hitches, and my mouth covers hers. This is my plan. We both need this release in order to concentrate later when I'll take my time after I ask her a very important question.

+ + +

When Dolores finishes her shift, she meets me at Magnolia's.

"Let's talk a walk." I haven't seen my dog, Wally, in these ten days and he's eager to run outside in the fresh June air. We start through the field which was plowed in the late winter by a local farmer. I don't know the first thing about farming but I'm not afraid to get my hands dirty and I supervised the whole thing. Hand to God, his name is Farmer Ted and he even let me drive the tractor.

"Is that…" Dolores voice falters as we continue walking. "…is that a yellow brick?"

She turns to glance at me, but I act as if I don't know what she's talking about. "Where?"

We approach the brick and Dolores notices another one a few feet ahead of us. Her head turns to me and once again I feign ignorance. Her hand has been tucked inside the crook of my elbow, but she releases me and begins to walk faster, following the bricks as they increase in quantity. Eventually, the bricks rest closer together until a small walk leads directly to a rundown gazebo on the edge of the property.

Dolores stops before the short trail hits the gazebo. "Garrett?" Her voice catches and I know she sees the item inside the old circular structure. She takes quick steps to close the distance and folds to her knees on the step.

"Garrett, what did you do?" Her voice squeaks but she's laughing as her hands scrub behind the ears of a puppy. The energy of the dog causes her to wiggle her backside and attempt to lick at Dolores's face which lowers to coo at the baby chocolate lab. "What's your name, smelly puppy?"

I shake my head and chuckle. That voice. "She's for you. You need to name her."

Dolores's head swivels to glance at me over her shoulder. "You bought me a dog?" Her voice drops as her gaze returns to the precious pup. If I'm honest, I knew it was a risk to purchase her a puppy. Dolores isn't a fan of dogs, and after mine ran into her last fall, she might have sworn off the animal forever. But deep down, Dolores loves Wally. She finds comfort in having him around when I can't be. She told me once, knowing she has Wally means I'll always come back to her, if for no other reason than to fetch my pet. It's silly, actually. I'll always come home to her.

"You should name her Toto," I say. Dolores hesitantly laughs and then stops petting the bouncing bundle. Her hand lowers for the giant woven container.

"It's a basket." Her voice fills with question and I move so I have a better angle of her face. "How did you do this?"

I didn't just plop the dog in a basket and set the poor thing in the antiquated gazebo to wait us out. "Magnolia." I recruited her grandmother to help me get the puppy in place. Dolores stands, scanning the fields behind us.

"Where is she?"

"I didn't send her alone. Kent Duncan helped her." Actually, the local hardware owner helped me, but Magnolia wanted to be part of the plan. Kent and I have become friends, and he helped me get the bricks painted and placed. He's also the one who found me the puppy. She's a cute little thing and seeing how Wally is bowing and sniffing, hoping to get near her I can see he's already smitten. *Sucker*. I know the feeling.

Dolores turns back to the puppy and lowers again for her new pet, scratching behind her ears and then she fingers the yellow silk tied around the dog's neck. Dolores's long fingers slide down the shiny fabric and pause under the dog's chin. Her palm flattens.

"Garrett." My name is spoke slow and purposeful, and full of question. When she shifts on the step to turn back to me, I'm down on one knee. Her breath hitches, and a hand covers her mouth.

"Dolores, from the moment I met you, I knew there was something special about you. Who else would call me out on leash jokes and entertain me with your love of classic movies?" She shakes her head as a smile hides behind her fingers. "This Tin Man feels his heart exploding whenever he looks at you. I know a lot happened all at once last winter, but you know I'm not a patient man and I'm finding it hard to wait any longer. I'd like you to be my wife."

Dolores's eyes drop to the ring still tied by a silky scarf around the neck of her puppy. Her thumb drags over the white gold band and the two carat, princess cut engagement ring.

"Will you marry me, Dorothy?"

She snorts on the nickname and her smile grows larger when she looks back up at me.

"Tin Man found a home with you. Let's make the yellow brick road go on forever."

Before I know it, Dolores lunges for me, wrapping her arms around me and knocking me over. The wind rushes out of me as I sprawl on my back, Dolores blanketing me. She's kissing me all over. My cheeks. My forehead. My eyes. My nose. It reminds me a little of when Wally plowed into her on our first meeting. Then her mouth covers mine, and I struggle to catch my breath and breathe her in.

My hands skate up her sides, outlining her body over mine. "Is that a yes?" I ask, pulling back for oxygen.

"That's undeniably a yes."

"Undeniable, you say?"

"Unbelievable," she mutters, chuckling over me. A dog yips in the background. Then another one does. Dolores slips off me and crawls back to her new dog. She unties the scarf around the pet's neck and then slips the ring off the yellow silk. As I watch her, I press up to sit and reach for the ring between her fingers.

"Allow me…" I cup her hand in mine and slide the ring on her third finger. We both stare at the diamond twinkling in the early evening sunshine.

"It's breathtaking," she mutters.

"It's stunning, like you."

Dolores glances up at me and curls her fingers under my chin. "You're stunning."

"We agree on something," I say with a laugh before I kiss her again. It isn't the heated kisses we normally give but one that tells me how she feels. She takes her time, expressing her gratitude and love in the linger of her lips on mine. When my tongue stretches for hers, she responds immediately to meet mine, but she doesn't rush. We dance—tango perhaps—taking the steps we need until we feel we've said it all with our lips and tongue.

"I love you, Garrett," she says once we pull apart. "And I love you, too," she says in that mocking tone reserved for dogs as she rubs over the head of the lab. The pup had begun to chew on the wicker container, impatient to be freed from the confines. Dolores lifts her out of the basket and sets the bundle of bounce in her lap.

"I love you too, stunner." I give her another quick kiss. "I know we talked about waiting for a wedding. And I tried to think of all kinds of special dates. First planting. First yield. First bottle of wine. But all of that will take too much time and I don't want to wait that long. I want to get married soon, right here, in this decrepit gazebo with the yellow bricks."

"Here?" She laughs. "Why here?"

"Because Magnolia told me this is where your great grandfather proposed to your great grandmother. Here he told her about they life he hoped to have on this land and here he promised her she'd be his partner. She'd own her own business selling eggs and chicken salad." It's the history of Dolores's maternal lineage and the birth of the eventual diner. "Here. In our own backyard is where I want to marry you."

Dolores's mouth pops open, surprise written in her expression, but I continue. "It also reminds me of my grandfather. He wanted land and he missed out." Dolores already knows he died when I was young and ambitious. His wife had preceded him in death. He lost it his dreams. I don't want to lose anything.

Dolores's hand cups my cheek, and she leans in for another brief kiss. "I'll marry you anywhere you want. Any time."

"Next week?" I sheepishly ask and her eyes widen.

"I…"

"If it's too soon, I can wait." But I'm lying. We don't really need to rush as I'm not going anywhere, and I believe Dolores isn't going anywhere either, but she knows my abandonment fears. I want to tie her to me in hopes they disappear.

"I think we can pull that off. I'll need a dress, but we can get married here. I can have the diner cater and we can—"

My mouth crushes hers once again, taking all her planning away. Her and her checklists. The only list I want her worried about is the one that places us at the top. She's my priority always and speaking of tying…

I pull back from her wicked mouth. "I think we should head back to the house and put this scarf to use." I slip my fingers over the silky material.

"What do you mean?" she asks innocent and ignorant, but I know my girl has not forgotten.

"Blindfold. You. Me. Now." I unfold from my seat on the rotten step and drag Dolores up with one hand. She still holds her new puppy, but then bends to set her on the ground. A leash is in the basket with a yellow collar. I can't have my gift running away on her first day with Dolores.

We walk back toward the house hand in hand as the puppy struggles against the leash and Wally teases her by running ahead.

"I need a good name for her," Dolores announces as we walk.

"Hmm…Wizard? Scarecrow? Lion?"

Dolores laughs at all my suggestions, and I sense her spinning with thought. "Rainbow."

"Rainbow?" I chuckle. "You can't call her that." It's too much of a little kid name.

"Why not?" Dolores defends. "I feel like I'm over one. Your proposal. The wedding. It's all a dream I didn't dare to dream for myself, Garrett."

This woman. That heart which was been missing before her? It swells again and I swallow the lump in my throat. "Rainbow," I repeat. "I love it."

"I love you," she whispers, the words filled with a deeper meaning. It's more than the surface. It's more than three words strung together. It's something neither one of us saw coming true for ourselves, and yet here it is…over the proverbial rainbow.

Garrett Fox has three sisters. Start their journeys with ***Hauling Ashe***

Turn the page for a nibble.

Ready for more sexy silver foxes in Blue Ridge? ***Silver Brewer***

Turn the page for a sip.

WINE & DINE

Thank you for taking the time to read WINE & DINE.
Please consider writing a review on major sales channels where ebooks
and paperbacks are sold and discussed.

more by L.B. Dunbar

Sterling Falls
Seven small-town siblings muddle their way through love over 40.
Sterling Heat
Sterling Brick
Sterling Streak
Sterling Clay
Sterling Fight
Sterling Touch
Sterling Stone

Chicago Anchors
When your eyes are on the silver fox coach, more than the ball.
Elevator Pitch
Catch the Kiss

Parentmoon
When the mother of the groom goes head-to-head with the single father
of the bride.

Holiday Hotties (Christmas novellas)
Holiday novellas certain to heat the season.
Scrooge-ish
Naughty-ish
Grouch-ish

Road Trips & Romance
Three sisters. Three destinations. All second chances at love over 40.
Hauling Ashe
Merging Wright
Rhode Trip

Lakeside Cottage
Four friends. Four summers. Shenanigans and love happen at the lake.

L.B. DUNBAR

Living at 40
Loving at 40
Learning at 40
Letting Go at 40

The Silver Foxes of Blue Ridge
Small mountain town, silver foxes. Brothers seeking love over 40.
Silver Brewer
Silver Player
Silver Mayor
Silver Biker

Sexy Silver Foxes
When sexy silver foxes meet the feisty vixens of their dreams.
After Care
Midlife Crisis
Restored Dreams
Second Chance
Wine&Dine

Collision novellas
A spin-off from After Care – the younger set/rock stars
Collide
Caught

The Sex Education of M.E.
The original sexy silver fox.
When a widowed professor decides she'd like to date again, and a local
fireman volunteers to give her lessons.

The Heart Collection
Small town, big hearts - stories of family and love.
Speak from the Heart
Read with your Heart
Look with your Heart
Fight from the Heart
View with your Heart

A Heart Collection Spin-off

The Heart Remembers

BOOKS IN OTHER AUTHOR WORLDS
Smartypants Romance (an imprint of Penny Reid)
Tales of the Winters sisters set in Green Valley.
Love in Due Time
Love in Deed
Love in a Pickle

The World of True North (an imprint of Sarina Bowen)
Welcome to Vermont! And the Busy Bean Café.
Cowboy
Studfinder

THE EARLY YEARS
The Legendary Rock Star Series
A classic tale with a modern twist of rockstar romance and suspense.

Paradise Stories
MMA romance. Two brothers. One fight.

The Island Duet
Intrigue and suspense. The island knows what you've done.

Modern Descendants – writing as elda lore
Magical realism. Modern myths of Greek gods.

nibble of

Hauling Ashe

1

PRE-TRIP

Playlist: "Unwritten" - Natasha Bedingfield

[Mae]

I'd been looking for a sign.

After stepping off the electric train affectionally known as the 'L' in downtown Chicago, I'd breathed in the fumes of the city on a warm summer day. The robotic voice of the conductor stated that the doors were closing and mixed with the chaotic sounds of people moving on the platform toward the stairs. The noise around me was different from my small hometown with its quiet afternoons of whispered breezes and chirping birds. I'd ridden the train in this dynamic city with my sister before, but never alone. And today's adventure had to be done on my own.

I'd stepped forward with the flow of people pressing toward the staircase like sugar grains filtering through a funnel and descended to the street below as the overhead train continued its loop through this city like a steel serpent, weaving in a perpetual circle around brick and mortar.

I have always loved the magnetism of this metropolis, but it wasn't home for me. My older sister Jane lived here, and it was a pit stop on the journey I was about to embark on.

My spirit trip awaited me. I was in search of renewing my soul and perhaps my heart, as mine had been shattered by Adam. My seventeen-year marriage was over. We'd been distant for some time and divorced for three years. After his first affair, I stayed with him. He made promises. He made plans. Now, I had a plan of my own. Eight states. Fourteen days. The open road. I'd hit the highlights as I went, where I pleased, when I pleased.

This was the starting point and that's why I was looking for a sign. An actual brown and white metal rectangle that signifies the beginning of something special. It marks the start of Route 66, the iconic highway from Chicago to Los Angeles. Using the GPS on my phone, I had worked my way to the corner of Wabash and Adams and then headed east on Adams toward Michigan Avenue. A coffee shop on the corner had distracted me and I reminded myself I was in no rush. Ahead of me were two weeks with no timetables and wide-open highway. The Mother Road was my destination and I wanted to plant my feet at the beginning.

When I entered the coffeeshop, I'd decided on the unusual. Instead of black coffee with limited cream and sugar, I ordered something that sounded fancy and fun.

"I'll take a mochaccino." Mocha-*ccino* had rolled off my tongue in a sassy, saucy way and I sashayed my hips a bit as I ordered. I wanted to be flirty. I wanted to be fun. I wanted to remember who I was before marriage and kids and commitments. I didn't begrudge those things in my life, but I was ready for…adventure. I hadn't really ever been anywhere, and I wanted to say I'd been somewhere. If I hadn't been in a coffeeshop on a street corner in Chicago, I might have broken out in song like Belle in Disney's *Beauty and the Beast*. Somehow, I didn't think the other patrons would appreciate me swinging out my arms and spinning in a circle in the cramped space singing off key about a great wide somewhere.

Once I'd exited the café, I popped the lid off my to-go cup and took a sip. The liquid was too hot to fully enjoy the chocolate-flavored zing I anticipated, so I took a short slurp and let the sweetness rush past my tongue in hopes of not burning it. Struggling to snap the lid back in place, I crossed the street obeying the crosswalk signal. The people around me acted like cattle herded over cement and I had laughed at the image since

I'd been in this town when the famous painted cow statues had been placed in various locations as decoration. A tourist mission at the time was to find all the cows.

Today's mission felt almost as daunting. Tons of signs on steel poles lined the sidewalks and as I hit the walkway opposite the coffee shop, I noticed the Art Institute on the other side of Michigan Avenue. I paused and spun in that circle like some animated peasant girl, trying to find my bearings. I pulled my phone from my oversized bag and struggled one handed to open the app where I had saved the coordinates while I stepped forward, looking at the device in my palm.

"Umph."

I slam into something hard but pliable before me. In fear of spilling my coffee, I was desperately trying not to bump into anyone on the packed city sidewalk. But the hot liquid washes over the front of me and something else. Or rather, down the impeccably tailored suit jacket stretched over the back of *someone* else.

"What the fu—" The remainder of the expletive spoken in a harsh, deep masculine tenor drones out like an echo at the end of its stream. Steel gray eyes lock on mine. For a moment I forget where I am, who I am, and what I'd been doing. Taking a moment to assess the damage, I notice the lid has popped off my cup resulting in hot liquid spilling over my wrist, splattering my once-white blouse, and dripping down my bare legs beneath the hem of my cut-off jean shorts. My sandaled feet are coated in mochaccino, and I step back from the person I've collided with.

But my foot slips off the raised sidewalk and I struggle once more with the uncovered cup in my hand. Attempting to balance the semi-full container, I'm off kilter with one foot down in the street and the other on the raised sidewalk.

"Easy there, sunshine." Long fingers catch my upper arm and yank me forward. The endearment throws me off balance even more and additional chocolate-flavored drink spurts from the cup like a sputtering fountain, sprinkling the front of his suit jacket.

"I'm so sorry." Not only is my skin hot, but I'm a hot mess, and of course, my savior and victim is a hot man. He looks like he stepped off a poster advertising professional business attire for men. His frame is a good half-foot taller than mine, with solid shoulders and long arms. His hair distracts me next as it's more salt than pepper. His cheekbones are clean-shaven cliffs but given a few days, I imagine the scruff on that firm jaw will match the coloring of the hair on his head. The potential ruggedness of ink and chrome facial hair in combination with that sharp jacket screams *sexy silver fox suit porn*. However, a sliver of leather and beads at his wrist hints there might be a rebel underneath that silk and gabardine material.

"Whatcha got in that cup?" His voice drips with insinuation. The playfulness of calling me sunshine dissipates a bit.

Sharp, silvery eyes ensnare mine and heat rushes across my cheeks because I'm caught staring. Forcing my gaze away from those eyes, I look at my cup. "Uh…nothing, anymore." He doesn't smile at my joke. "I wasn't drinking," I defend next, although I feel a little drunk just looking at him.

I'm always stupid around good-looking people, especially handsome men. I'd like to say I'm out of practice—with men, flirting and otherwise. However, I can hold my own with the best of flirty people. I'm the one with teasing comments at work or subtle remarks under my breath in public, but today I'm off my witty comebacks game.

Releasing my arm, he shakes out his, flicking droplets of coffee off the expensive-looking coat in a summer khaki color. He tips his head, attempting to glance over his shoulder, and spins in a circle like a dog chasing his tail. The sight of such a handsome man twirling around causes me to giggle like a schoolgirl. Then again, the rhythmic squeak could be the sudden anxiety rippling up my center.

I just spilled coffee on a hot man.

He abruptly stops twirling and his gaze falls to my lips. The corner of his mouth hints at a potential grin. "What's so funny?" His warm voice washes over me like the drink still soaking my thin shirt. His cadence is lyrical, like a classic rock star or maybe someone in a blues band.

Shaking my head, I apologize a second time. "Let me get your suit cleaned for you." Suddenly, I have visions of him stripping out of that suit right here on the street and my breath hitches at the possibility. *The lazy removal, slowly shrugging the jacket down his arms. The pop of buttons on his dress shirt. The quiet snick of his suit pants zipper.* Another part of me strums to life and I clench my thighs. *What is happening to me?* Is this a hot flash? I thought I wasn't due for them for another ten years.

Deciding I need his phone number, and that I can figure out the logistics of getting him out of his suit…I mean, getting his suit *from him* later, I realize I've dropped my phone and I begin my own tailspin, scanning the cement at my feet.

"My phone." Spotting the device in the street, I step down off the curb, and my ankle twists, throbbing as a result of my earlier slip. I wince as I bend at the waist, pitching forward at the last second to retrieve my phone. With my backside in the air, aimed at my coffee-spill victim, I pick up the device at the same time he grips my hips and tugs me back up onto the sidewalk. A taxi driver wails on his horn as the yellow vehicle zips past us.

"Sunshine, you're a real hazard to yourself." The rough sound near my ear sends shivers down my spine.

I spin to face him, forcing his hands to release me, and my face heats once more at the flirtatious endearment and sensual voice. We stand closer than two people who don't know one another should. I definitely do not look like sunshine. I'm a forty-three-year-old brunette with hints of gray; a mother of two with a belly scarred like a taxi ran over my midsection; and an exhausted business owner who has bags under her eyes packed with sorrow and stress.

"I was looking for a sign," I say to him for some reason, as if that explains knocking into him, spilling coffee, dropping my phone, and fumbling—*twice*—into the street.

He tilts his head, assessing me, perhaps wondering once more if I'd been day-drinking instead of savoring syrupy chocolate mixed with coffee.

He takes a cautious step backward. "Maybe you need some…help." His tone mocks me a bit, deepening in concern for my mental stability.

Holding my phone in my hand, I swipe the screen against my hip to wipe off the street dirt. "Let me get your number."

His chiseled face shutters to stillness. "Now you're hitting on me?" Incredulity fills his voice. His brows arch and the corner of his pale red lips twitch. The grin is more forced than flirtatious. He thinks I'm a nut.

"I wasn't… I mean, I'm not… I never… I just want to have your suit cleaned." Well, that pretty much covers it all. In my line of work, a pleasant attitude helps sales. The customer is always right, so I've learned how to master words and a wink to soothe someone who is disgruntled. Of course, a little banter never hurt anyone and some of my best customers enjoy the repartee. The innocent jesting might even be the reason they return to my garden center. But in the case of this encounter, I'm surprisingly flustered.

"It's a thousand-dollar suit. A mere dry-cleaning won't salvage this mess." He glances down at the arm of his jacket and at the once-white shirt he wore, now looking like freckles dot the material. The underscore to his statement resonates louder than the hint of his concern I was hitting on him. He's not joking about the cost and his expression tightens even more. Disgust and disappointment etch his fine cheekbones.

"Made of gold-laden thread?" I joke, hoping to lighten the moment, but in return those silver eyes pinch. His gaze becomes colder, matching the metallic posts holding up a variety of signs along this street.

"Something like that." His voice is suddenly devoid of all emotion, monotone and dry, which is everything opposite my clothing still soaked with coffee. Absentmindedly, I reach for the middle of my peasant blouse and squeeze the material, which looks like I've tried to tea-stain fabric at home. Warm liquid seeps over my fist like I've wrung out a sponge. His eyes follow the motion, and narrow when his gaze reaches my chest. I look like I've entered a wet T-shirt contest.

Without another word, he reaches into his suit coat and pulls out his own phone. My breath hitches for some reason, momentarily thinking he'll ask me for my number. Instead, he stabs the device with a forceful finger and lifts it to his ear. His eyes peer upward, locking on mine once more before he abruptly turns and walks away.

"Hope your day gets better," I holler after him, taking a mental snapshot of him walking away. He shoots me a one-handed wave over his shoulder, then closes his fingers leaving only the one in the middle upright.

Well.

My gaze falls to his backside. The slightly lifted jacket in his single arm salute gives me a clear view of firm globes in form-fitting suit pants. Those thousand dollars were well spent to accentuate him there. However, a man with a fine ass does not make him a fine man. It normally just makes him an ass.

Too bad. He was nice to look at.

On that note, I glance around me, taking in the rush of the 'L' down the block, racing over Wabash Avenue. Brakes screech and horns honk as all types of vehicles come to a stop at the red light down the street ahead of me. I scan the tall buildings shadowing the walkway and then I see it.

A brown and white sign marked with the iconic emblem for Route 66.

Underneath the landmark rectangle is another sign with one word. BEGIN.

Continue reading Mae and Tucker's story in ***Hauling Ashe***

a sip of
<u>Silver Brewer</u>

A Long and Winding Road

[Letty]

Where the hell am I?

I'm losing the GPS on my phone, and I feel as though I've passed the same copse of trees three times.

Who can tell?

Birches, maples, and cedars surround me, and those are the trees I recognize. Everything is a sea of thick bark and greenery, but soon, this forest will be ablaze with golds, reds, and oranges. The changing season is the reason for my rush. I need to secure the property before winter so the ground can be broken first thing next spring.

Working for Mullen Realty, I've climbed my way up from assistant office manager to assistant seller to commercial real estate agent. Not exactly my career choice but it's been a steady income. When I didn't have a job at twenty-four using my college degree in English, my mom made me go to work for my uncle, a real estate mogul in Chicago. I'm now forty, so I guess you could say I settled into the family business. Uncle Frank prides himself on buying and selling, and what he wants is to buy this godforsaken property in Georgia and sell it to a hotel company who wants the space for their next lodge-like resort and spa.

As the only vehicle in sight while I wind through the curving roads, I'm waiting for Jason to jump out with his creepy hockey mask and start swinging a chainsaw at me at any second. I might have mixed a few horror movies together, but that's the scene in my head as I weave along the narrow drive. I'm not even certain I'm in the correct county, let alone the right state anymore. I need Blue Ridge, Georgia, but all I've seen for miles is tree trunks and foliage, and occasionally, the inconspicuous marking for a turnoff. From the office, Marcus tries to assure me I'm in the correct place.

"There are only two tire tracks leading to nowhere," I say into the phone, struggling to drive the rented Jetta over the rough terrain.

"That's it. You're in the right place. Don't mess this up," his gruff voice barks through the speaker.

I hit a bump, and the phone jostles out of the cup holder to the floor. *Dammit.*

I can't risk reaching for it, and I'm too afraid to stop until I see the place I'm destined to find.

Harrington cabin.

I'm not certain what I expect. I've been told it's rustic, but I don't know if that means quaint or just plain rough. Either way, Mullen Real Estate wants the property.

"I think I'm almost there," I shout, as the phone lies facedown on the passenger side floor. I can't hear Marcus's reply. He's not only my assistant but one of my best friends, and he knows this acquisition is important to me. I'd prove myself as a skilled real estate buyer if I can book this deal. I'd also solidify my position in the company and earn myself a cut of the business.

Partner.

The word echoes through my head. The sound has a nice ring to it.

Olivet Pierson. Partner.

As the dirt road narrows, I see light at the end of the tunnel of trees. A clearing of sorts opens before me, and I slow even more than the five miles per hour I've been driving. As I break through the lane, a vision of masculinity stands before me. With his shirt off, the bare back of a muscular being slings an ax over his shoulder, splitting a piece of wood standing upright on another log. The thwack isn't heard inside the car, but the thunderous power in which he cracks the wood seems to vibrate under my vehicle and into my foot. I'm frozen at the appearance of his rippling back, sweaty spine, and low-slung pants that suggest he wears boxer briefs by the sliver of waistband exposed. In red. The hair on top of his head is short, trimmed close but not military style to his skull, while a bush of facial hair covers his jaw. My eyes focus on his profile as he stands and straightens, then quickly turns to see my car. Deep, dark eyes narrow, zeroing in on me in anger. He drops the ax and raises his hands, his mouth opening, but I don't hear what he says.

I'm blinded by the gleam of sunlight bouncing off his firm chest, a sprinkle of hair in the shape of a V between the flat plains of his pecs and above the slow hills of his abs. More hair leads south, dipping into the red band exposed above his waistline, and my mouth waters until two large hands hit the hood of my rental car, and I notice his mouth move as he shouts.

"Stop."

Oh. My. God.

My foot slams on the brake, causing me to jolt forward and narrowly missing the bridge of my nose on the steering wheel. I stare out the front windshield, taking in the appearance of the man I almost hit. He's a mountain of a man, someone I envision people wrote tales about long ago. He's lumbersexual by modern standards, and then I note his hair again. Cropped and charcoal. It isn't black but more like the smoky color before the coals are ready. A perfect blend of dusty silver covers his head and jaw. He's a silver fox, but from the size of him, he looks more like an angry grizzly.

"I'm so sorry," I mutter as I place the car in park and scramble to remove myself from the rental. My ankles twist as the heels I wear can't balance on the uneven dirt beneath my feet. I clutch the open driver's door for support, expecting to fall and knock my chin. How many stitches would I need? Is there even a doctor out here? A hospital nearby? Oh God, I might bleed to death.

Then I take note of the puzzled man before me, still leaning against my hood.

Staring at him, I'd die a happy woman.

However, the vibe coming off him is anything but pleased. His chest heaves as his eyes nearly disappear while he squints at me.

"Who are you?" He emphasizes each word as he speaks. I certainly can't use the statement "I was in the neighborhood" because I doubt you'd find another human being within miles.

Oh Lord, if I screamed, would anyone hear me? If a tree falls in the woods, does it make a sound if no one is around to hear it? My thoughts are out of control.

"I'm Olivet Pierson, and I'm looking for George Harrington the second. Is this the Harrington cabin?"

I'm here for the land, but the cabin catches my sight. The two-story building is of medium size, balanced with a window on either side of a single front door, standing open and inviting. A heavy metal overhang shadows the porch, which runs the full length of the cabin. The weathered gray structure with the deep black shingled roof doesn't look worn. It appears brand new. With a small yard and a forestry backdrop, the place looks quite homey.

"How did you get here?" His gruff voice returns my attention to him. His curiosity causes him to look up over the back of my car, staring down the pinched lane I traveled.

"Are you George Harrington?"

His head swings back to me, and his lips twist. Pressing off my car, he turns for a cloth on the pile of wood and wipes his face with it. Absentmindedly, he travels down his chest, or rather purposely, as he must know I'm watching his every move. I'm practically salivating as he takes his time to swipe across his broad pecs and dip to the trail leading lower. He pats himself with the cloth over the zipper region of his pants, and I flinch. My eyes flick upward, and his lips mockingly smirk.

I can't say it's a smile. His face looks far too serious for such a thing. Crinkles mark the edges of his eyes, and his cheekbones are well-defined. He might have been teasing me, but his face gives nothing away.

"So…" I repeat. "Are you George?"

"You must be looking for my father," he states, tossing what I realize is a white T-shirt back onto the pile of wood. He picks up the ax, and I try to catch my breath. I'm gripping the open door for support, peering at him as he turns his back on me and lifts the wood-chopping instrument. The sound of a splintering log resonates loudly around us, echoing in the deep quiet. I take a second to look around me, no longer lost in the woods, but noticing the beauty of various shades of green. Steeples of pines and broad sweeps of maple whisper in the breeze with a glorious blue sky as its backdrop. The landscape is breathtaking, and the silence reminds me this is the perfect location for a spa and resort. Secluded. Rustic. Peaceful.

Thwack.

Another log splits, and I shift my attention back to Mr. Lumbersexy.

"Do you know anything about the property?" I ask, interrupting him mid-swing. He doesn't miss the log, but it doesn't crack. The ax bounces back, and the log topples to its side. When he turns on me, the move is aggressive in nature, yet I find I don't fear him. His mouth opens, but I speak.

"I'm told it's owned by George Harrington II. A Miss Elaina Harrington on Mountain Spring Lane told me how to get here. Told me I'd find him here." I pause as he glares at me. I stopped at the original address given to me by the office. Mountain Spring Lane was a dirt strip with three impressive antebellum homes along the private drive. Old money covered the white paint of each house.

When he doesn't speak, I continue. "It's a beautiful piece of property." I turn my head as if I'm noticing the land, but all I can concentrate on is the weight of his eyes on me, knowing he's following the twist of my neck as I gaze around me.

"What do you want?" he snaps. The gruffness of his tone snaps my attention back to him. Maybe Grumpy is a better name for him instead of Sexy Lumberjack.

"I'm looking to discuss purchasing the land."

The ax slips from his hand while his other hand fists into a ball of knuckles. He's scary, but again, I don't fear him for some reason.

"It's not for sale."

"Everything's for sale, Mr...." He still doesn't offer his name, but I'm sensing I'm in the right place, so he must be George Harrington.

"Listen…" He pauses, and I offer my name.

"Olivet Pierson. Mullen Realty," I say, walking around my door and closing it. Reaching forward for his hand, I realize my palm already sweats with the anticipation of touching the paw of his. The closer I get to him, he appears even bigger, and we stand in contrast to one another. He's bare chested in wood shaving-covered pants and rustic work boots while I'm wobbling in my heels with a pencil skirt, blazer, and uncomfortable blouse.

His eyes glance down at my hand, but he doesn't reciprocate and reach for mine. Instead, he crosses his arms, puffing out his barrel chest and producing two large biceps, flexed in warning.

"Cricket," he begins, but I correct him.

"Olivet."

"This place isn't for sale, so you can just reverse out of here, hopefully without backing into an unsuspecting tree, and return to wherever you came from." All those words in his definitive tone add up to one: *Leave.* But I'm not going anywhere without the security of this property signed on a dotted line.

"Now Mr. Harrington," I say. Lowering my hand, I place both on the hood of my car. The problem is I'm still looking *up* at him, so I'm not really in a position of authority to talk him down. This always looks good in the movies, but it's clearly not working with my five-foot-seven stature compared to his six-foot-plus-too-many-extra-inches height.

"Giant," he states, and I stop.

"Excuse me?"

"Everyone calls me Giant."

"Well, Mr. Giant—"

"What do you want with the land?" he interjects, his voice still thunder deep but not so menacing.

"I work for Mullen Realty in Chicago, and we'd like to acquire this property for a resort—"

"A resort?" he huffs, his arms falling to his sides as he interrupts me. He turns his large head to the side, giving me a view of his profile. Strong facial features, a sharp nose broken at least once, and a tic to his jaw as he concentrates on something in the distance. "Do you know anything about this property, Cricket?"

"Olivet," I correct. "And yes, I do. I know it's a fine piece of land situated perfectly for a beautiful resort that will offer people peace and tranquility away from their hectic lives." I ramble off the future brochure sure to include such words to entice potential visitors. The serenity around us reminds me I'm not far off from my speculation.

He harrumphs, crossing his arms again. Not as fierce as the first time and more casual in nature, he shakes his head as though he's laughing at me. Only he isn't laughing. "It's not for sale."

I dismiss his words, considering what he would look like with laughter on his face. Would his cheeks glow? His mouth spread? I bet he has white teeth. A smile and a good chuckle might set him on fire. He's already larger than life in size, but with a good guffaw, he'd be bigger than thunder. A Greek god of sound and stature.

He's staring at me, and I realize I've taken too long to respond. I eye the cabin behind him. Rustic is one word for it. Cozy, graying, inviting. I rid the possibility of seeing the inside from my head. *He probably hides bodies under the porch.* I chuckle with the thought. He's fierce but not fearsome. There's just something about him. My head tilts, and my eyes pinch. I decide to change tactics. A new appeal.

"If it's a matter of money—"

"I don't need money." He scoffs, cutting me off and glaring at me again with a look of offense. "There isn't enough money in the world for me to give up this place."

My mouth pops open. "So, you are George Harrington the second?"

"I told you, I'm Giant, and I think we're done here, Cricket."

"Now, Mr. Harrington—"

He turns his back to me, that beautifully muscular back. My mouth waters, and I want to kiss up the river of his spine and along the flexing plains of his shoulder blades, which is absolutely ridiculous, considering he's a stranger. Besides, I've sworn off men. Pretty men with fancy names. *No thank you.* Although this man isn't pretty. He's weathered and worn like the cabin behind him, and for once, I'd like to be a little less straitlaced and buttoned-up. The collar of my blouse itches.

"Name your price, Mr. Harrington," I shout to his retreating back. He's abandoned the wood pile and stalks toward the low porch. Without touching the first stair, he steps up to the platform, swallowed by the shade of the overhang. My eyes are fixated on two firm globes filling out his Carhartt pants. *Oh my.* Within seconds, he's disappeared inside the cabin, closing the door on my proposal.

Well, that certainly didn't go as planned.

Continue reading Giant and Letty's story in ***Silver Brewer***

about the author

www.lbdunbar.com

L.B. Dunbar loves sexy silver foxes, second chances, and small towns. If you enjoy older characters in your romance reads, including a hero with a little silver in his scruff and a heroine rediscovering her worth, then welcome to romance for those over 40. L.B. Dunbar's signature works include women and men in their prime taking another turn at love and happily ever. Along with her #sexysilverfox collection, she's made Amazon Top 10 in Later in Life Romance with her Lakeside Cottage and Road Trips & Romance series. She is also a *USA Today Bestseller*. L.B. lives in Chicago with her own sexy silver fox.

To get all the scoop about the self-proclaimed queen of silver fox romance, join her on Facebook at Loving L.B. or receive her monthly newsletter, Love Notes.

+ + +

connect with L.B. Dunbar